PLANTS VS. ZOMBIES

THE GARDEN PATH

Written by **PAUL TOBIN**
Art by **KIERON DWYER**
Colors by **HEATHER BRECKEL**
Letters by **STEVE DUTRO**
Cover by **KIERON DWYER**

DARK HORSE BOOKS

Plants vs. Zombies
THE GARDEN PATH

President and Publisher **MIKE RICHARDSON**
Senior Editor **PHILIP R. SIMON**
Assistant Editor **JOSHUA ENGLEDOW**
Designer **BRENNAN THOME**
Digital Art Technician **ALLYSON HALLER**

Special thanks to A.J. Rathbun, Kristen Star, Joshua Franks, Jessica Leung, and everyone at PopCap Games and EA Games.

First Edition: June 2020
ISBN 978-1-50671-306-9

10 9 8 7 6 5 4 3 2 1
Printed in Canada

DarkHorse.com
PopCap.com

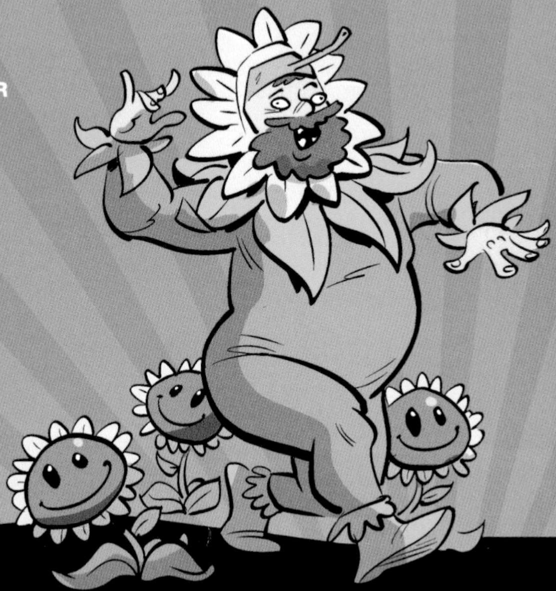

No plants were harmed in the making of this graphic novel. However, several confused zombies wound up with "bad endings"—probably because they followed Zomboss's orders. So many choices! So many different garden paths! In order to avoid "bad endings," too, the editorial team for this graphic novel followed Kristen Star's intuitions. (Always follow the right "star"!) And we all made it out of this adventure just fine! Now on to building the next graphic novel, while you have fun finding all the endings in this one!

PLANTS vs. ZOMBIES: THE GARDEN PATH | Published by Dark Horse Books, a division of Dark Horse Comics LLC. 10956 SE Main Street, Milwaukie, OR 97222 | To find a comics shop in your area, visit comicshoplocator.com |

Library of Congress Cataloging-in-Publication Data

Names: Tobin, Paul, writer. | Dwyer, Kieron, artist. | Breckel, Heather, colourist. | Dutro, Steve, letterer.
Title: The garden path / written by Paul Tobin ; art by Kieron Dwyer ; colors by Heather Breckel ; letters by Steve Dutro.
Description: First edition. | Milwaukie, OR : Dark Horse Books, 2020. | Series: Plants vs. Zombies vol. 16 | Audience: Ages 8+ | Audience: Grades 2-3 | Summary: ""Our story begins with Dr. Zomboss' latest plan of evil genius - disguising his zombies as each other, in an effort to confuse plants and plant pals Crazy Dave, Nate, and Patrice. Can the friendly fronds get past these dastardly disguises before the zombies sneak into Neighborville tourist attractions - and even Watson Elementary school - to unleash their hungry ways? Every major decision along the path will be made by you and determine if our horticultural heroes end up facing their unfortunate demise . . . or victory! Eisner Award-winning writer Paul Tobin (Bandette, Genius Factor) collaborates with artist Kieron Dwyer (Captain America, The Avengers) for a brand-new, interactive Plants vs. Zombies journey!"--Provided by publisher"-- Provided by publisher.
Identifiers: LCCN 2019059204 (print) | LCCN 2019059205 (ebook) | ISBN 9781506713069 (hardcover) | ISBN 9781506713151 (ebook)
Subjects: LCSH: Graphic novels. | CYAC: Graphic novels. | Humorous stories. | Zombies--Fiction. | Plants--Fiction.
Classification: LCC PZ7.7.T62 Gar 2020 (print) | LCC PZ7.7.T62 (ebook) | DDC 741.5/973--dc23
LC record available at https://lccn.loc.gov/2019059204
LC ebook record available at https://lccn.loc.gov/2019059205

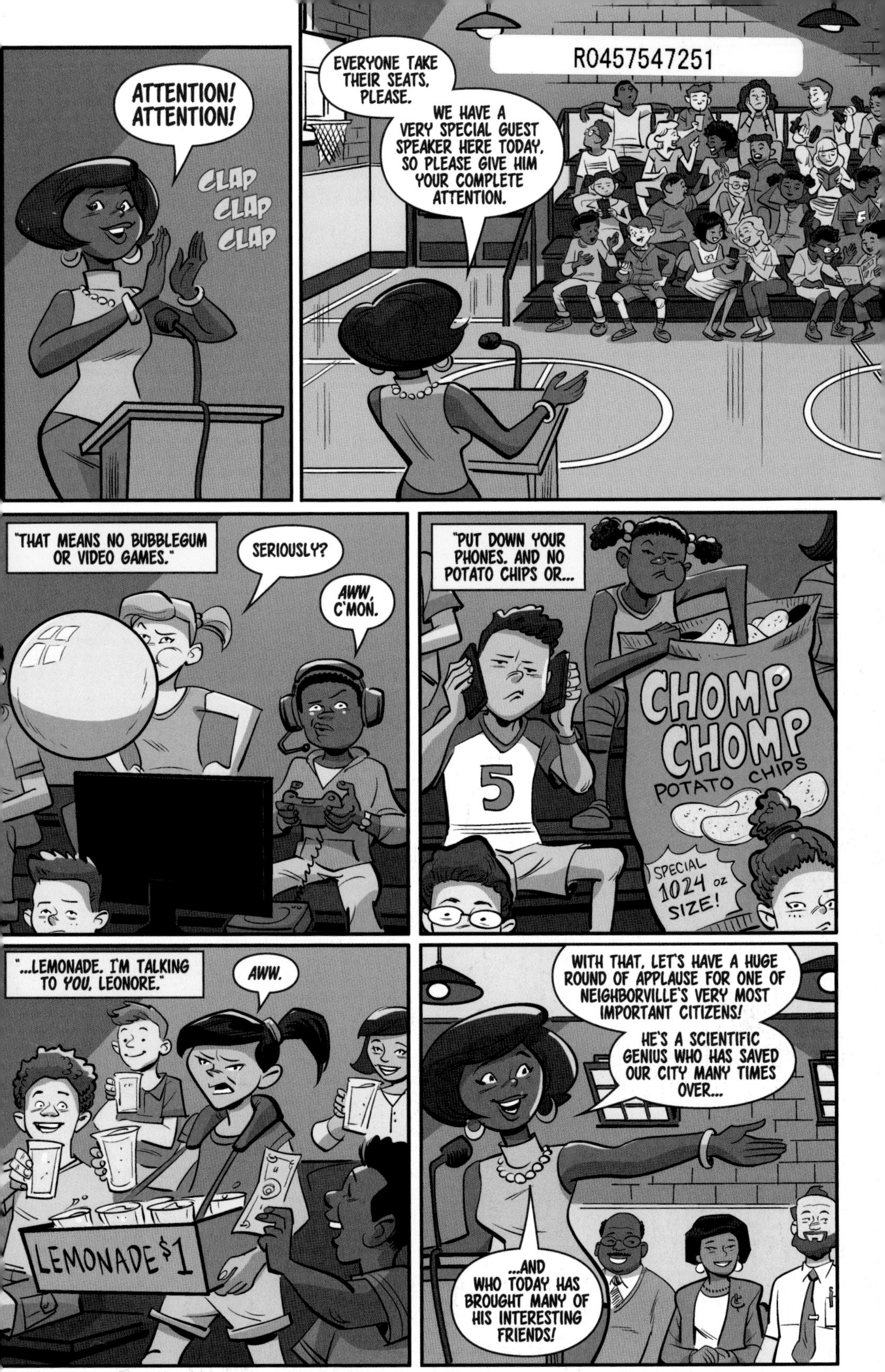
ATTENTION! ATTENTION!
CLAP CLAP CLAP
R0457547251
EVERYONE TAKE THEIR SEATS, PLEASE.
WE HAVE A VERY SPECIAL GUEST SPEAKER HERE TODAY, SO PLEASE GIVE HIM YOUR COMPLETE ATTENTION.
"THAT MEANS NO BUBBLEGUM OR VIDEO GAMES."
SERIOUSLY?
AWW, C'MON.
"PUT DOWN YOUR PHONES. AND NO POTATO CHIPS OR...
CHOMP CHOMP POTATO CHIPS
SPECIAL 1024 oz SIZE!
"...LEMONADE. I'M TALKING TO YOU, LEONORE."
AWW.
LEMONADE $1
WITH THAT, LET'S HAVE A HUGE ROUND OF APPLAUSE FOR ONE OF NEIGHBORVILLE'S VERY MOST IMPORTANT CITIZENS!
HE'S A SCIENTIFIC GENIUS WHO HAS SAVED OUR CITY MANY TIMES OVER...
...AND WHO TODAY HAS BROUGHT MANY OF HIS INTERESTING FRIENDS!

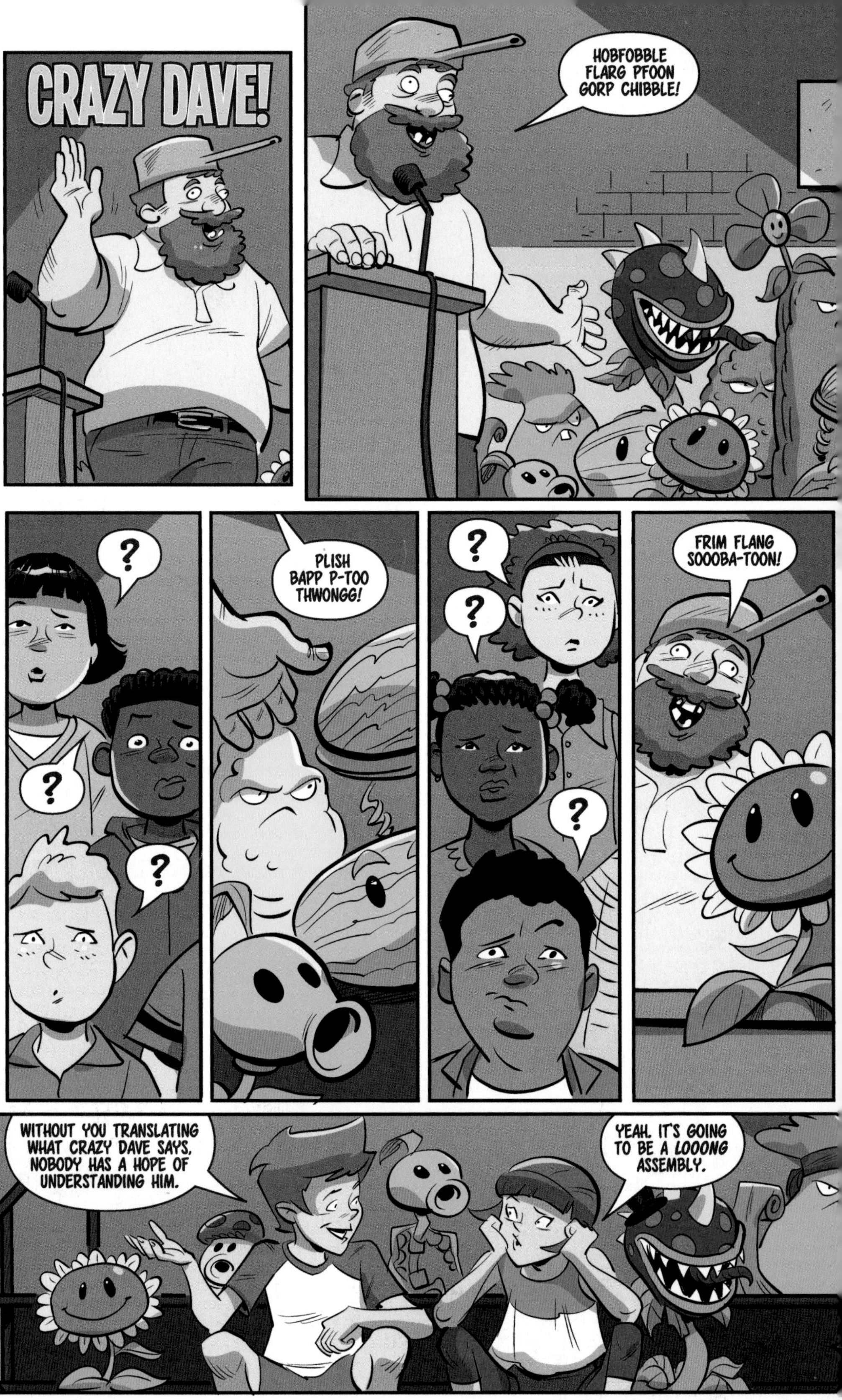

CRAZY DAVE!
HOBFOBBLE FLARG PFOON GORP CHIBBLE!
?
?
?
PLISH BAPP P-TOO THWONGG!
?
?
?
FRIM FLANG SOOOBA-TOON!
WITHOUT YOU TRANSLATING WHAT CRAZY DAVE SAYS, NOBODY HAS A HOPE OF UNDERSTANDING HIM.
YEAH. IT'S GOING TO BE A *LOOONG* ASSEMBLY.

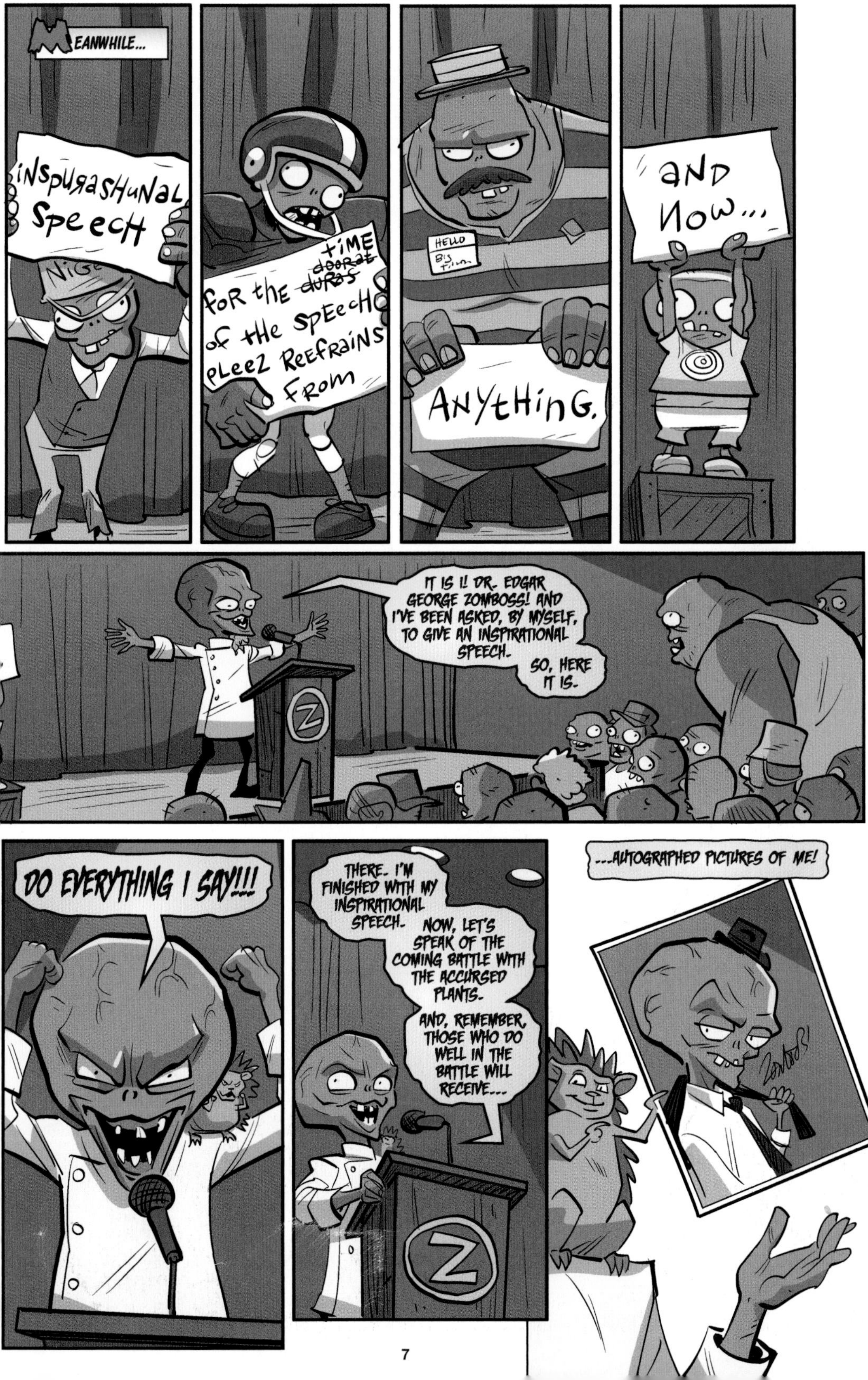
MEANWHILE...
INSPURASHUNAL SPEECH
FOR THE TIME OF THE SPEECH PLEEZ REEFRAINS FROM
ANYTHING.
AND NOW...
IT IS I! DR. EDGAR GEORGE ZOMBOSS! AND I'VE BEEN ASKED, BY MYSELF, TO GIVE AN INSPIRATIONAL SPEECH.
SO, HERE IT IS.
DO EVERYTHING I SAY!!!
THERE. I'M FINISHED WITH MY INSPIRATIONAL SPEECH.
NOW, LET'S SPEAK OF THE COMING BATTLE WITH THE ACCURSED PLANTS.
AND, REMEMBER, THOSE WHO DO WELL IN THE BATTLE WILL RECEIVE...
...AUTOGRAPHED PICTURES OF ME!

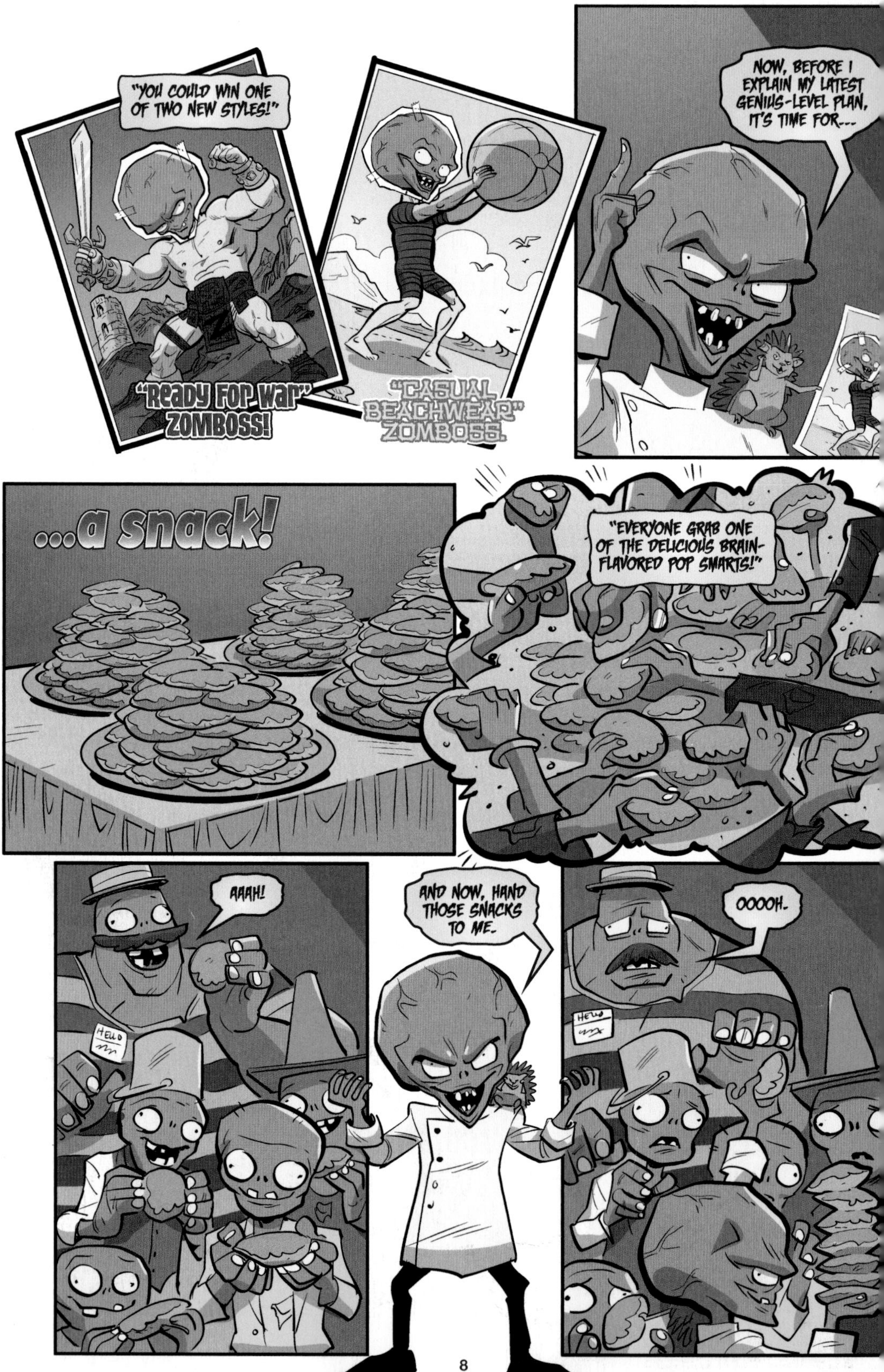
"YOU COULD WIN ONE OF TWO NEW STYLES!"
"Ready For War" ZOMBOSS!
"CASUAL BEACHWEAR" ZOMBOSS.
NOW, BEFORE I EXPLAIN MY LATEST GENIUS-LEVEL PLAN, IT'S TIME FOR...
...a snack!
"EVERYONE GRAB ONE OF THE DELICIOUS BRAIN-FLAVORED POP SMARTS!"
AAAH!
AND NOW, HAND THOSE SNACKS TO ME.
OOOOH.

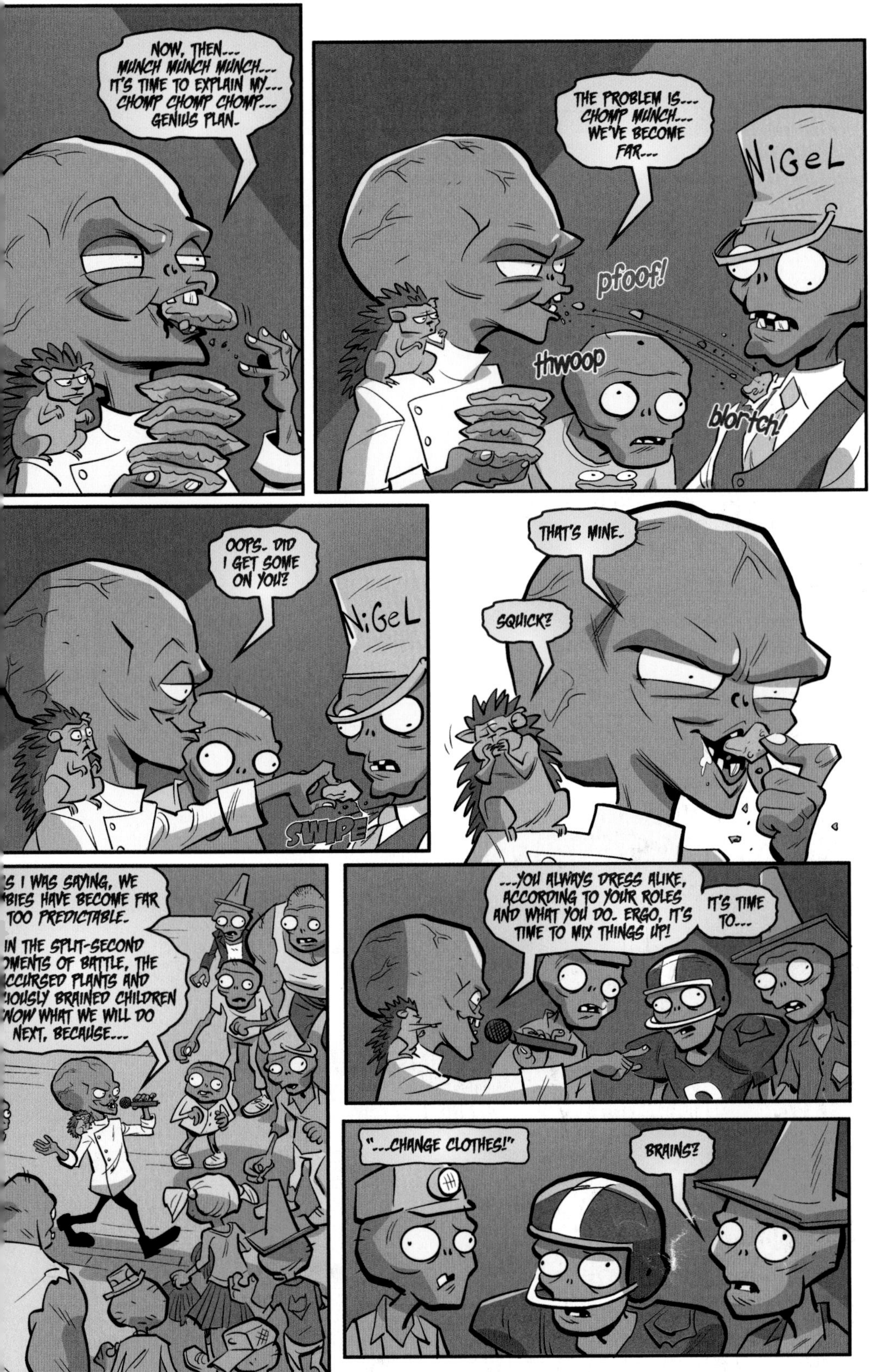
NOW, THEN... MUNCH MUNCH MUNCH... IT'S TIME TO EXPLAIN MY... CHOMP CHOMP CHOMP... GENIUS PLAN.
THE PROBLEM IS... CHOMP MUNCH... WE'VE BECOME FAR...
NiGeL
pfoof!
thwoop
blortch!
OOPS. DID I GET SOME ON YOU?
NiGeL
SWIPE
THAT'S MINE.
SQUICK?
S I WAS SAYING, WE BIES HAVE BECOME FAR TOO PREDICTABLE.
IN THE SPLIT-SECOND OMENTS OF BATTLE, THE CCURSED PLANTS AND CIOUSLY BRAINED CHILDREN NOW WHAT WE WILL DO NEXT, BECAUSE...
...YOU ALWAYS DRESS ALIKE, ACCORDING TO YOUR ROLES AND WHAT YOU DO. ERGO, IT'S TIME TO MIX THINGS UP!
IT'S TIME TO...
"...CHANGE CLOTHES!"
BRAINS?

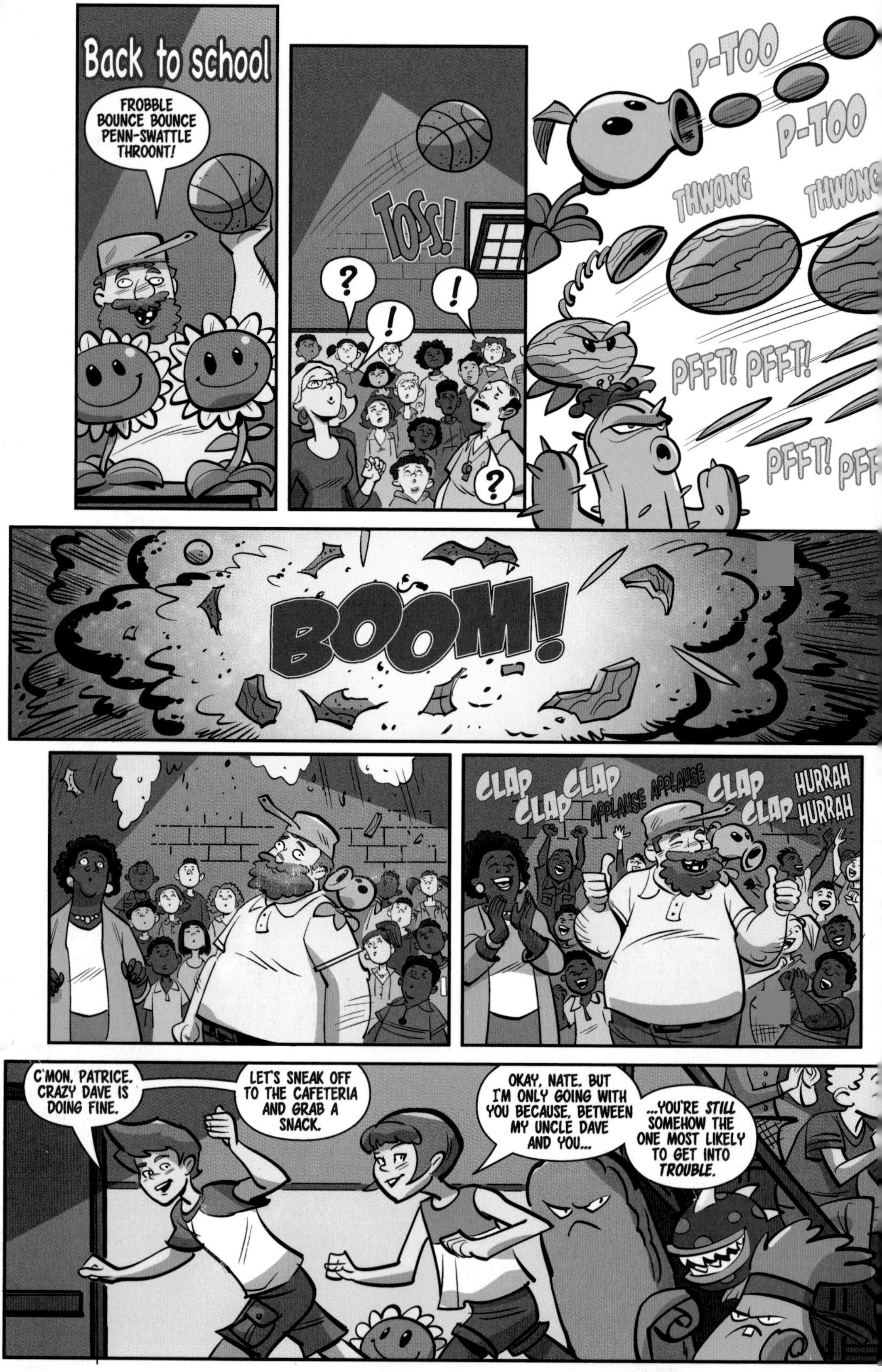
Back to school
FROBBLE BOUNCE BOUNCE PENN-SWATTLE THROONT!
TOSS!
?
!
!
?
P-TOO
P-TOO
THWONG
THWONG
PFFT! PFFT!
PFFT!
BOOM!
CLAP CLAP CLAP
APPLAUSE APPLAUSE
CLAP CLAP
HURRAH HURRAH
C'MON, PATRICE. CRAZY DAVE IS DOING FINE.
LET'S SNEAK OFF TO THE CAFETERIA AND GRAB A SNACK.
OKAY, NATE. BUT I'M ONLY GOING WITH YOU BECAUSE, BETWEEN MY UNCLE DAVE AND YOU...
...YOU'RE *STILL* SOMEHOW THE ONE MOST LIKELY TO GET INTO *TROUBLE*.

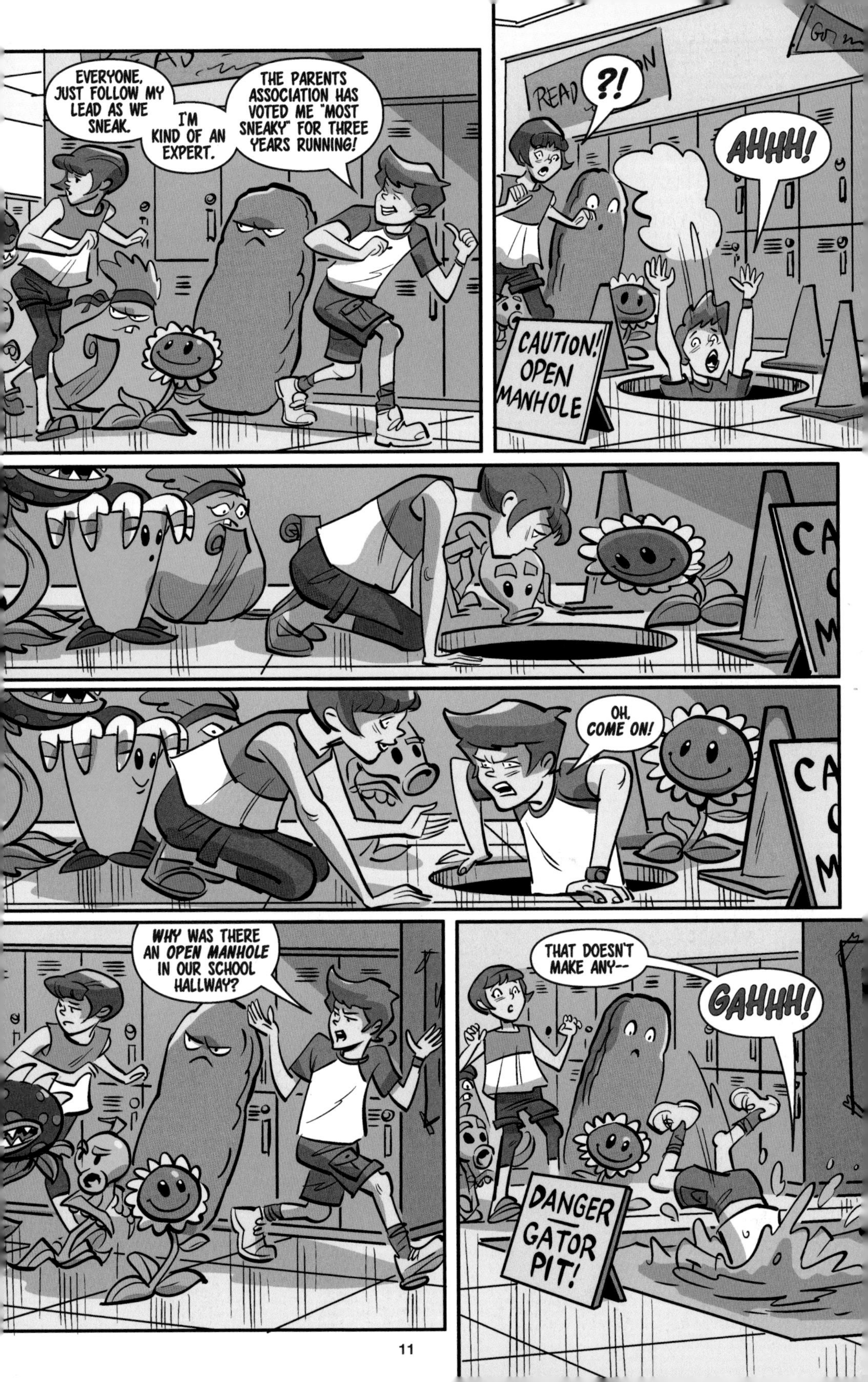
READ
EVERYONE, JUST FOLLOW MY LEAD AS WE SNEAK.
I'M KIND OF AN EXPERT.
THE PARENTS ASSOCIATION HAS VOTED ME "MOST SNEAKY" FOR THREE YEARS RUNNING!
READ
?!
AHHH!
CAUTION! OPEN MANHOLE
OH, COME ON!
WHY WAS THERE AN OPEN MANHOLE IN OUR SCHOOL HALLWAY?
THAT DOESN'T MAKE ANY--
GAHHH!
DANGER GATOR PIT!

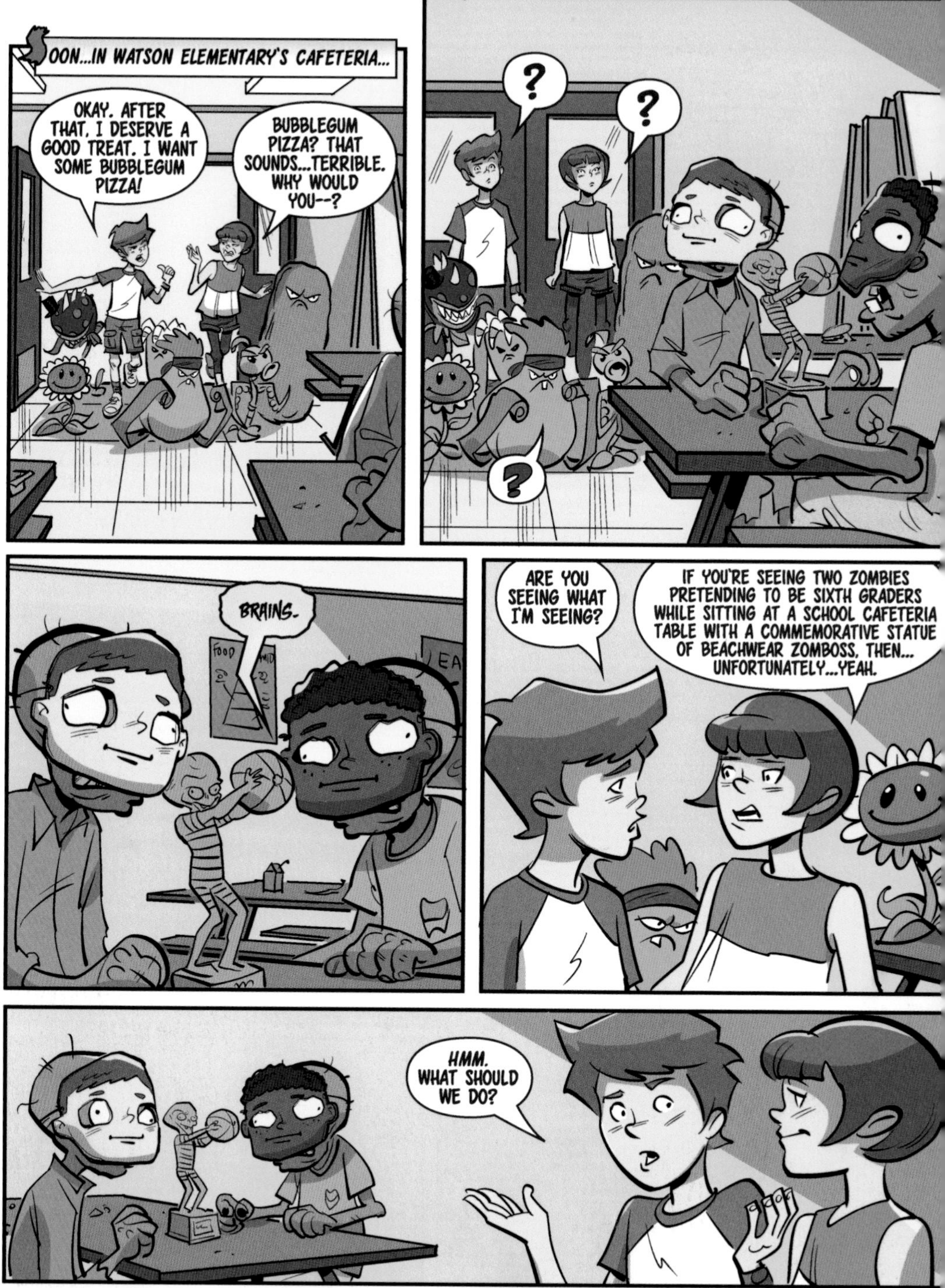
SOON...IN WATSON ELEMENTARY'S CAFETERIA...
OKAY. AFTER THAT, I DESERVE A GOOD TREAT. I WANT SOME BUBBLEGUM PIZZA!
BUBBLEGUM PIZZA? THAT SOUNDS...TERRIBLE. WHY WOULD YOU--?
?
?
?
BRAINS.
ARE YOU SEEING WHAT I'M SEEING?
IF YOU'RE SEEING TWO ZOMBIES PRETENDING TO BE SIXTH GRADERS WHILE SITTING AT A SCHOOL CAFETERIA TABLE WITH A COMMEMORATIVE STATUE OF BEACHWEAR ZOMBOSS, THEN... UNFORTUNATELY...YEAH.
HMM. WHAT SHOULD WE DO?

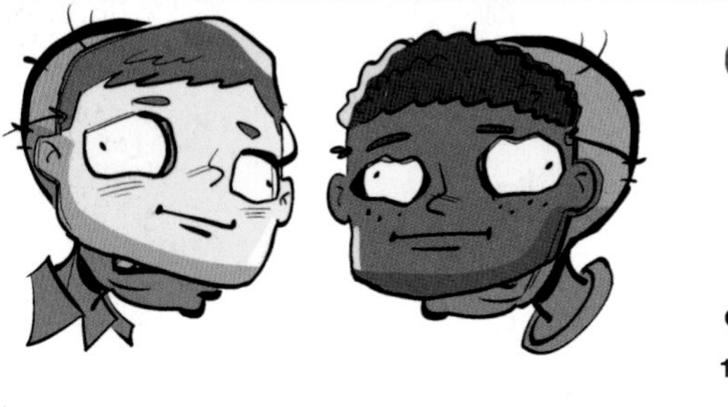

FIND THE GARDEN PATH:

Should Patrice and Nate confront the zombies, or let them stay?

LEAVE THEM ALONE! ZOMBIES NEED AN EDUCATION TOO!: Go to next page!

CONFRONT THE ZOMBIES: Turn to page 15!

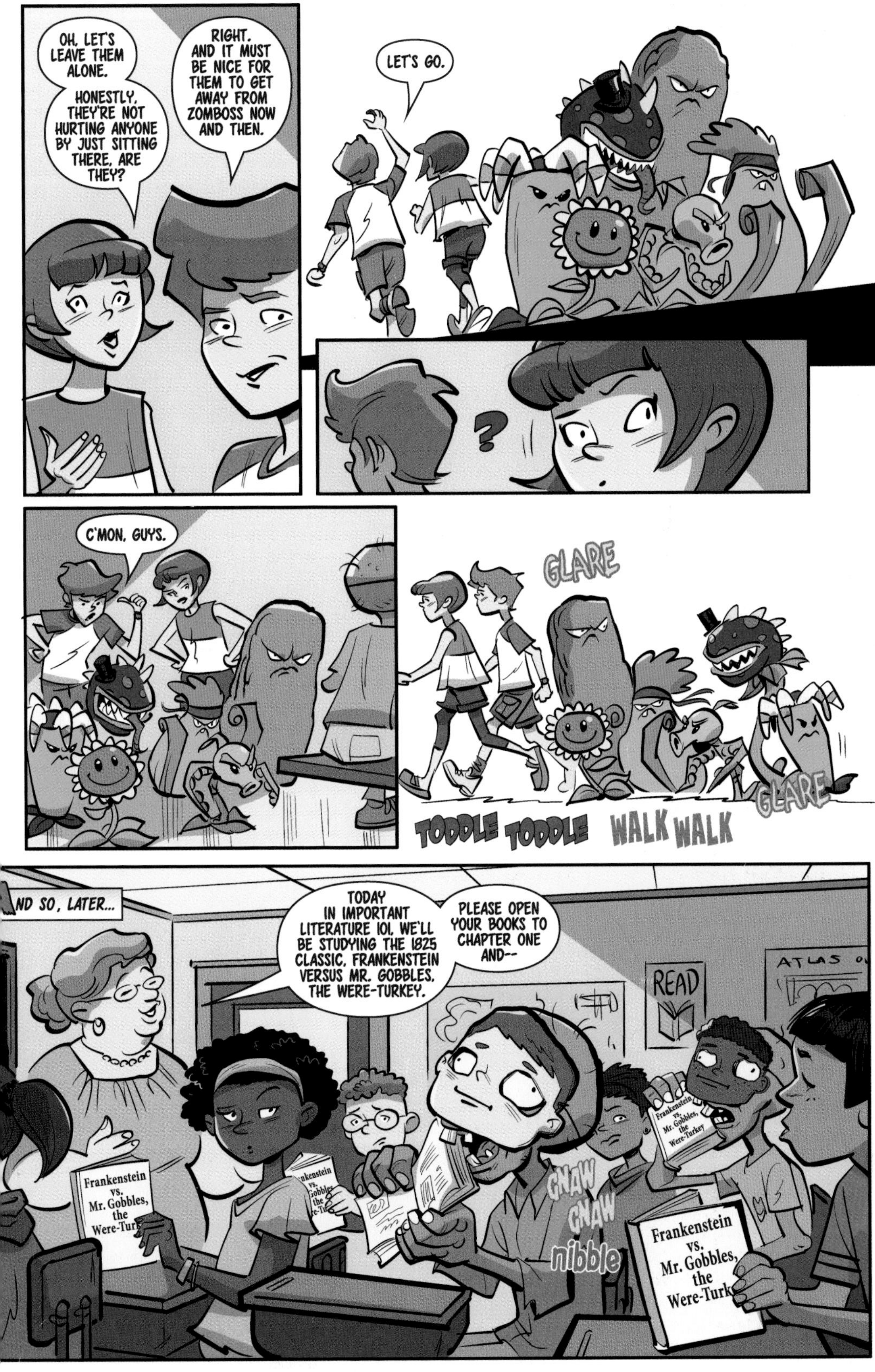
OH, LET'S LEAVE THEM ALONE.
HONESTLY, THEY'RE NOT HURTING ANYONE BY JUST SITTING THERE, ARE THEY?
RIGHT. AND IT MUST BE NICE FOR THEM TO GET AWAY FROM ZOMBOSS NOW AND THEN.
LET'S GO.
?
C'MON, GUYS.
GLARE
GLARE
TODDLE TODDLE WALK WALK
...ND SO, LATER...
TODAY IN IMPORTANT LITERATURE 101, WE'LL BE STUDYING THE 1825 CLASSIC, FRANKENSTEIN VERSUS MR. GOBBLES, THE WERE-TURKEY.
PLEASE OPEN YOUR BOOKS TO CHAPTER ONE AND--
READ
Frankenstein vs. Mr. Gobbles, the Were-Turk
GNAW
GNAW
nibble
Frankenstein vs. Mr. Gobbles, the Were-Turkey
Frankenstein vs. Mr. Gobbles, the Were-Turk

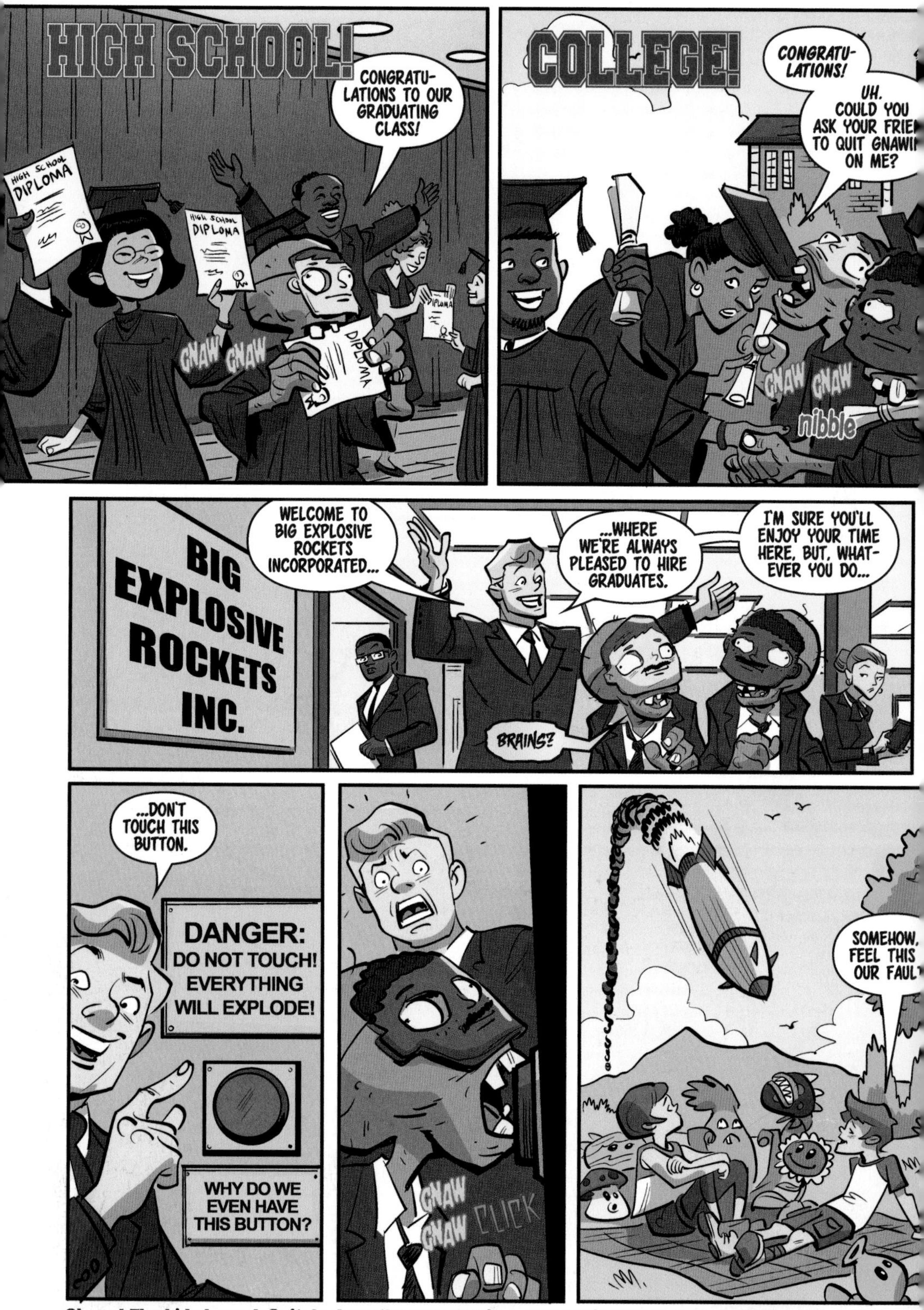
HIGH SCHOOL!
CONGRATULATIONS TO OUR GRADUATING CLASS!
HIGH SCHOOL DIPLOMA
HIGH SCHOOL DIPLOMA
DIPLOMA
DIPLOMA
GNAW GNAW
COLLEGE!
CONGRATULATIONS!
UH. COULD YOU ASK YOUR FRIE
TO QUIT GNAWI
ON ME?
GNAW GNAW
nibble
BIG EXPLOSIVE ROCKETS INC.
WELCOME TO BIG EXPLOSIVE ROCKETS INCORPORATED...
...WHERE WE'RE ALWAYS PLEASED TO HIRE GRADUATES.
I'M SURE YOU'LL ENJOY YOUR TIME HERE, BUT, WHATEVER YOU DO...
BRAINS?
...DON'T TOUCH THIS BUTTON.
DANGER: DO NOT TOUCH! EVERYTHING WILL EXPLODE!
WHY DO WE EVEN HAVE THIS BUTTON?
GNAW GNAW CLICK
SOMEHOW,
FEEL THIS
OUR FAUL

Oh, no! The kids have definitely done the wrong thing. Bad ending! Return to page 12 and start again!

Continued from page 12:

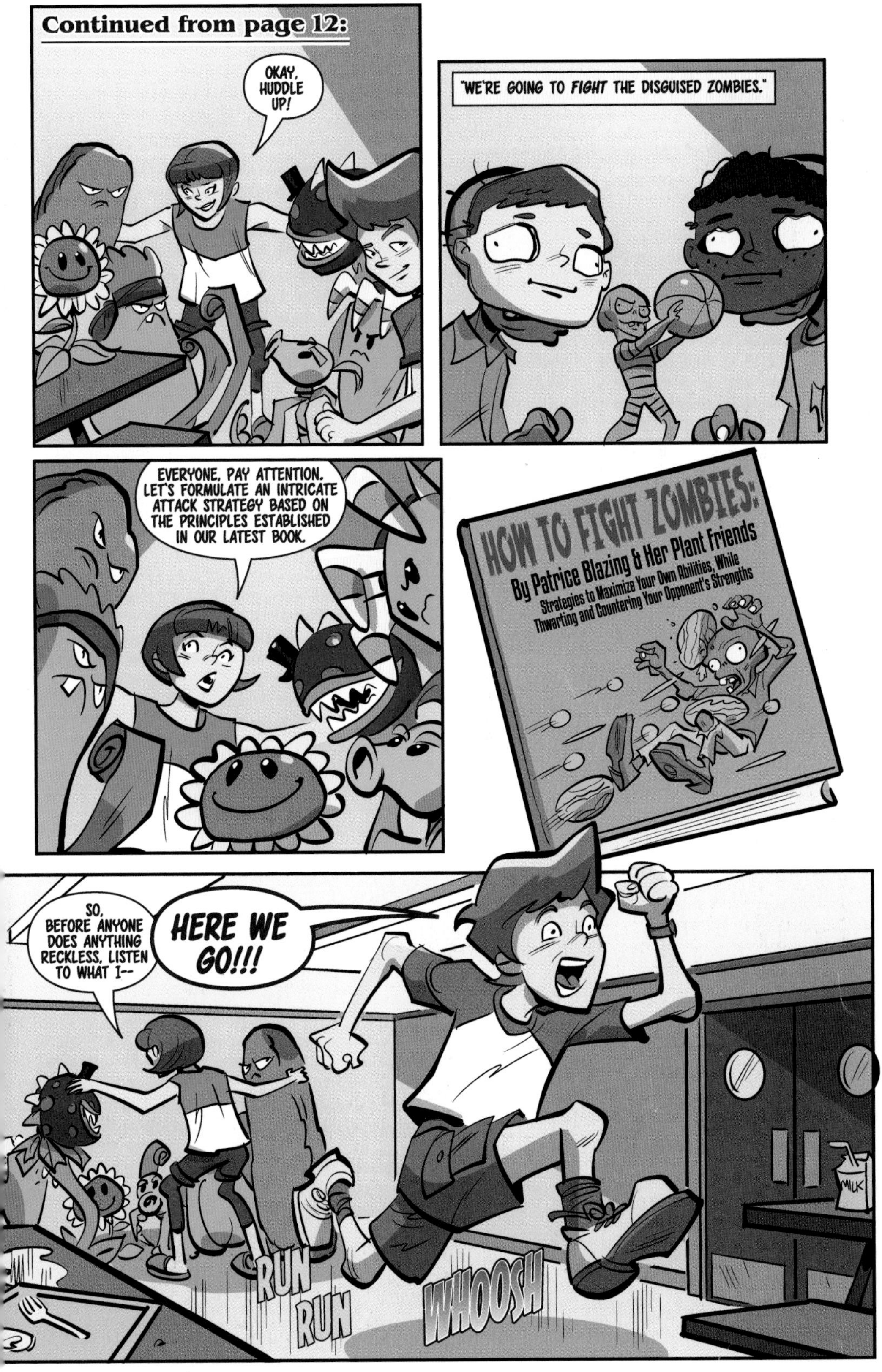
OKAY, HUDDLE UP!
"WE'RE GOING TO FIGHT THE DISGUISED ZOMBIES."
EVERYONE, PAY ATTENTION. LET'S FORMULATE AN INTRICATE ATTACK STRATEGY BASED ON THE PRINCIPLES ESTABLISHED IN OUR LATEST BOOK.
HOW TO FIGHT ZOMBIES:
By Patrice Blazing & Her Plant Friends
Strategies to Maximize Your Own Abilities, While Thwarting and Countering Your Opponent's Strengths
SO, BEFORE ANYONE DOES ANYTHING RECKLESS, LISTEN TO WHAT I--
HERE WE GO!!!
RUN
RUN
WHOOSH
MILK

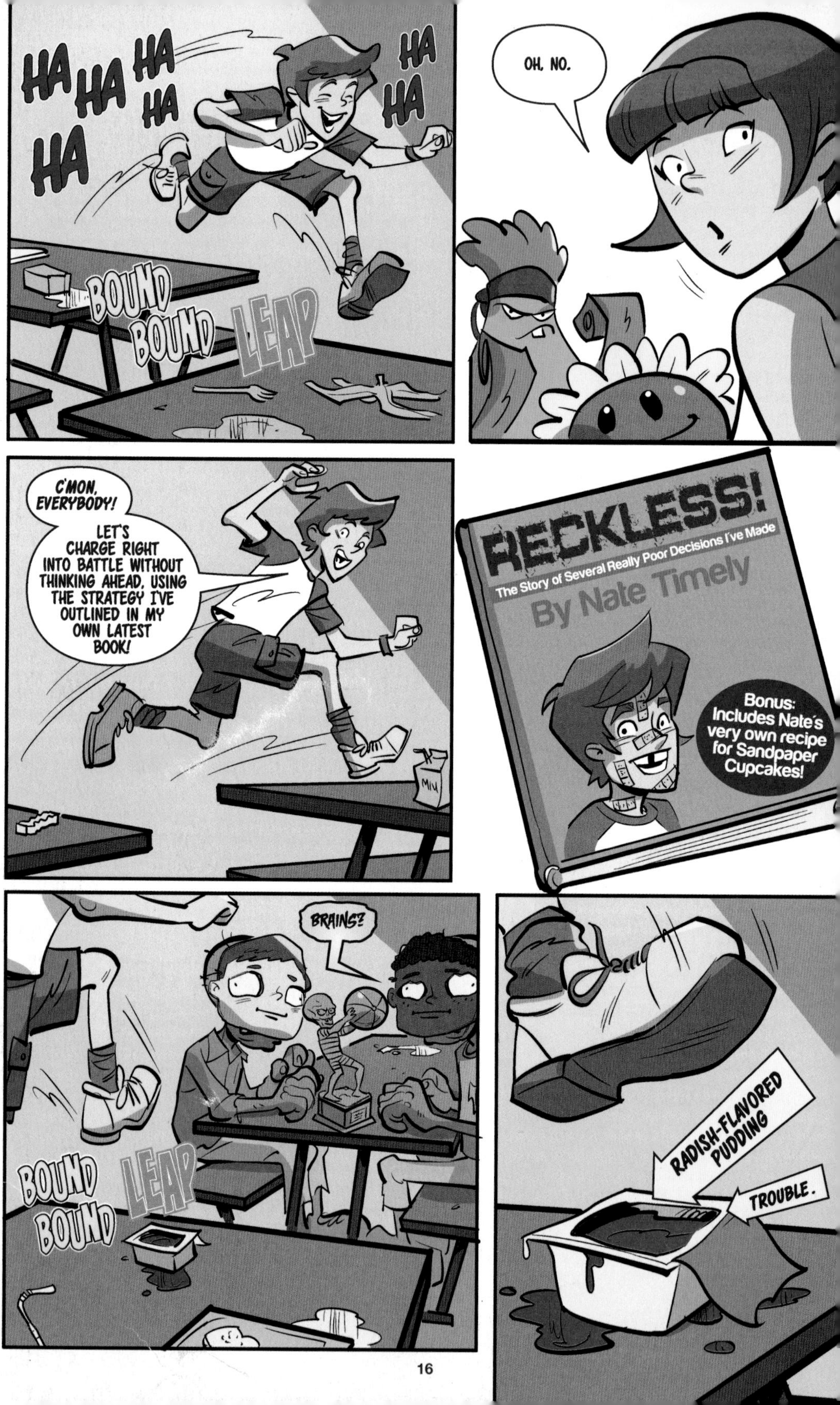
HA HA HA HA HA
HA HA
OH, NO.
BOUND BOUND LEAP
C'MON, EVERYBODY!
LET'S CHARGE RIGHT INTO BATTLE WITHOUT THINKING AHEAD, USING THE STRATEGY I'VE OUTLINED IN MY OWN LATEST BOOK!
MLK
RECKLESS!
The Story of Several Really Poor Decisions I've Made
By Nate Timely
Bonus: Includes Nate's very own recipe for Sandpaper Cupcakes!
BRAINS?
BOUND BOUND LEAP
RADISH-FLAVORED PUDDING
TROUBLE.

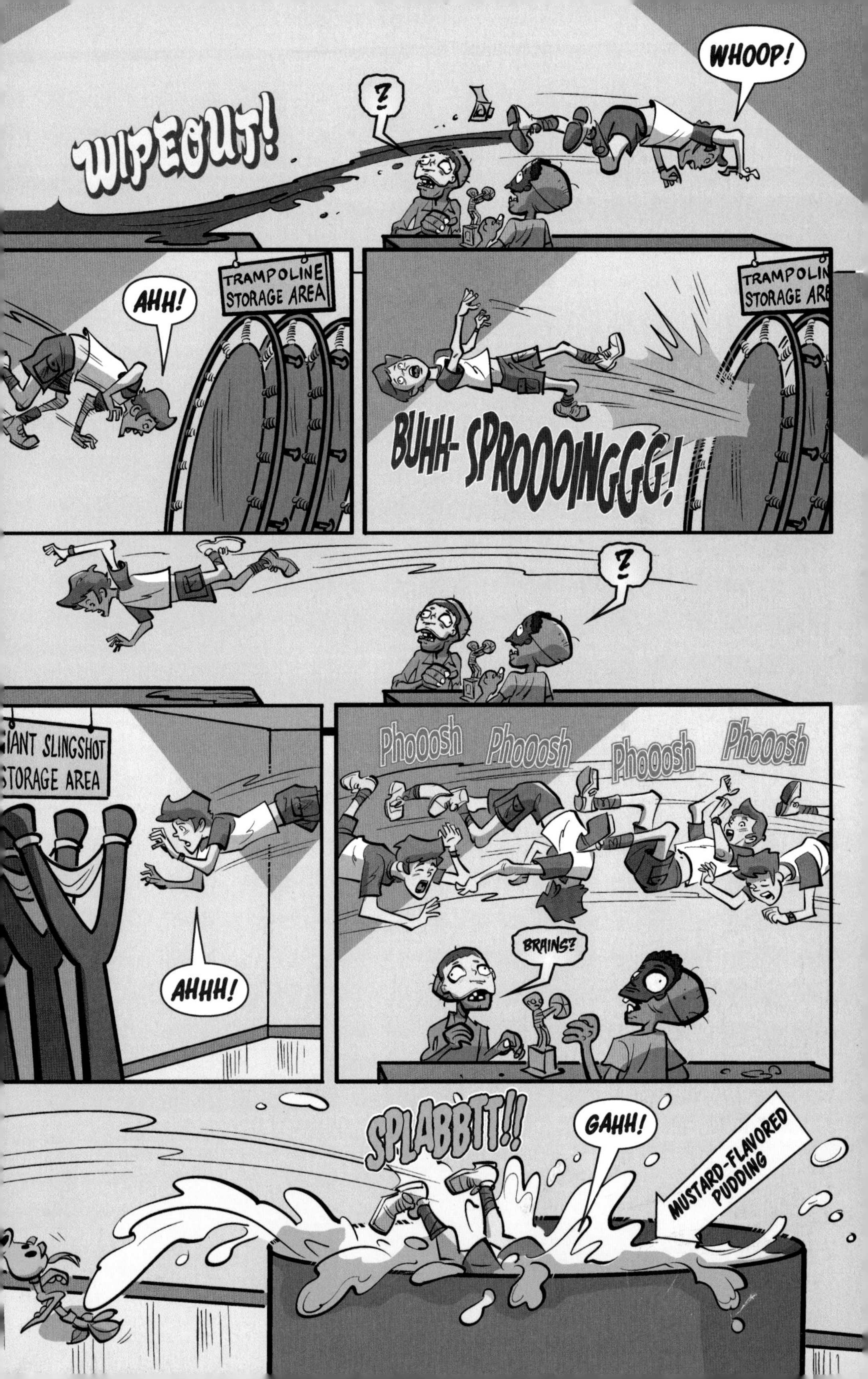

WIPEOUT!
?
WHOOP!
AHH!
TRAMPOLINE STORAGE AREA
TRAMPOLIN STORAGE ARE
BUHH- SPROOOINGGG!
?
GIANT SLINGSHOT STORAGE AREA
AHHH!
Phooosh Phooosh Phooosh Phooosh
BRAINS?
SPLABBTT!!
GAHH!
MUSTARD-FLAVORED PUDDING

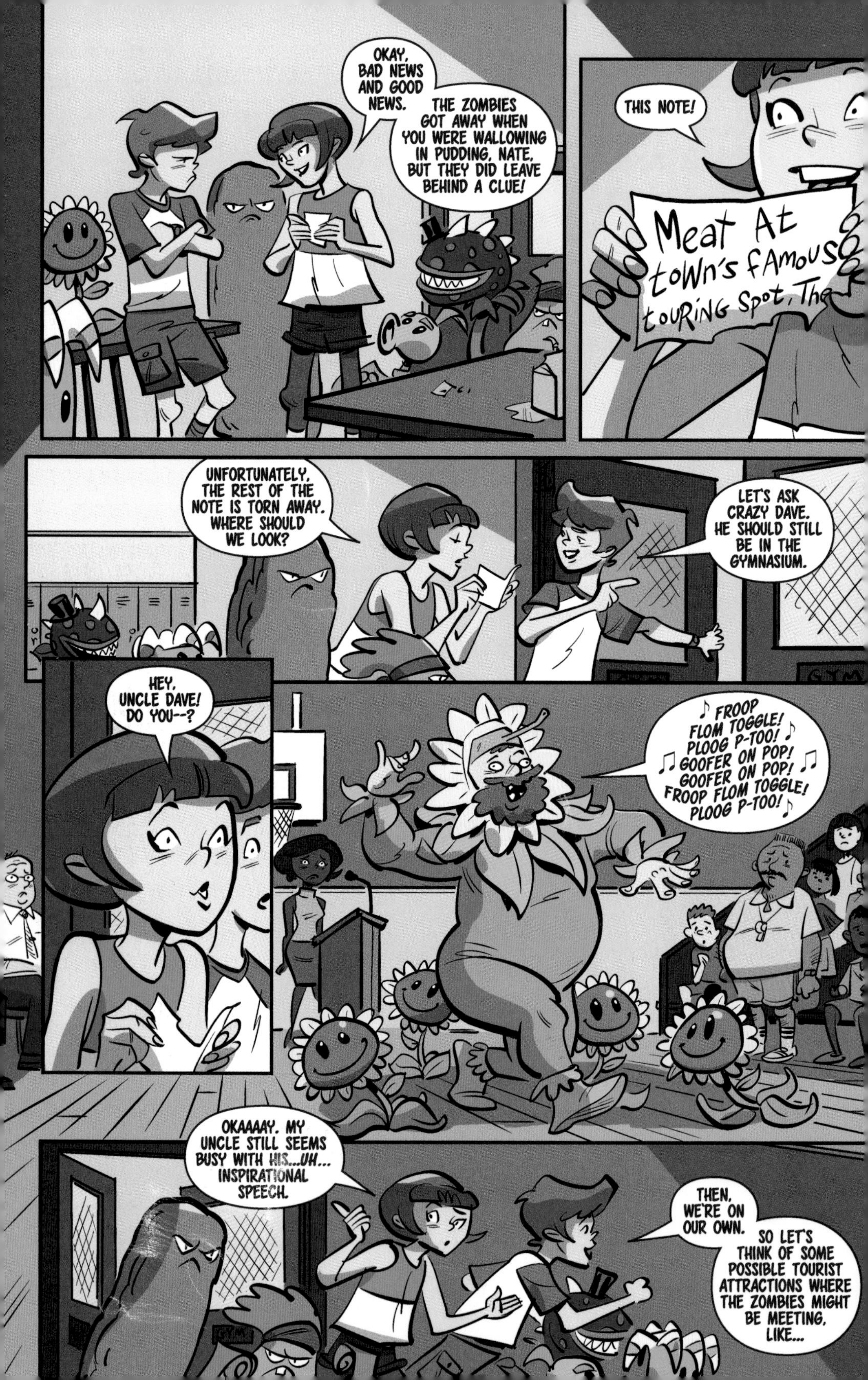
OKAY, BAD NEWS AND GOOD NEWS.
THE ZOMBIES GOT AWAY WHEN YOU WERE WALLOWING IN PUDDING, NATE, BUT THEY DID LEAVE BEHIND A CLUE!
THIS NOTE!
Meat At town's famous touring Spot, The
UNFORTUNATELY, THE REST OF THE NOTE IS TORN AWAY. WHERE SHOULD WE LOOK?
LET'S ASK CRAZY DAVE. HE SHOULD STILL BE IN THE GYMNASIUM.
HEY, UNCLE DAVE! DO YOU--?
♪ FROOP FLOM TOGGLE! PLOOG P-TOO! ♪ ♫ GOOFER ON POP! GOOFER ON POP! ♫ FROOP FLOM TOGGLE! PLOOG P-TOO! ♪
OKAAAAY. MY UNCLE STILL SEEMS BUSY WITH HIS...UH... INSPIRATIONAL SPEECH.
THEN, WE'RE ON OUR OWN.
SO LET'S THINK OF SOME POSSIBLE TOURIST ATTRACTIONS WHERE THE ZOMBIES MIGHT BE MEETING, LIKE...

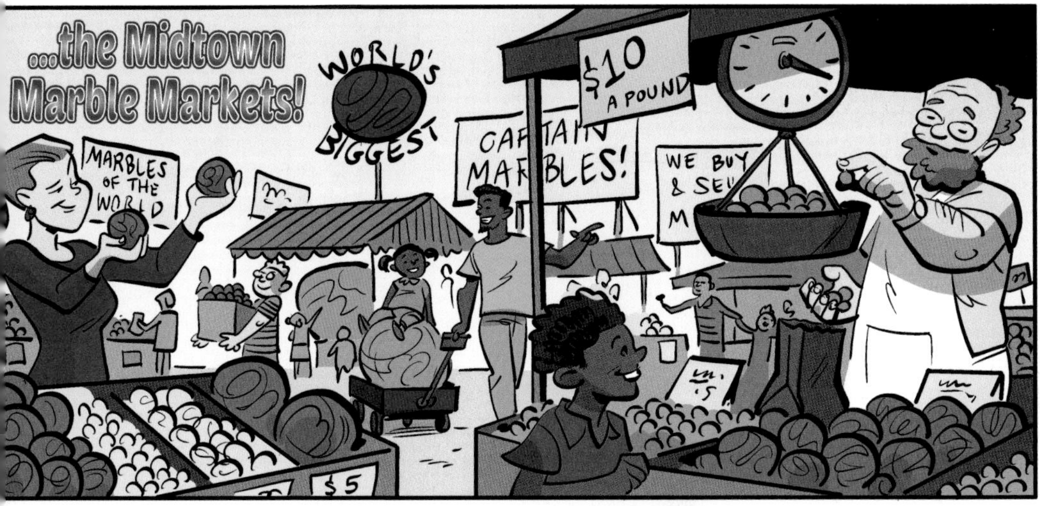
...the Midtown Marble Markets!
WORLD'S BIGGEST
$10 A POUND
CAPTAIN MARBLES!
MARBLES OF THE WORLD
WE BUY & SELL M
$5

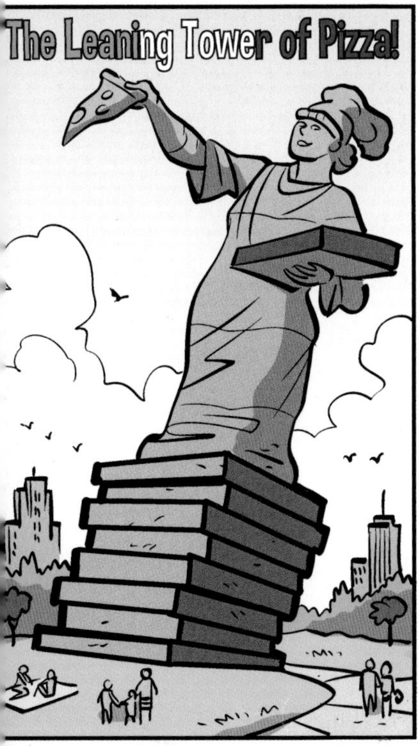
The Leaning Tower of Pizza!

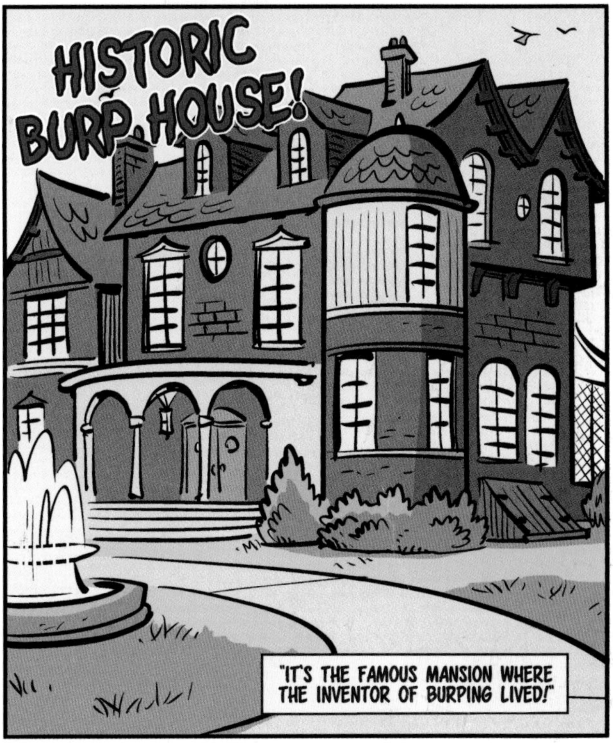
HISTORIC BURP HOUSE!
"IT'S THE FAMOUS MANSION WHERE THE INVENTOR OF BURPING LIVED!"

FIND THE GARDEN PATH:

So, where should the kids go?

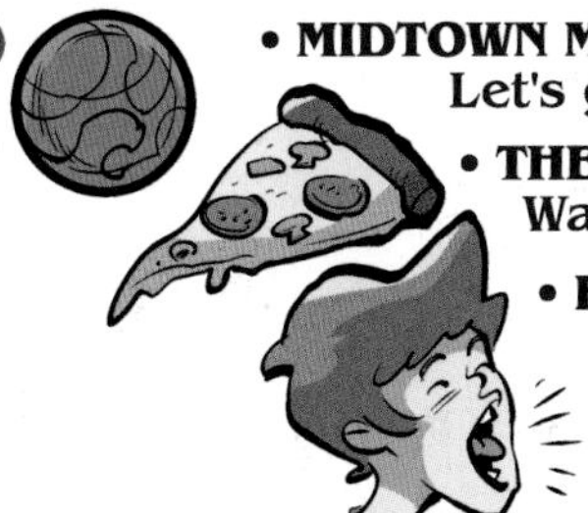

- **MIDTOWN MARBLE MARKETS:** Let's get rolling! Go to next page!
- **THE LEANING TOWER OF PIZZA:** Want a slice of this? Turn to Page 25!
- **BURP HOUSE:** Sounds good! Turn to page 30!

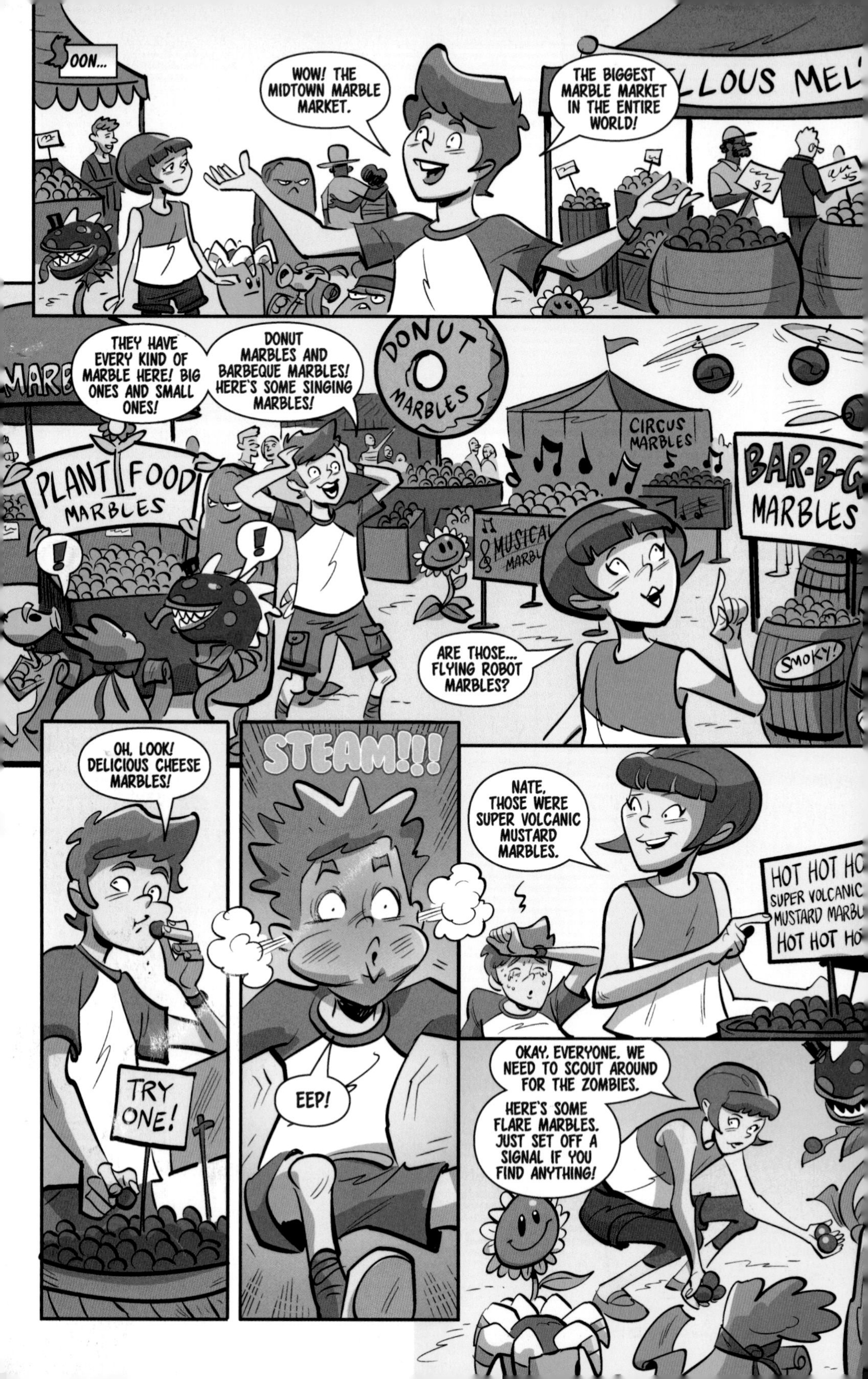
SOON...
WOW! THE MIDTOWN MARBLE MARKET.
THE BIGGEST MARBLE MARKET IN THE ENTIRE WORLD!
...LLOUS MEL'
THEY HAVE EVERY KIND OF MARBLE HERE! BIG ONES AND SMALL ONES!
DONUT MARBLES AND BARBEQUE MARBLES! HERE'S SOME SINGING MARBLES!
DONUT MARBLES
CIRCUS MARBLES
PLANT FOOD MARBLES
MUSICAL MARBLES
BAR-B-Q MARBLES
SMOKY!
ARE THOSE... FLYING ROBOT MARBLES?
OH, LOOK! DELICIOUS CHEESE MARBLES!
TRY ONE!
STEAM!!!
EEP!
NATE, THOSE WERE SUPER VOLCANIC MUSTARD MARBLES.
HOT HOT HO
SUPER VOLCANIC
MUSTARD MARBL
HOT HOT HO
OKAY, EVERYONE. WE NEED TO SCOUT AROUND FOR THE ZOMBIES.
HERE'S SOME FLARE MARBLES. JUST SET OFF A SIGNAL IF YOU FIND ANYTHING!

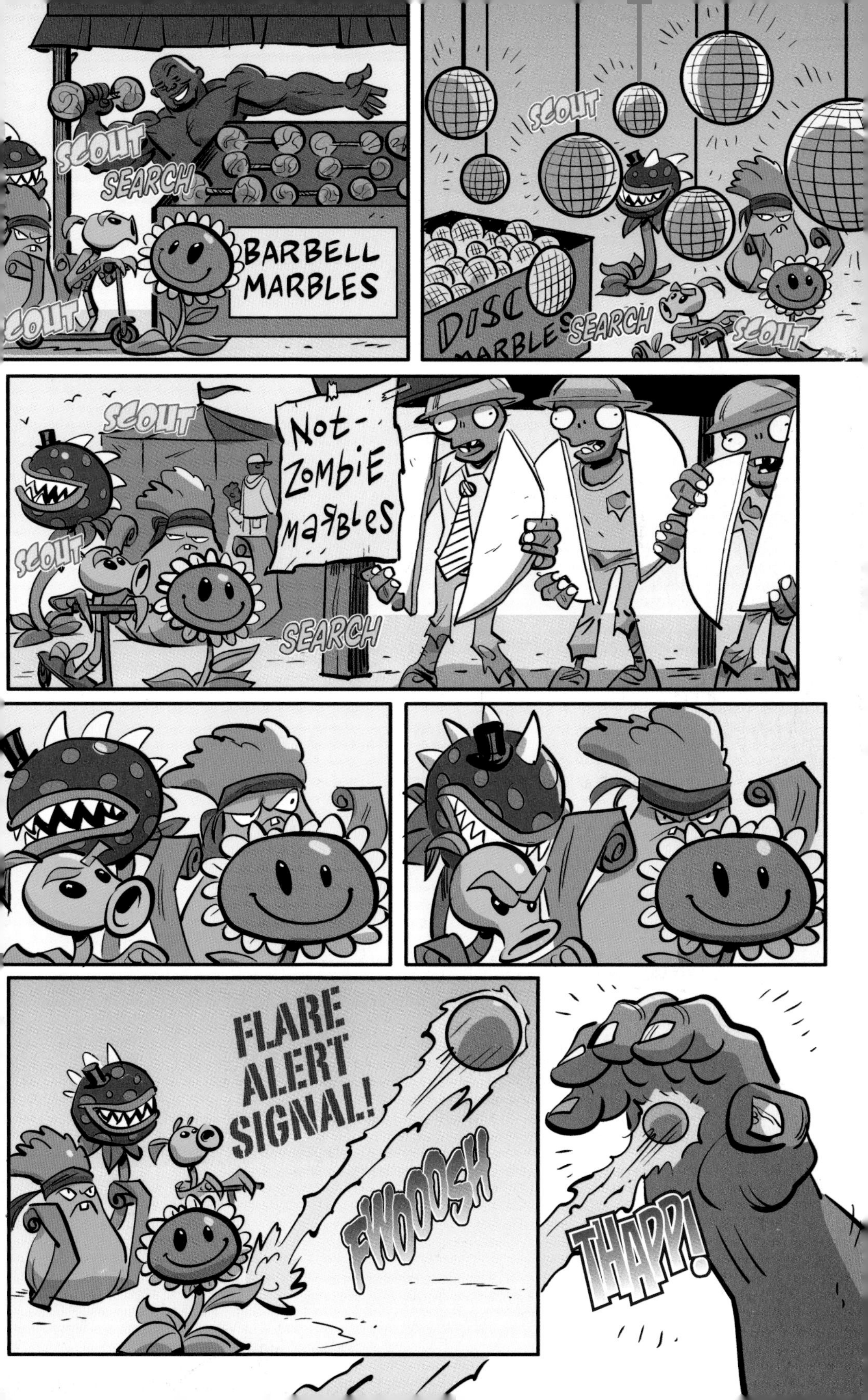
SCOUT
SEARCH
BARBELL MARBLES
SCOUT
SCOUT
DISC MARBLES
SEARCH
SCOUT
SCOUT
Not-Zombie Marbles
SCOUT
SEARCH
FLARE ALERT SIGNAL!
FWOOOSH
THAPP!

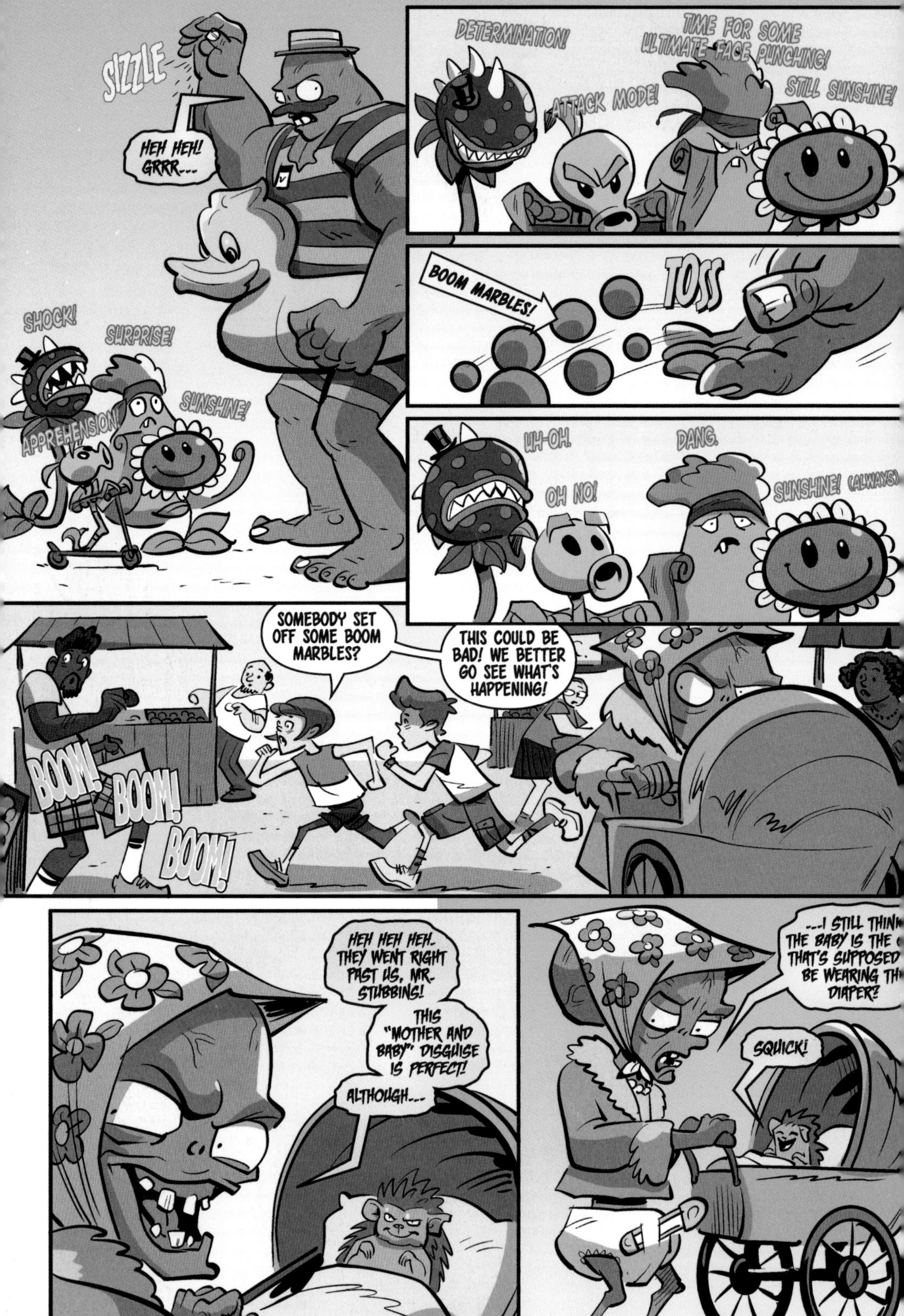
SIZZLE
HEH HEH! GRRR...
SHOCK!
SURPRISE!
APPREHENSION!
SUNSHINE!
DETERMINATION!
TIME FOR SOME ULTIMATE FACE PUNCHING!
ATTACK MODE!
STILL SUNSHINE!
BOOM MARBLES!
TOSS
UH-OH.
DANG.
OH NO!
SUNSHINE! (ALWAYS)
SOMEBODY SET OFF SOME BOOM MARBLES?
THIS COULD BE BAD! WE BETTER GO SEE WHAT'S HAPPENING!
BOOM!
BOOM!
BOOM!
HEH HEH HEH. THEY WENT RIGHT PAST US, MR. STUBBINS!
THIS "MOTHER AND BABY" DISGUISE IS PERFECT!
ALTHOUGH...
SQUICK!

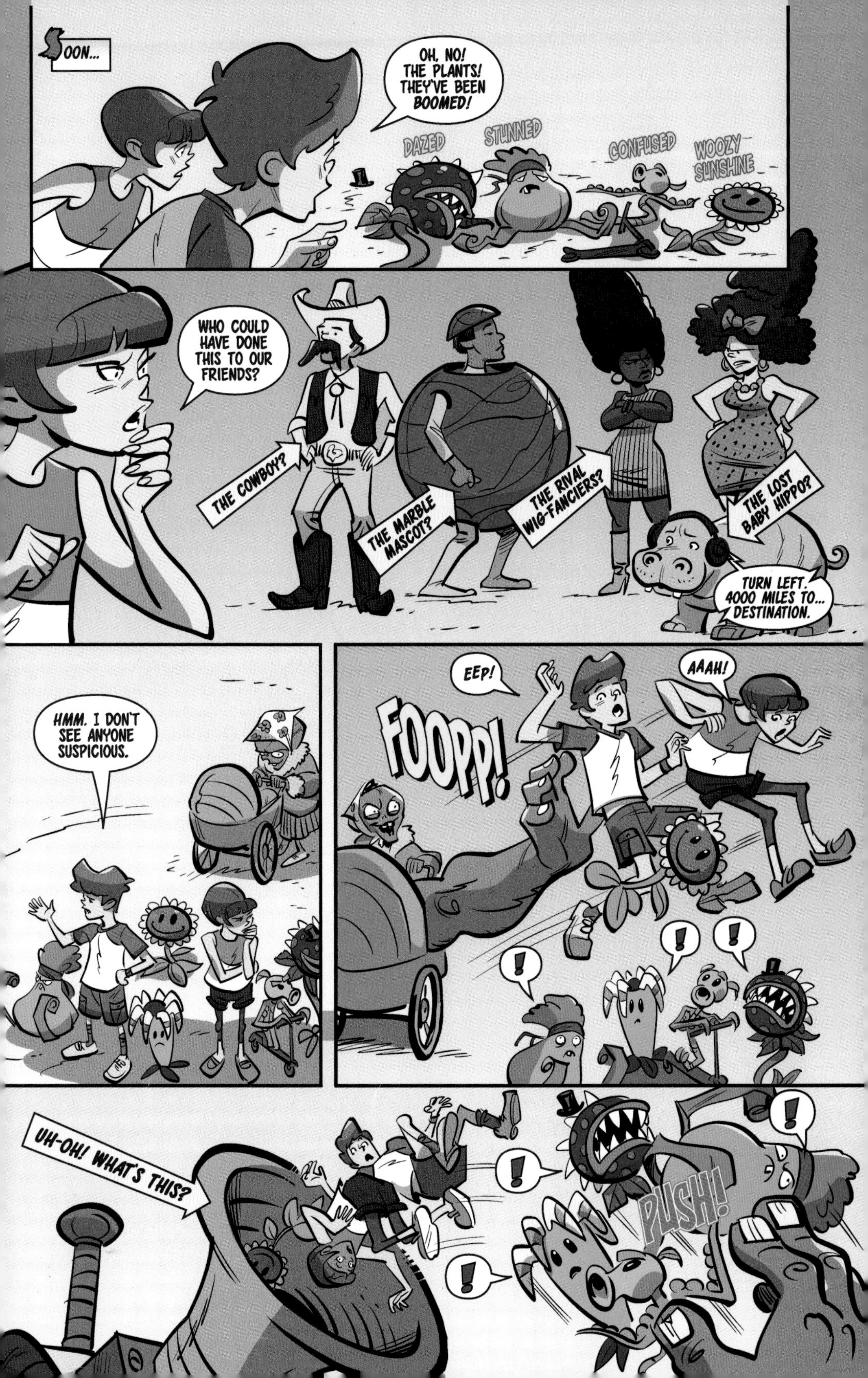
SOON...
OH, NO! THE PLANTS! THEY'VE BEEN BOOMED!
DAZED
STUNNED
CONFUSED
WOOZY SUNSHINE
WHO COULD HAVE DONE THIS TO OUR FRIENDS?
THE COWBOY?
THE MARBLE MASCOT?
THE RIVAL WIG-FANCIERS?
THE LOST BABY HIPPO?
TURN LEFT. 4000 MILES TO... DESTINATION.
HMM. I DON'T SEE ANYONE SUSPICIOUS.
EEP!
AAAH!
FOOPP!
!
!
!
UH-OH! WHAT'S THIS?
!
!
!
PUSH!

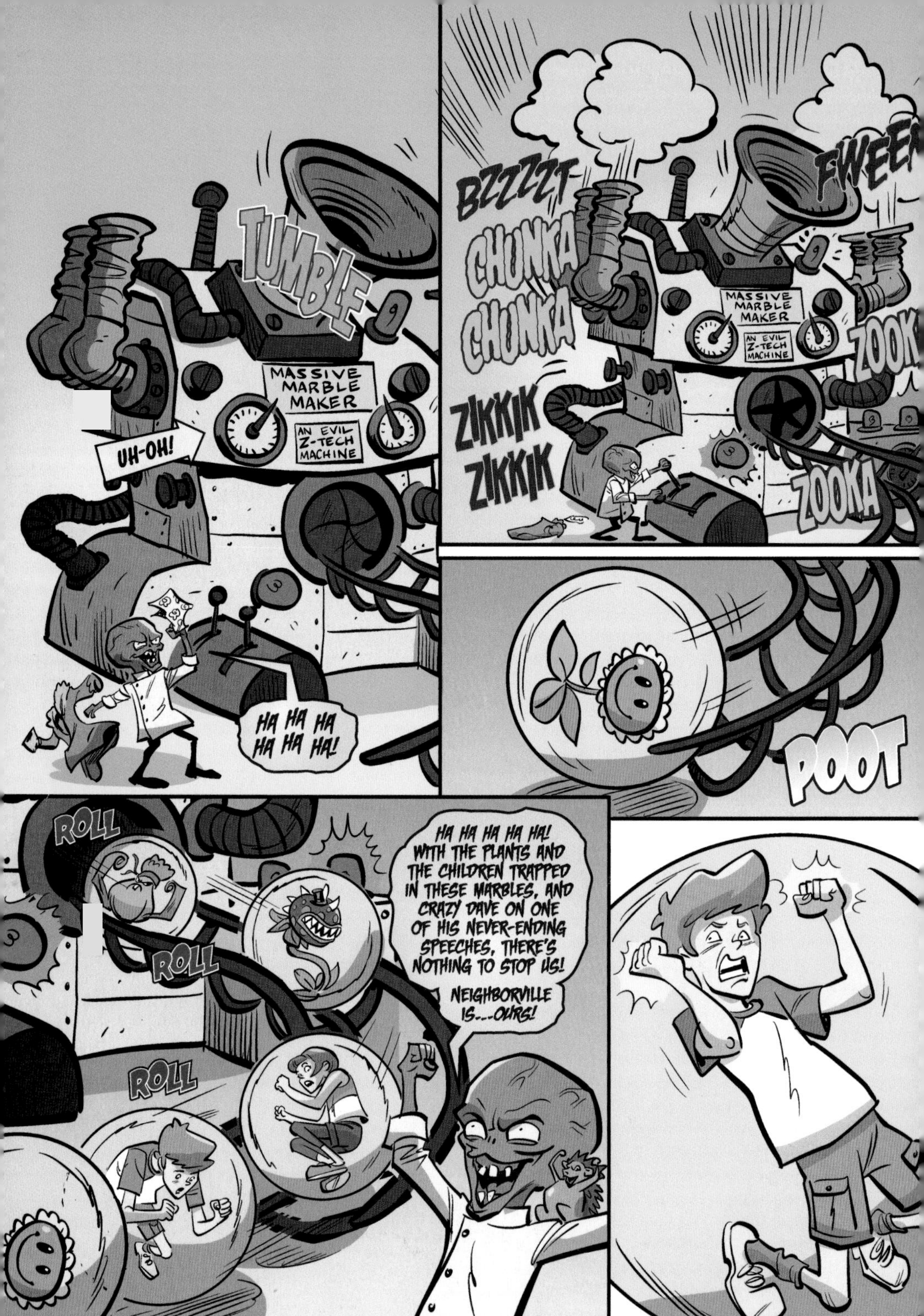
TUMBLE
MASSIVE MARBLE MAKER
AN EVIL Z-TECH MACHINE
UH-OH!
HA HA HA HA HA HA!
BZZZZT
CHUNKA CHUNKA
ZIKKIK ZIKKIK
MASSIVE MARBLE MAKER
AN EVIL Z-TECH MACHINE
FWEE
ZOOK
ZOOKA
POOT
ROLL
ROLL
ROLL
HA HA HA HA HA! WITH THE PLANTS AND THE CHILDREN TRAPPED IN THESE MARBLES, AND CRAZY DAVE ON ONE OF HIS NEVER-ENDING SPEECHES, THERE'S NOTHING TO STOP US!
NEIGHBORVILLE IS...OURS!

UH OH! BAD ENDING!

Go back to page 19 and try again!

Continued from page 19:

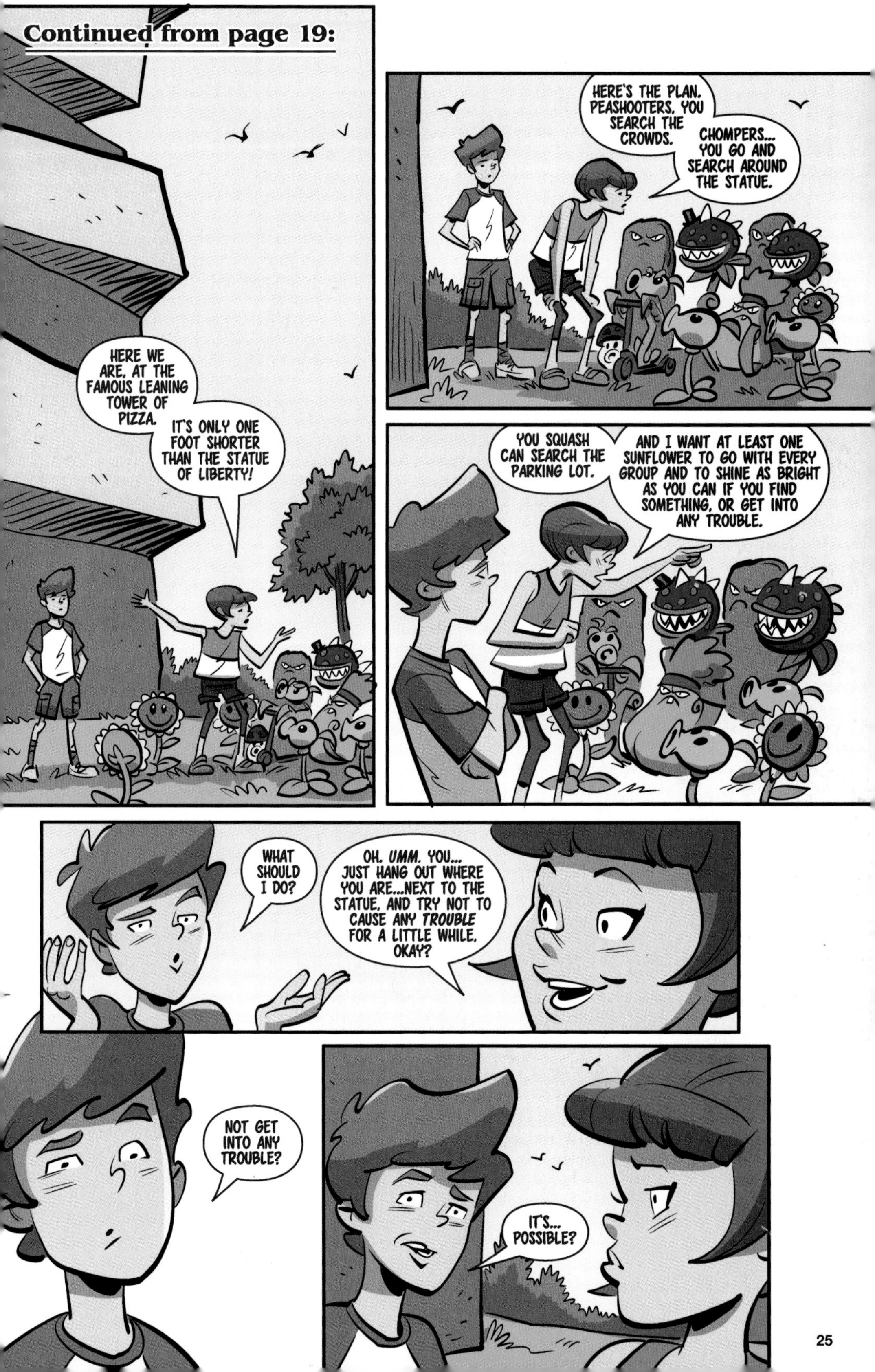
HERE WE ARE, AT THE FAMOUS LEANING TOWER OF PIZZA.
IT'S ONLY ONE FOOT SHORTER THAN THE STATUE OF LIBERTY!
HERE'S THE PLAN. PEASHOOTERS, YOU SEARCH THE CROWDS.
CHOMPERS... YOU GO AND SEARCH AROUND THE STATUE.
YOU SQUASH CAN SEARCH THE PARKING LOT.
AND I WANT AT LEAST ONE SUNFLOWER TO GO WITH EVERY GROUP AND TO SHINE AS BRIGHT AS YOU CAN IF YOU FIND SOMETHING, OR GET INTO ANY TROUBLE.
WHAT SHOULD I DO?
OH, UMM. YOU... JUST HANG OUT WHERE YOU ARE...NEXT TO THE STATUE, AND TRY NOT TO CAUSE ANY TROUBLE FOR A LITTLE WHILE, OKAY?
NOT GET INTO ANY TROUBLE?
IT'S... POSSIBLE?

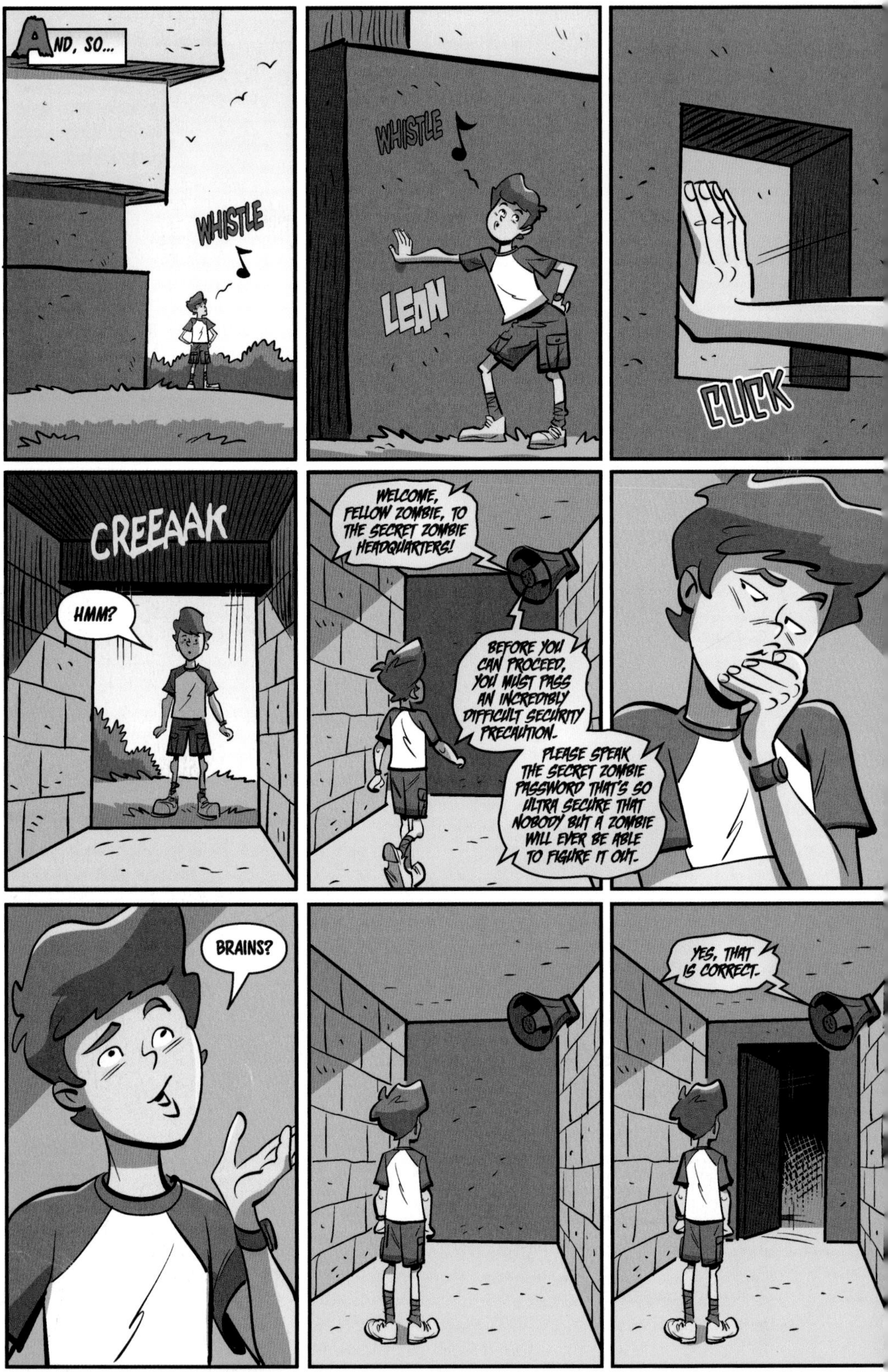
AND, SO...
WHISTLE
WHISTLE
LEAN
CLICK
CREEAAK
HMM?
WELCOME, FELLOW ZOMBIE, TO THE SECRET ZOMBIE HEADQUARTERS!
BEFORE YOU CAN PROCEED, YOU MUST PASS AN INCREDIBLY DIFFICULT SECURITY PRECAUTION.
PLEASE SPEAK THE SECRET ZOMBIE PASSWORD THAT'S SO ULTRA SECURE THAT NOBODY BUT A ZOMBIE WILL EVER BE ABLE TO FIGURE IT OUT.
BRAINS?
YES, THAT IS CORRECT.

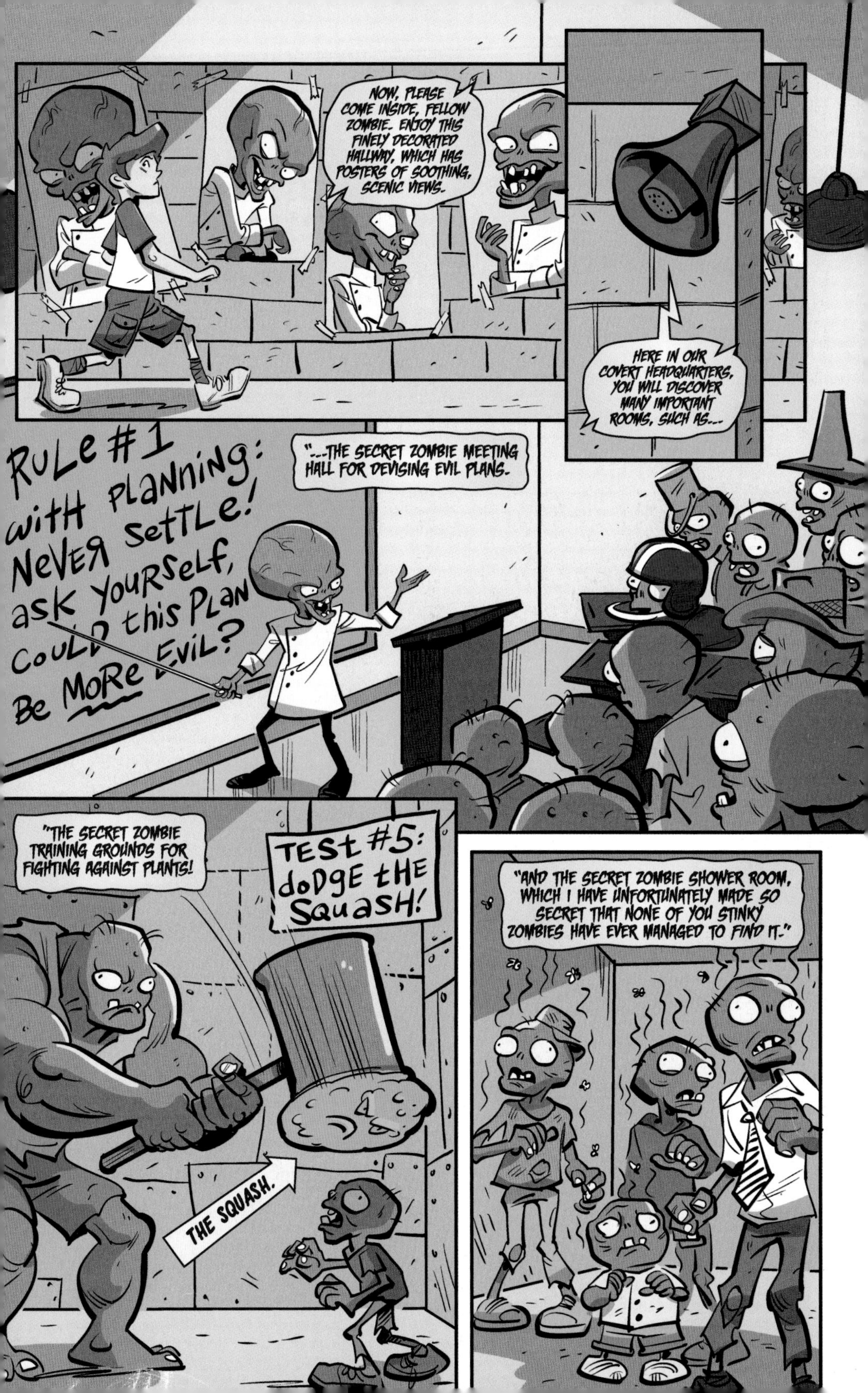

NOW, PLEASE COME INSIDE, FELLOW ZOMBIE. ENJOY THIS FINELY DECORATED HALLWAY, WHICH HAS POSTERS OF SOOTHING, SCENIC VIEWS.
HERE IN OUR COVERT HEADQUARTERS, YOU WILL DISCOVER MANY IMPORTANT ROOMS, SUCH AS...
"...THE SECRET ZOMBIE MEETING HALL FOR DEVISING EVIL PLANS.
RULE #1 with PLANNING: NEVER settLe! ask YOURSELF, COULD this PLAN Be MORE EVIL?
"THE SECRET ZOMBIE TRAINING GROUNDS FOR FIGHTING AGAINST PLANTS!
TEST #5: dodge tHE SQUASH!
THE SQUASH.
"AND THE SECRET ZOMBIE SHOWER ROOM, WHICH I HAVE UNFORTUNATELY MADE SO SECRET THAT NONE OF YOU STINKY ZOMBIES HAVE EVER MANAGED TO FIND IT."

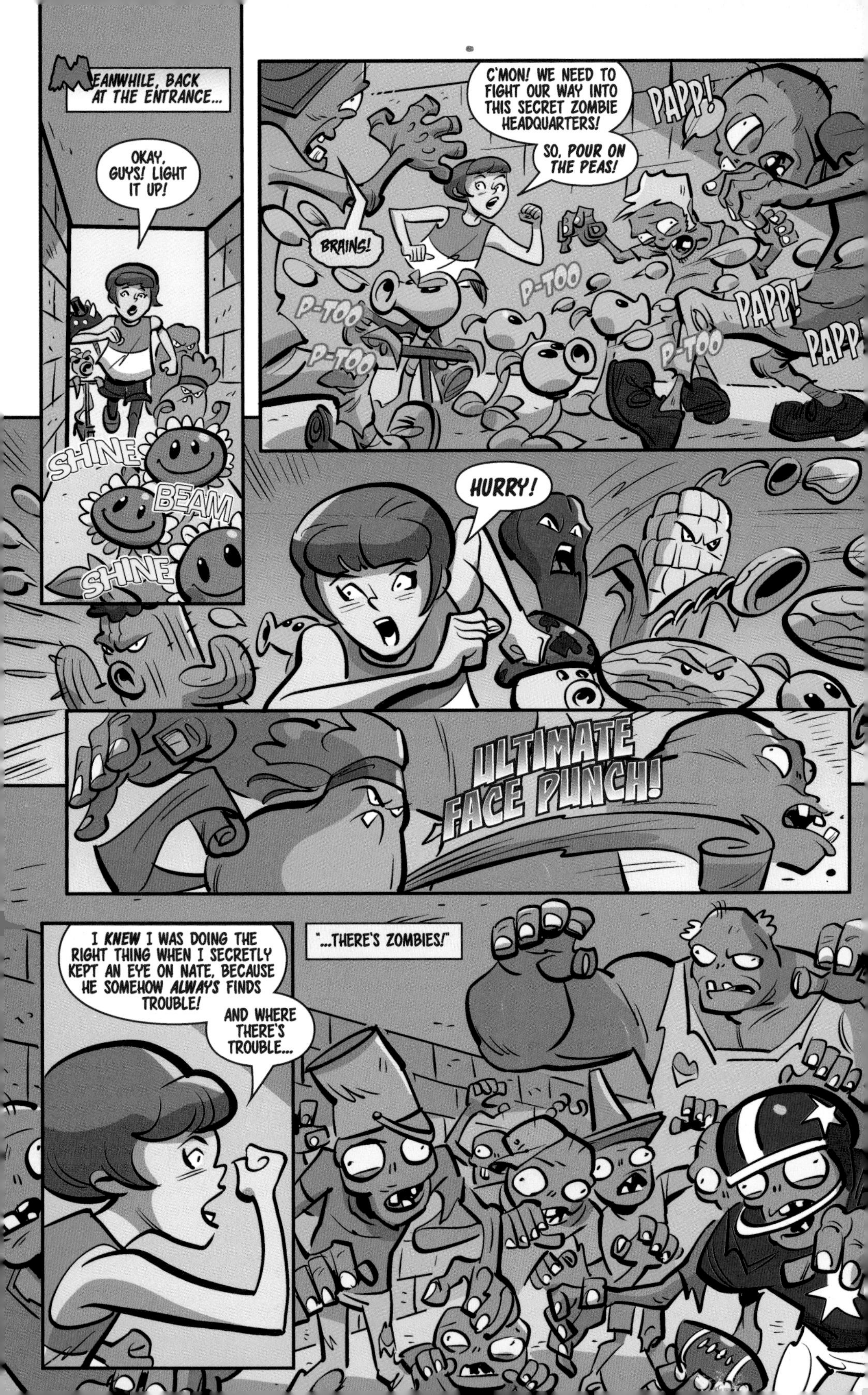
MEANWHILE, BACK AT THE ENTRANCE...
OKAY, GUYS! LIGHT IT UP!
SHINE
BEAM
SHINE
C'MON! WE NEED TO FIGHT OUR WAY INTO THIS SECRET ZOMBIE HEADQUARTERS!
SO, POUR ON THE PEAS!
BRAINS!
PAPP!
P-TOO
P-TOO
P-TOO
P-TOO
PAPP!
PAPP!
HURRY!
ULTIMATE FACE PUNCH!
I KNEW I WAS DOING THE RIGHT THING WHEN I SECRETLY KEPT AN EYE ON NATE, BECAUSE HE SOMEHOW ALWAYS FINDS TROUBLE!
AND WHERE THERE'S TROUBLE...
"...THERE'S ZOMBIES!"

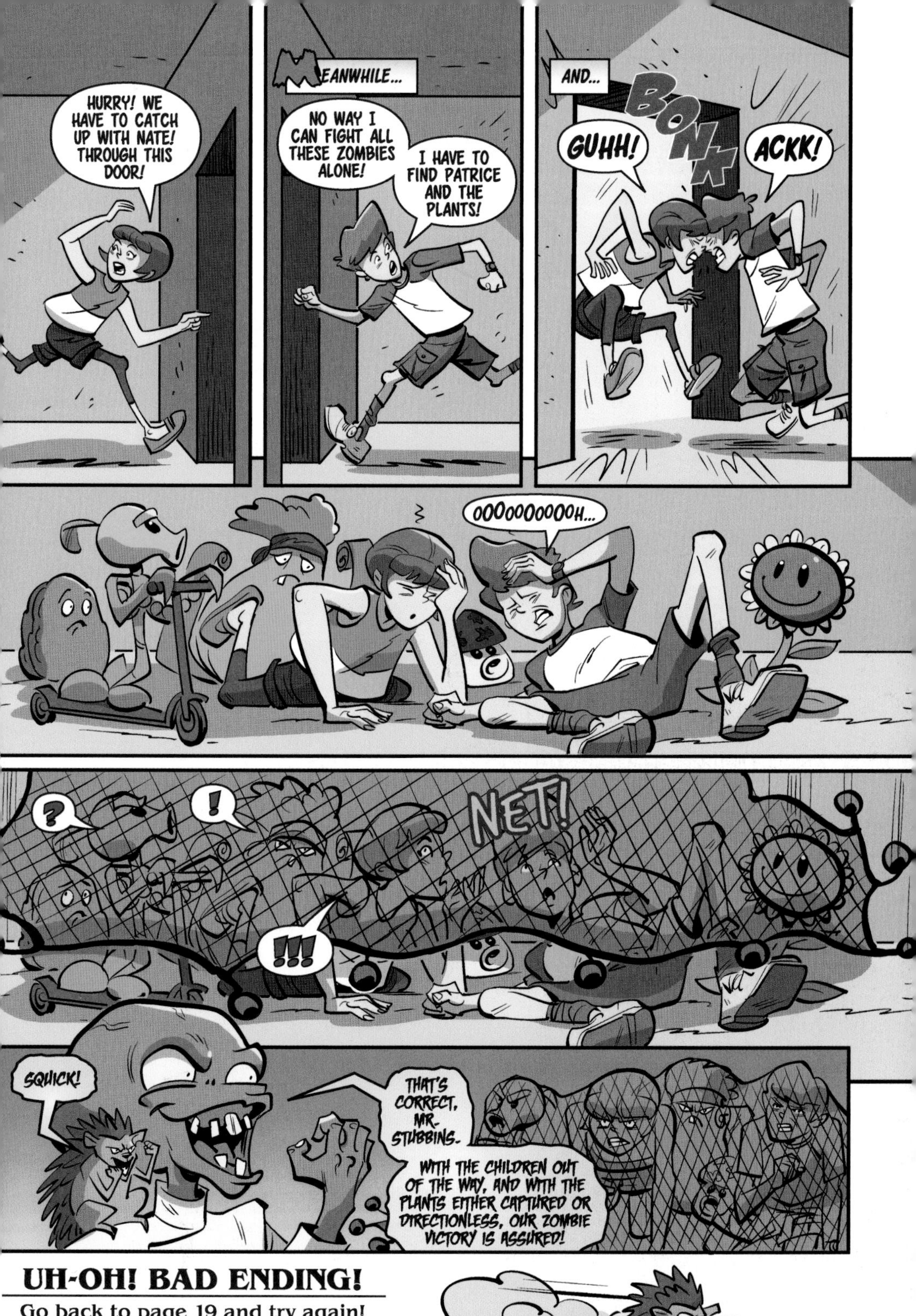
HURRY! WE HAVE TO CATCH UP WITH NATE! THROUGH THIS DOOR!
MEANWHILE...
NO WAY I CAN FIGHT ALL THESE ZOMBIES ALONE!
I HAVE TO FIND PATRICE AND THE PLANTS!
AND...
BONK
GUHH!
ACKK!
OOOOOOOOOOH...
?
!
NET!
!!!
SQUICK!
THAT'S CORRECT, MR. STUBBINS.
WITH THE CHILDREN OUT OF THE WAY, AND WITH THE PLANTS EITHER CAPTURED OR DIRECTIONLESS, OUR ZOMBIE VICTORY IS ASSURED!

UH-OH! BAD ENDING!

Go back to page 19 and try again!
(Unless you're on the zombies' side, in which case, you win! **BUT WHY ARE YOU ON THE ZOMBIES' SIDE?!?!?)**

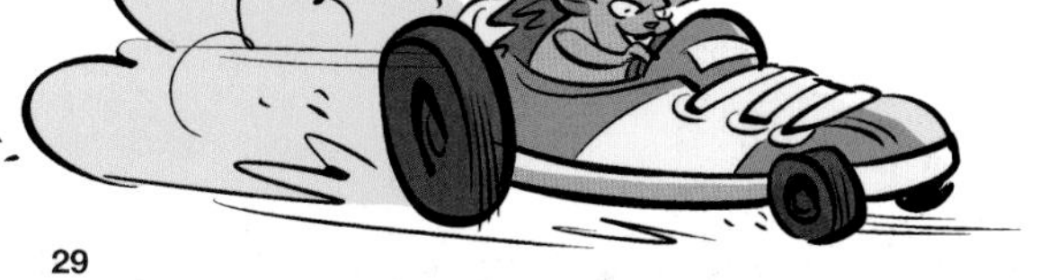

Continued from page 19:

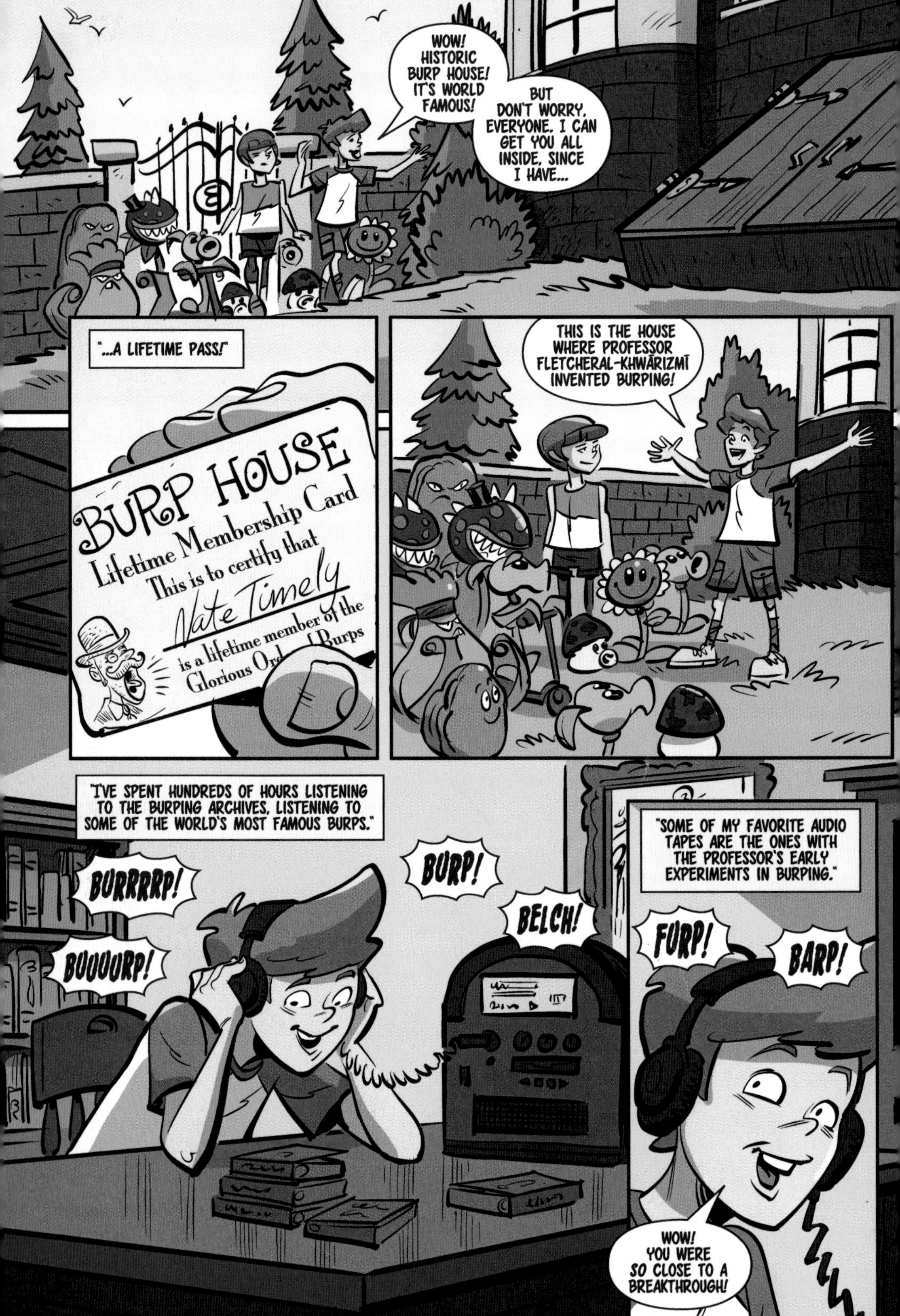
WOW! HISTORIC BURP HOUSE! IT'S WORLD FAMOUS!
BUT DON'T WORRY, EVERYONE. I CAN GET YOU ALL INSIDE, SINCE I HAVE...
"...A LIFETIME PASS!"
BURP HOUSE
Lifetime Membership Card
This is to certify that
Nate Timely
is a lifetime member of the
Glorious Ord l Burps
THIS IS THE HOUSE WHERE PROFESSOR FLETCHERAL-KHWĀRIZMĪ INVENTED BURPING!
"I'VE SPENT HUNDREDS OF HOURS LISTENING TO THE BURPING ARCHIVES, LISTENING TO SOME OF THE WORLD'S MOST FAMOUS BURPS."
BURRRRP!
BURP!
BELCH!
BUUUURP!
"SOME OF MY FAVORITE AUDIO TAPES ARE THE ONES WITH THE PROFESSOR'S EARLY EXPERIMENTS IN BURPING."
FURP!
BARP!
WOW! YOU WERE SO CLOSE TO A BREAKTHROUGH!

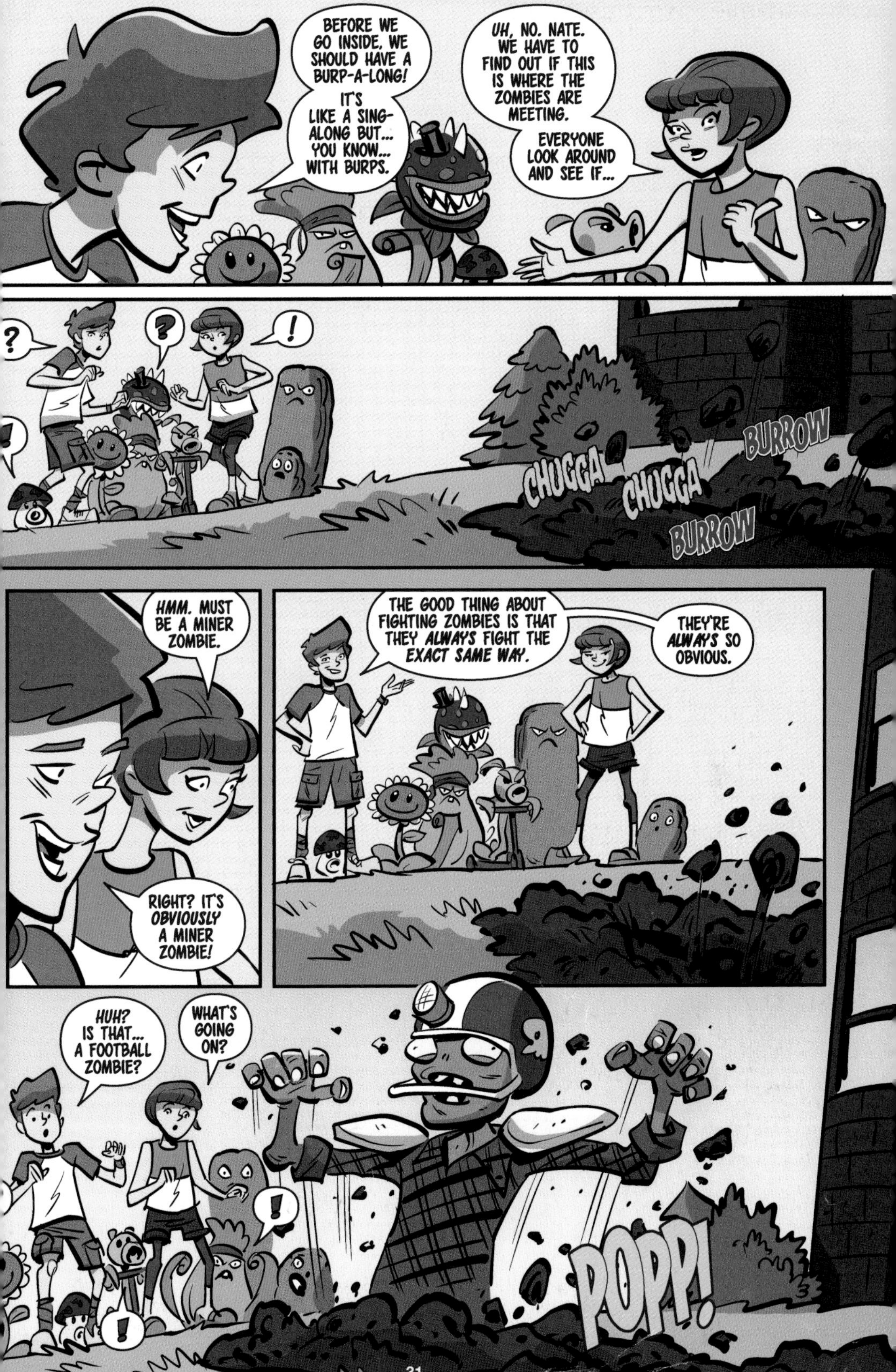
BEFORE WE GO INSIDE, WE SHOULD HAVE A BURP-A-LONG!
IT'S LIKE A SING-ALONG BUT... YOU KNOW... WITH BURPS.
UH, NO. NATE. WE HAVE TO FIND OUT IF THIS IS WHERE THE ZOMBIES ARE MEETING.
EVERYONE LOOK AROUND AND SEE IF...
?
?
!
!
CHUGGA
CHUGGA
BURROW
BURROW
HMM. MUST BE A MINER ZOMBIE.
RIGHT? IT'S OBVIOUSLY A MINER ZOMBIE!
THE GOOD THING ABOUT FIGHTING ZOMBIES IS THAT THEY ALWAYS FIGHT THE EXACT SAME WAY.
THEY'RE ALWAYS SO OBVIOUS.
HUH? IS THAT... A FOOTBALL ZOMBIE?
WHAT'S GOING ON?
!
!
POPP!

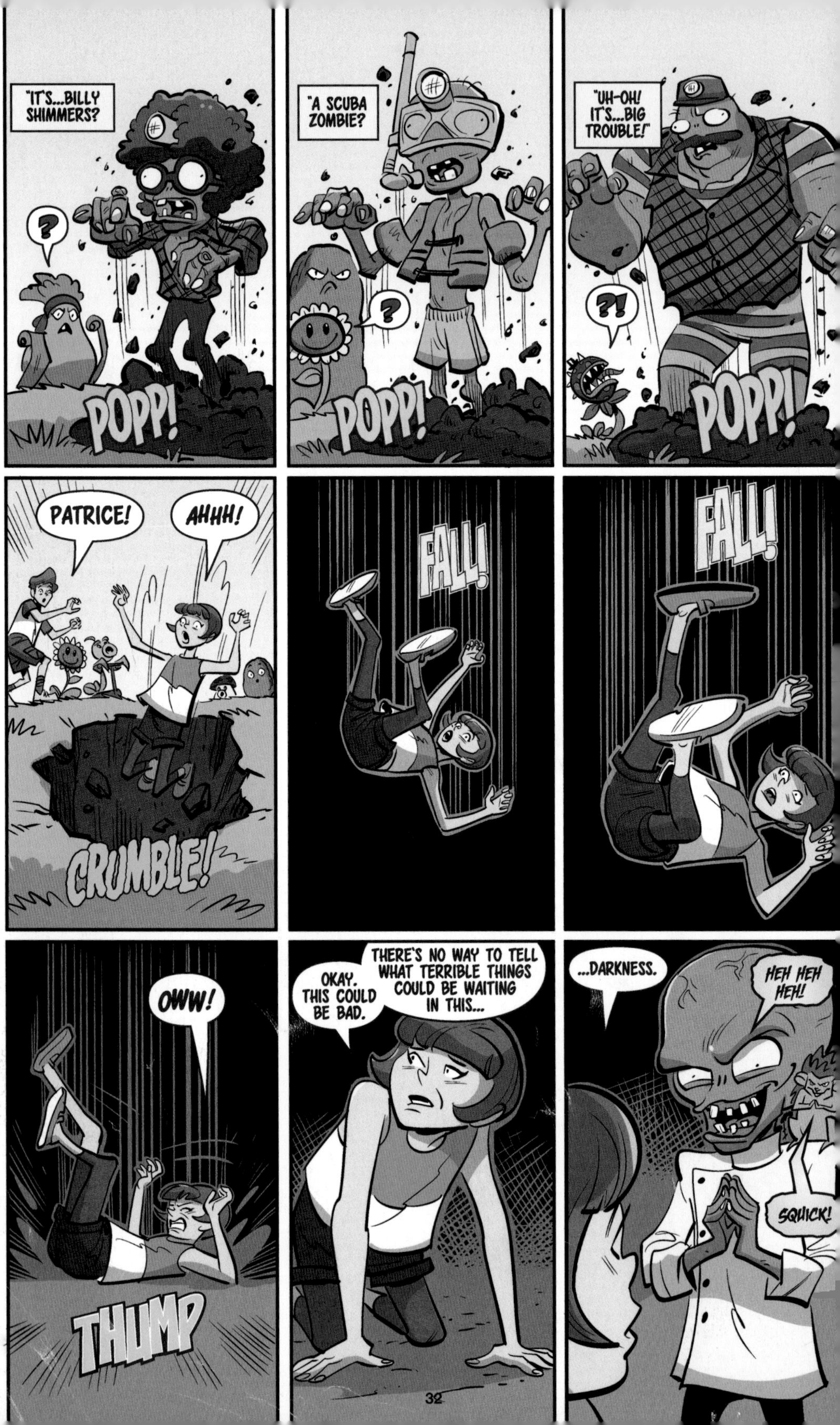
"IT'S...BILLY SHIMMERS?
?
POPP!
"A SCUBA ZOMBIE?
?
POPP!
"UH-OH! IT'S...BIG TROUBLE!"
?!
POPP!
PATRICE!
AHHH!
CRUMBLE!
FALL!
FALL!
OWW!
THUMP
OKAY. THIS COULD BE BAD.
THERE'S NO WAY TO TELL WHAT TERRIBLE THINGS COULD BE WAITING IN THIS...
...DARKNESS.
HEH HEH HEH!
SQUICK!

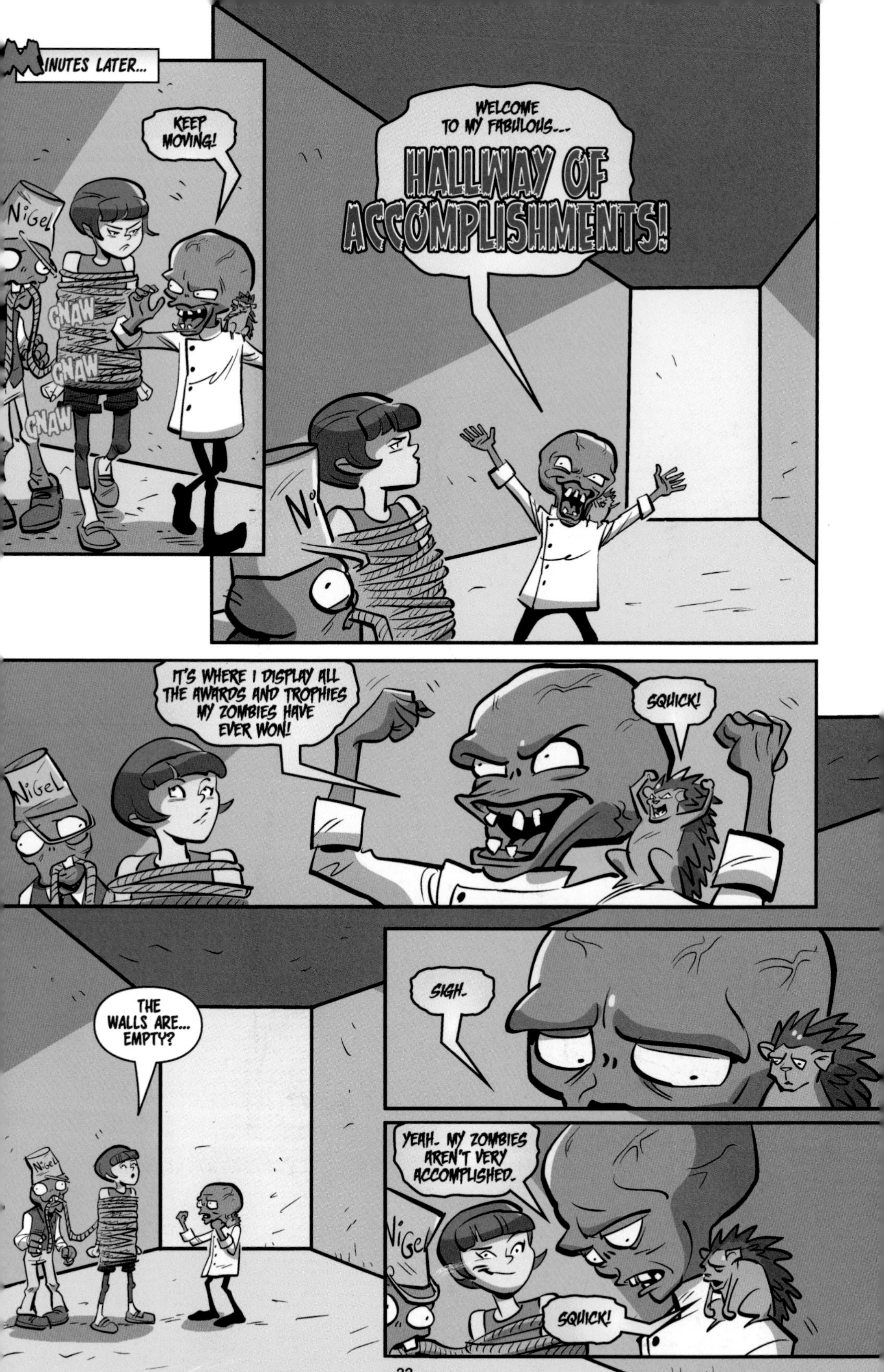
MINUTES LATER...
KEEP MOVING!
GNAW
GNAW
GNAW
WELCOME TO MY FABULOUS...
HALLWAY OF ACCOMPLISHMENTS!
IT'S WHERE I DISPLAY ALL THE AWARDS AND TROPHIES MY ZOMBIES HAVE EVER WON!
SQUICK!
THE WALLS ARE... EMPTY?
SIGH.
YEAH. MY ZOMBIES AREN'T VERY ACCOMPLISHED.
SQUICK!

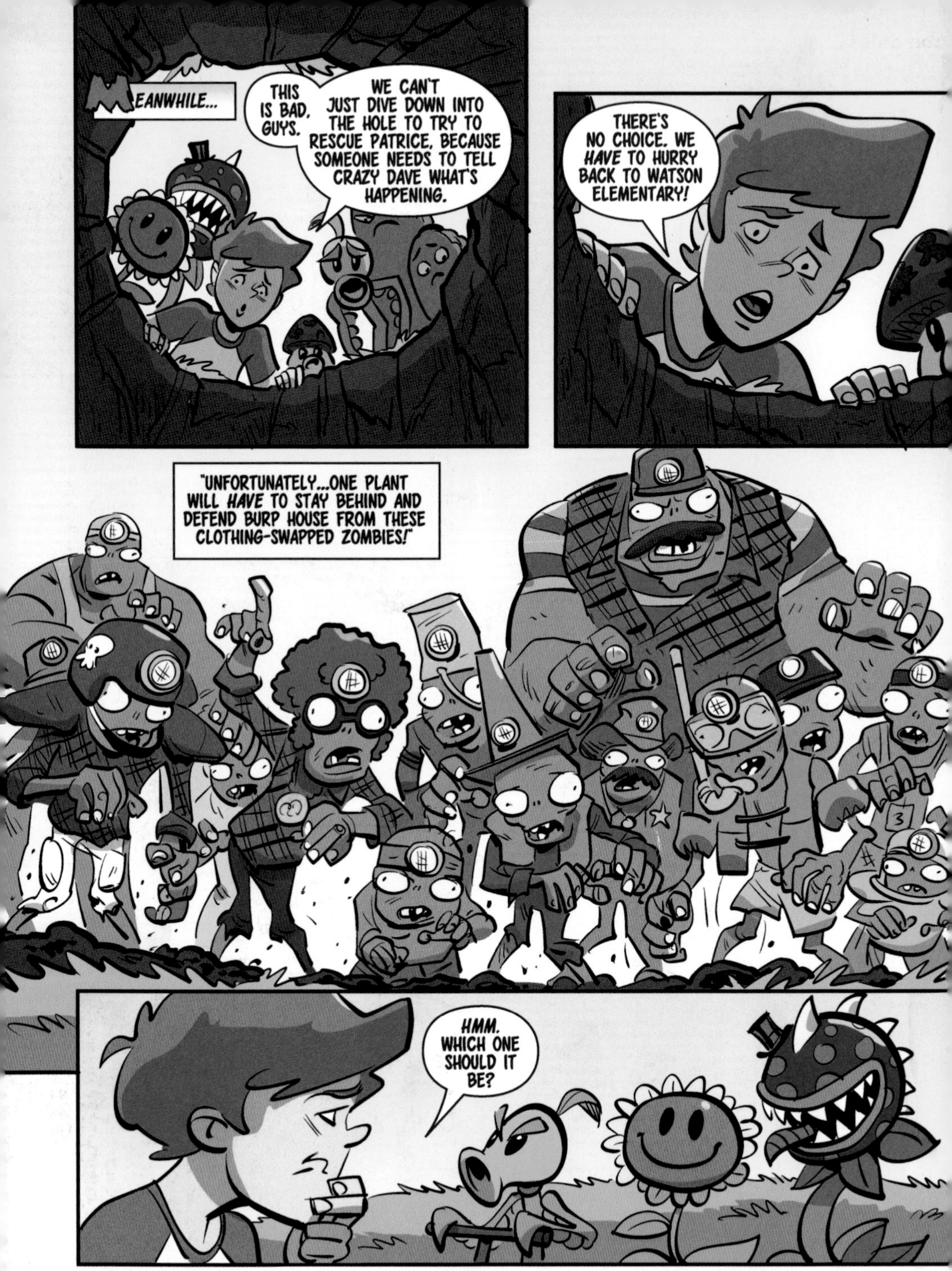
MEANWHILE...
THIS IS BAD, GUYS.
WE CAN'T JUST DIVE DOWN INTO THE HOLE TO TRY TO RESCUE PATRICE, BECAUSE SOMEONE NEEDS TO TELL CRAZY DAVE WHAT'S HAPPENING.
THERE'S NO CHOICE. WE *HAVE* TO HURRY BACK TO WATSON ELEMENTARY!
"UNFORTUNATELY...ONE PLANT WILL *HAVE* TO STAY BEHIND AND DEFEND BURP HOUSE FROM THESE CLOTHING-SWAPPED ZOMBIES!"
HMM. WHICH ONE SHOULD IT BE?

FIND THE GARDEN PATH:

Help Nate choose ONE plant to stay behind and fight the strange zombies!

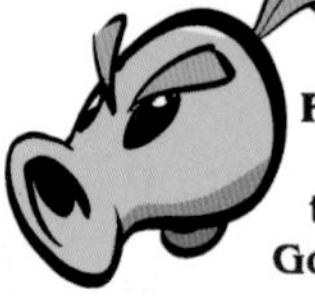

PEASHOOTER
(Let's give this a shot!):
Go to next page!

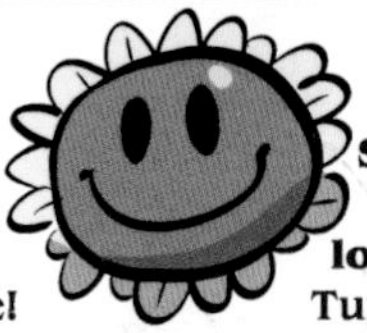

SUNFLOWER
(The future looks bright!):
Turn to page 36!

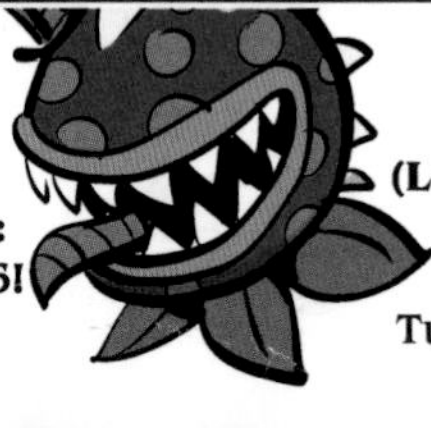

CHOMPER
(Let's take a bite out of those zombies!):
Turn to page 37

You chose...
PEASHOOTER!

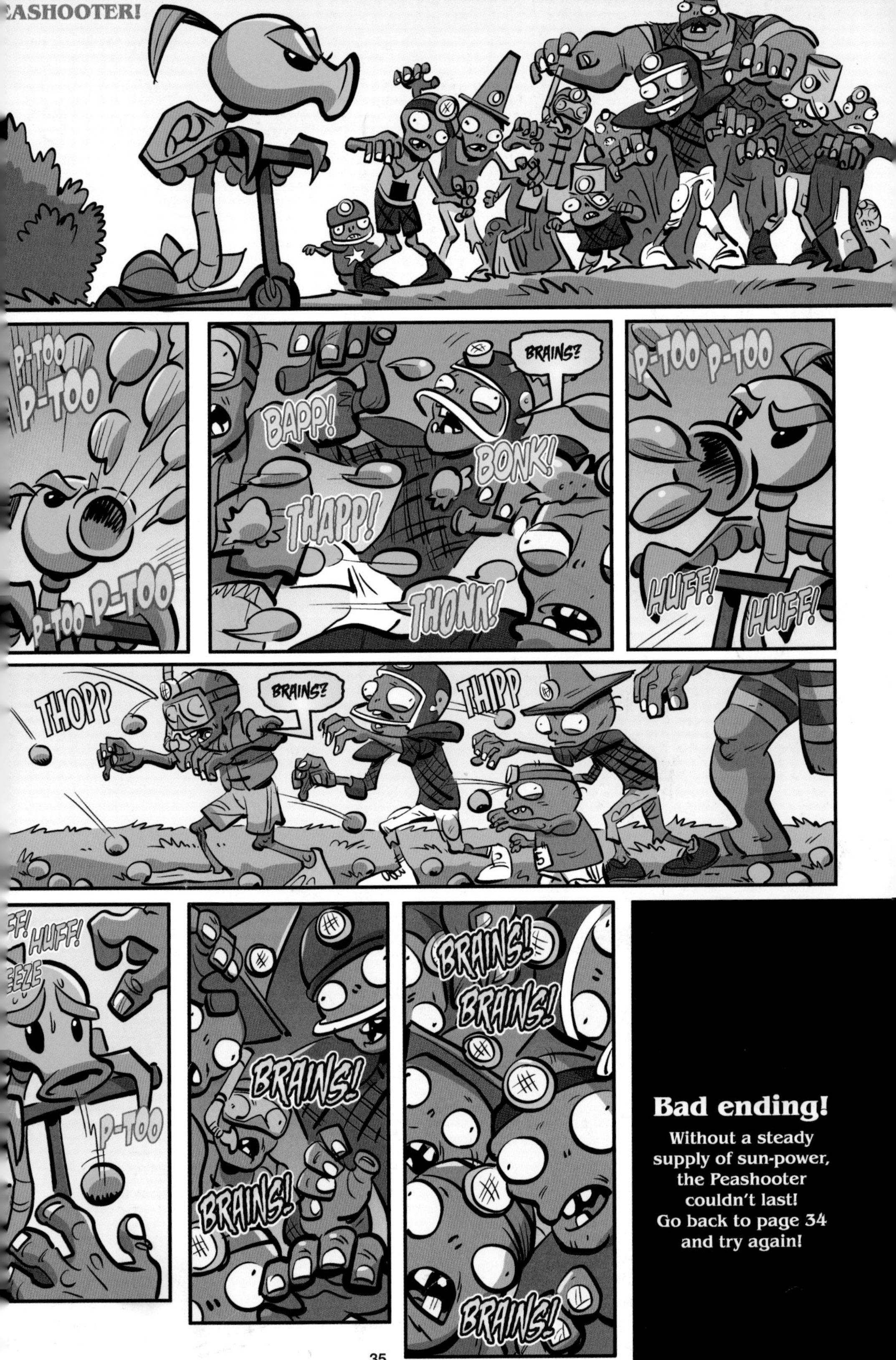

P-TOO
P-TOO
P-TOO P-TOO
BAPP!
BRAINS?
BONK!
THAPP!
THONK!
P-TOO P-TOO
HUFF!
HUFF!
THOPP
BRAINS?
THIPP
HUFF!
P-TOO
BRAINS!
BRAINS!
BRAINS!
BRAINS!
BRAINS!

Bad ending!

Without a steady supply of sun-power, the Peashooter couldn't last!
Go back to page 34 and try again!

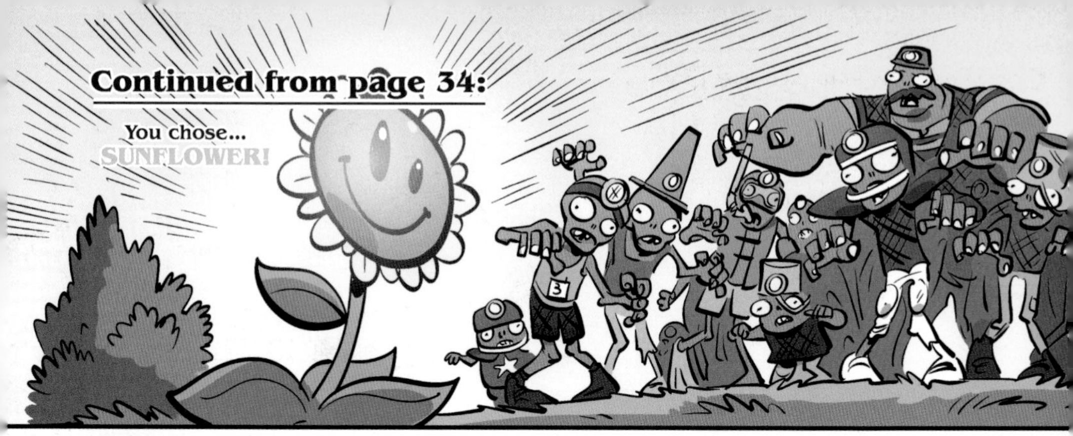
Continued from page 34:
You chose...
SUNFLOWER!

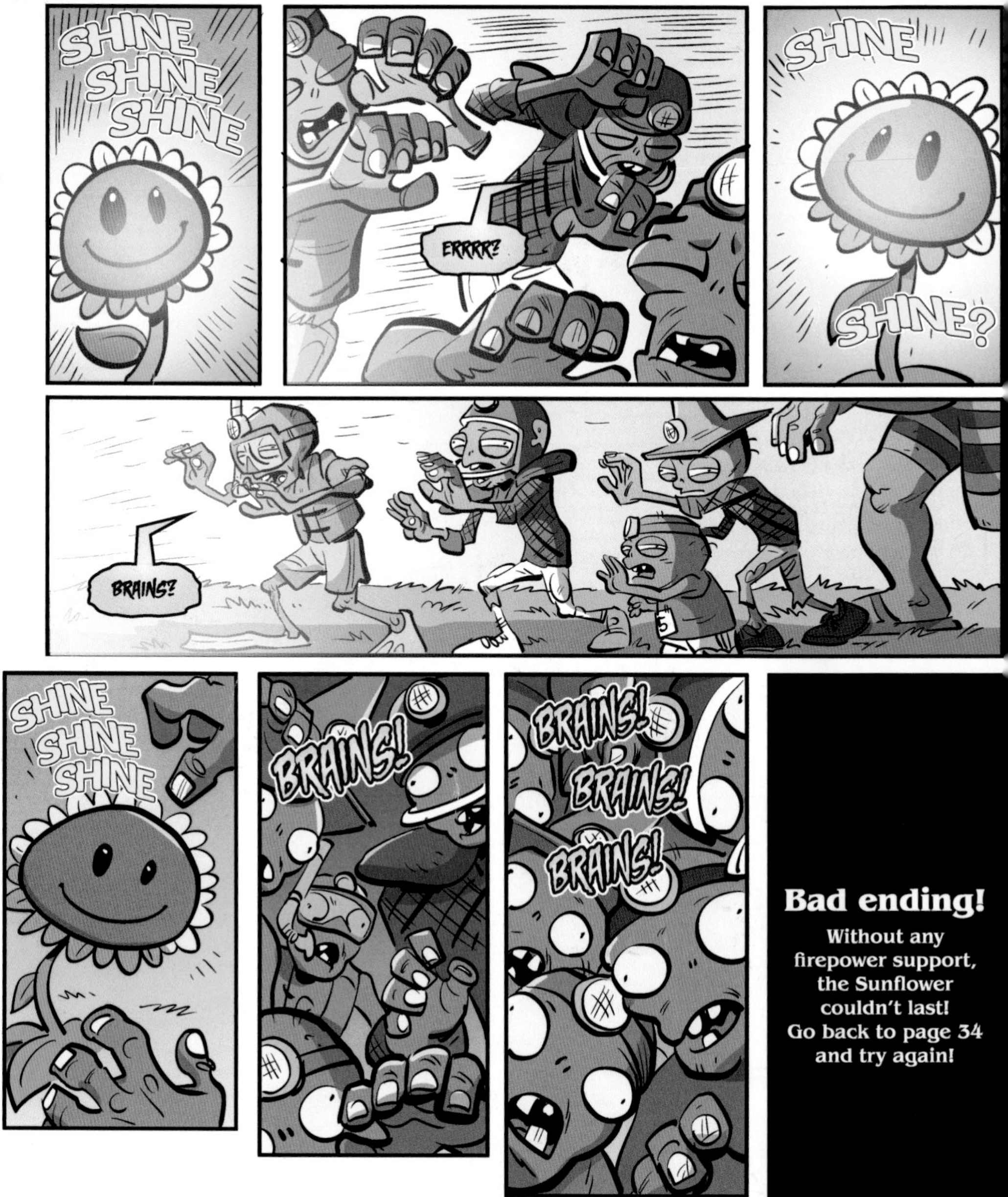
SHINE SHINE SHINE
ERRRR?
SHINE
SHINE?
BRAINS?
SHINE SHINE SHINE
BRAINS!
BRAINS!
BRAINS!
BRAINS!

Bad ending!

Without any firepower support, the Sunflower couldn't last! Go back to page 34 and try again!

Continued from page 34:

You chose...
CHOMPER!

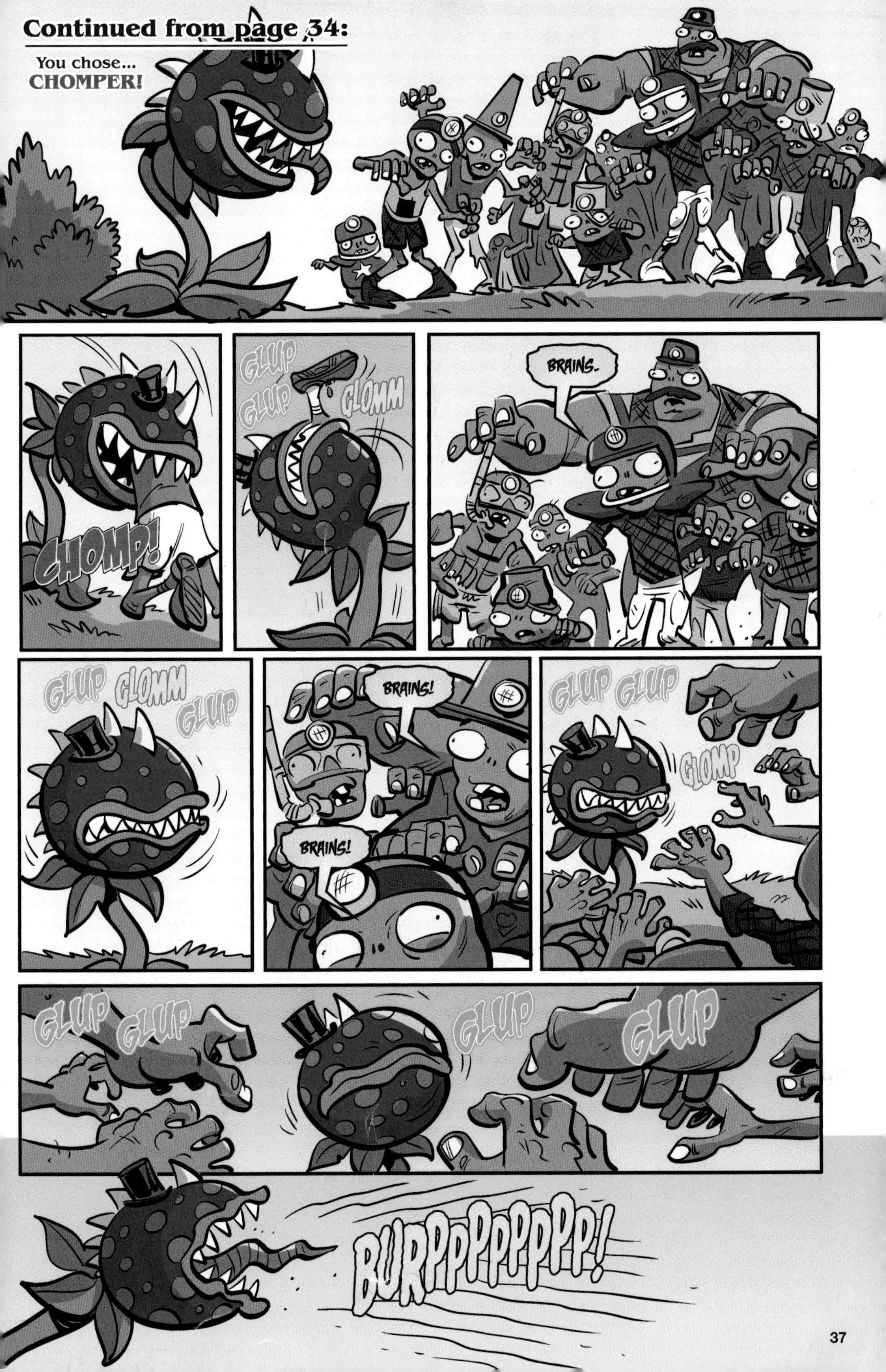

CHOMP!
GLUP
GLUP
GLOMM
BRAINS.
GLUP
GLOMM
GLUP
BRAINS!
BRAINS!
GLUP
GLUP
GLOMP
GLUP
GLUP
GLUP
GLUP
BURPPPPPPPP!

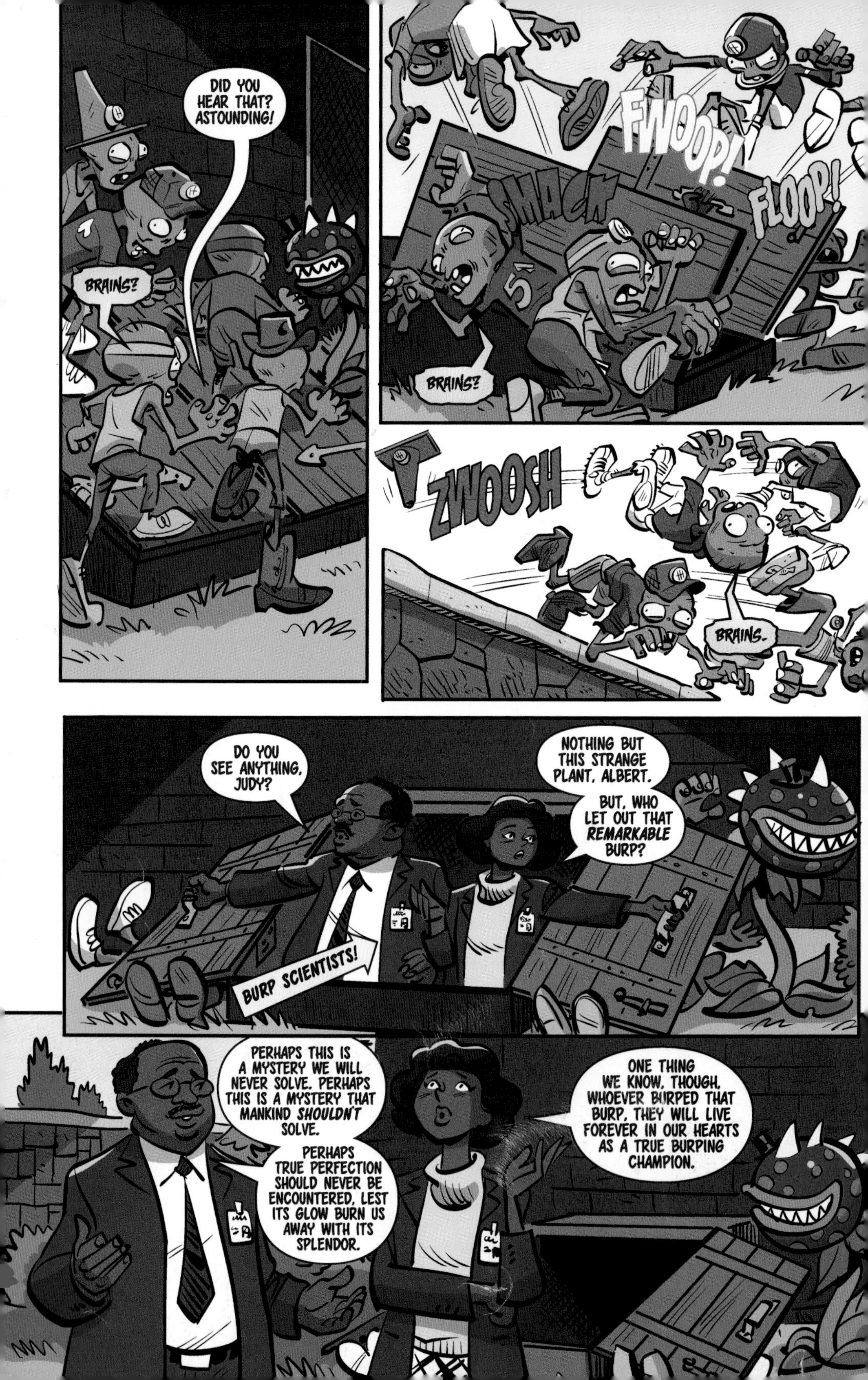
DID YOU HEAR THAT? ASTOUNDING!
BRAINS?
FWOOP!
SMACK
FLOOP!
BRAINS?
ZWOOSH
BRAINS.
DO YOU SEE ANYTHING, JUDY?
NOTHING BUT THIS STRANGE PLANT, ALBERT.
BUT, WHO LET OUT THAT REMARKABLE BURP?
BURP SCIENTISTS!
PERHAPS THIS IS A MYSTERY WE WILL NEVER SOLVE. PERHAPS THIS IS A MYSTERY THAT MANKIND SHOULDN'T SOLVE.
PERHAPS TRUE PERFECTION SHOULD NEVER BE ENCOUNTERED, LEST ITS GLOW BURN US AWAY WITH ITS SPLENDOR.
ONE THING WE KNOW, THOUGH. WHOEVER BURPED THAT BURP, THEY WILL LIVE FOREVER IN OUR HEARTS AS A TRUE BURPING CHAMPION.

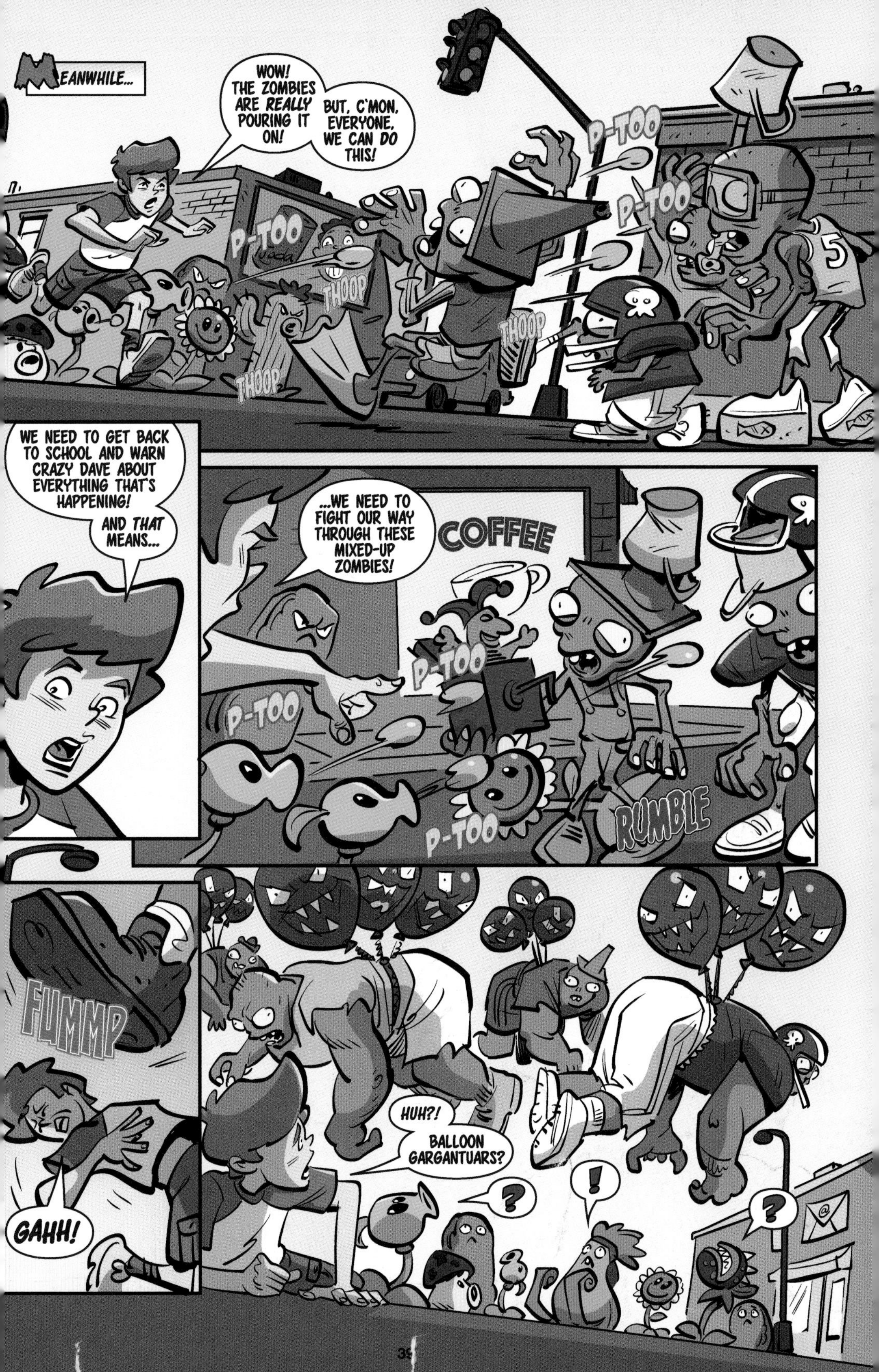
MEANWHILE...
WOW! THE ZOMBIES ARE REALLY POURING IT ON!
BUT, C'MON, EVERYONE, WE CAN DO THIS!
P-TOO
P-TOO
P-TOO
THOOP
THOOP
THOOP
WE NEED TO GET BACK TO SCHOOL AND WARN CRAZY DAVE ABOUT EVERYTHING THAT'S HAPPENING!
AND THAT MEANS...
...WE NEED TO FIGHT OUR WAY THROUGH THESE MIXED-UP ZOMBIES!
COFFEE
P-TOO
P-TOO
P-TOO
RUMBLE
FUMMP
GAHH!
HUH?!
BALLOON GARGANTUARS?
?
!
?

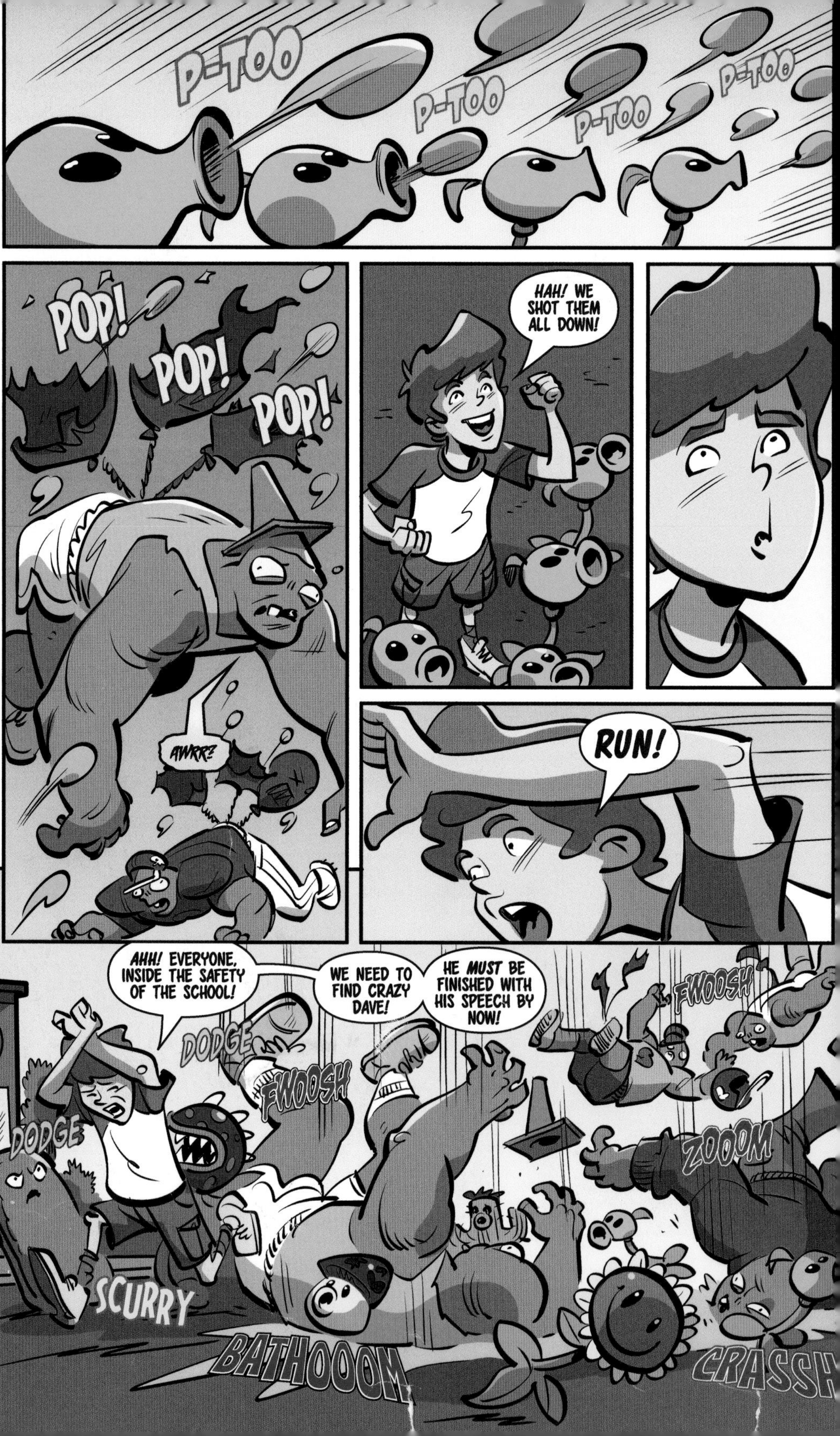
P-TOO
P-TOO
P-TOO
P-TOO
POP!
POP!
POP!
AWRR?
HAH! WE SHOT THEM ALL DOWN!
RUN!
AHH! EVERYONE, INSIDE THE SAFETY OF THE SCHOOL!
WE NEED TO FIND CRAZY DAVE!
HE MUST BE FINISHED WITH HIS SPEECH BY NOW!
DODGE
FWOOSH
FWOOSH
DODGE
ZOOOM
SCURRY
BATHOOOM
CRASSH

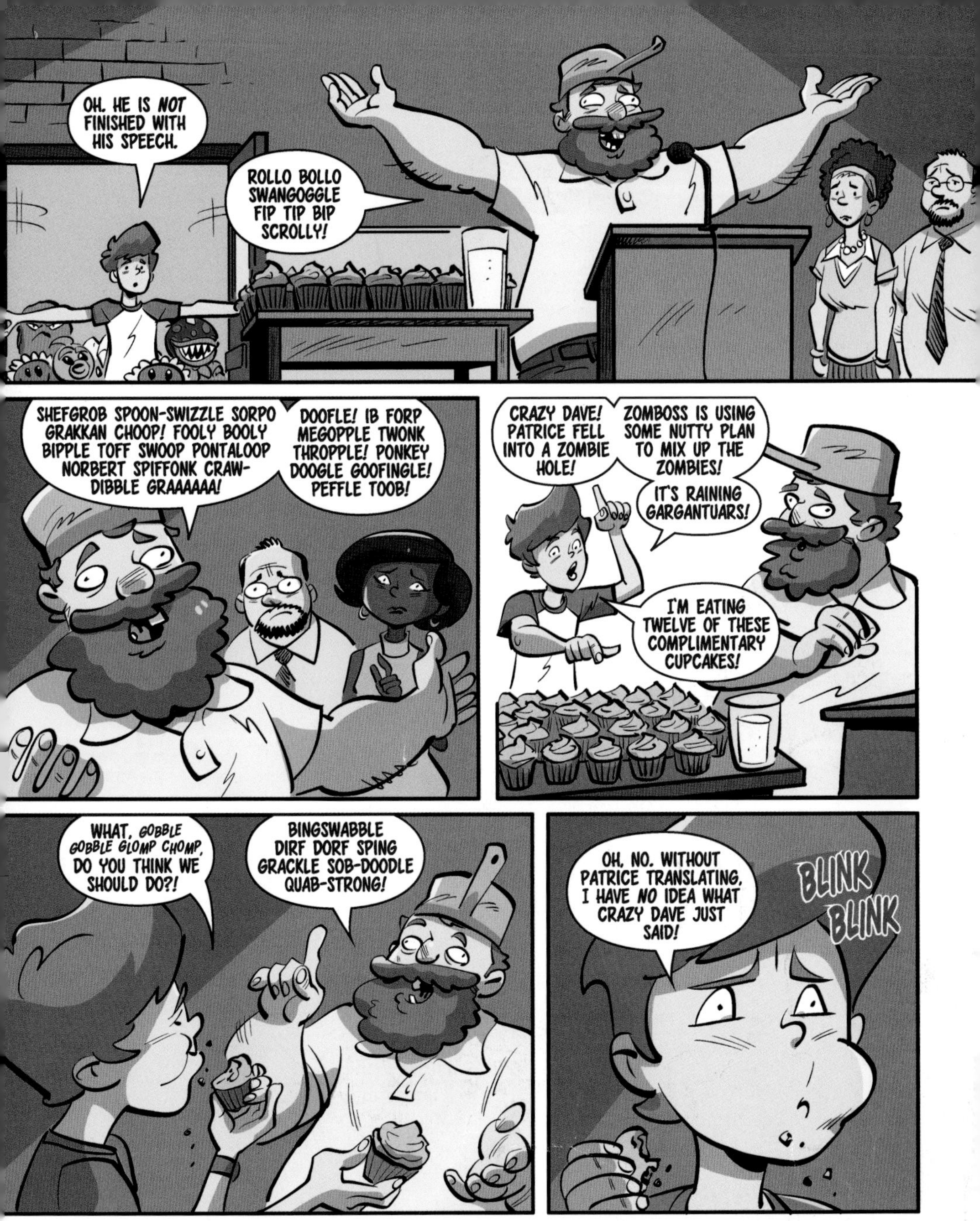
OH, HE IS NOT FINISHED WITH HIS SPEECH.
ROLLO BOLLO SWANGOGGLE FIP TIP BIP SCROLLY!
SHEFGROB SPOON-SWIZZLE SORPO GRAKKAN CHOOP! FOOLY BOOLY BIPPLE TOFF SWOOP PONTALOOP NORBERT SPIFFONK CRAW-DIBBLE GRAAAAAA!
DOOFLE! IB FORP MEGOPPLE TWONK THROPPLE! PONKEY DOOGLE GOOFINGLE! PEFFLE TOOB!
CRAZY DAVE! PATRICE FELL INTO A ZOMBIE HOLE!
ZOMBOSS IS USING SOME NUTTY PLAN TO MIX UP THE ZOMBIES!
IT'S RAINING GARGANTUARS!
I'M EATING TWELVE OF THESE COMPLIMENTARY CUPCAKES!
WHAT, GOBBLE GOBBLE GLOMP CHOMP, DO YOU THINK WE SHOULD DO?!
BINGSWABBLE DIRF DORF SPING GRACKLE SOB-DOODLE QUAB-STRONG!
OH, NO. WITHOUT PATRICE TRANSLATING, I HAVE NO IDEA WHAT CRAZY DAVE JUST SAID!
BLINK
BLINK

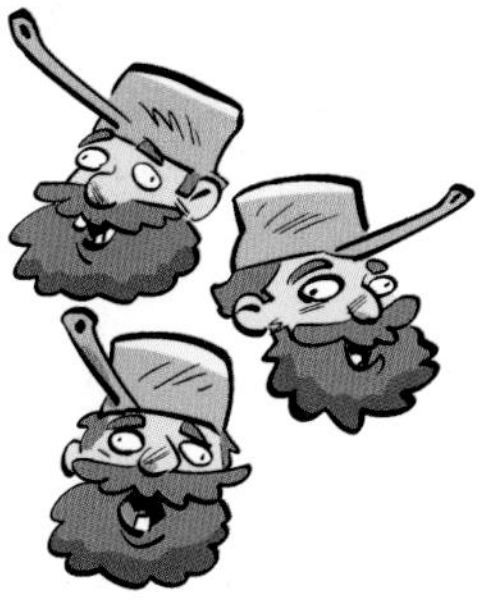

FIND THE GARDEN PATH:

What do YOU think Crazy Dave said?

- **"Let's go to my garage, and I'll make a cool INVENTION!"** Go to next page!
- **"We need to gather all the plants we can, and go FIGHT!"** Turn to page 43!
- **"You should eat more cupcakes and then let's DISCO!"** Turn to page 48!

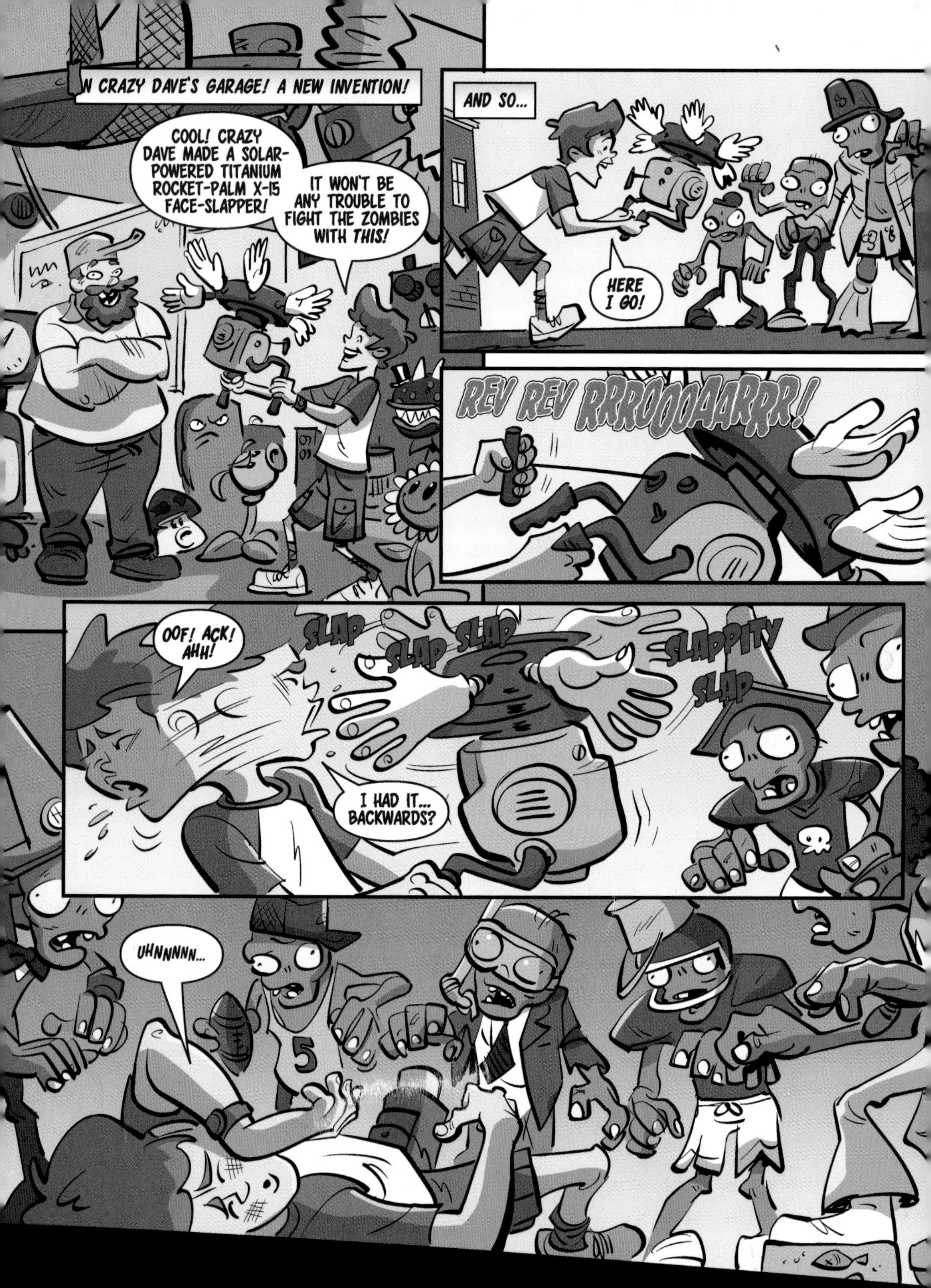
N CRAZY DAVE'S GARAGE! A NEW INVENTION!
COOL! CRAZY DAVE MADE A SOLAR-POWERED TITANIUM ROCKET-PALM X-15 FACE-SLAPPER!
IT WON'T BE ANY TROUBLE TO FIGHT THE ZOMBIES WITH *THIS*!
AND SO...
HERE I GO!
REV REV RRROOOAARRR!
OOF! ACK! AHH!
SLAP
SLAP SLAP
SLAPPITY SLAP
I HAD IT... BACKWARDS?
UHNNNNN...

OOPS! YOU GOT SLAPPED WITH A BAD ENDING!

Go back to page 41 and try again!

Continued from page 41!

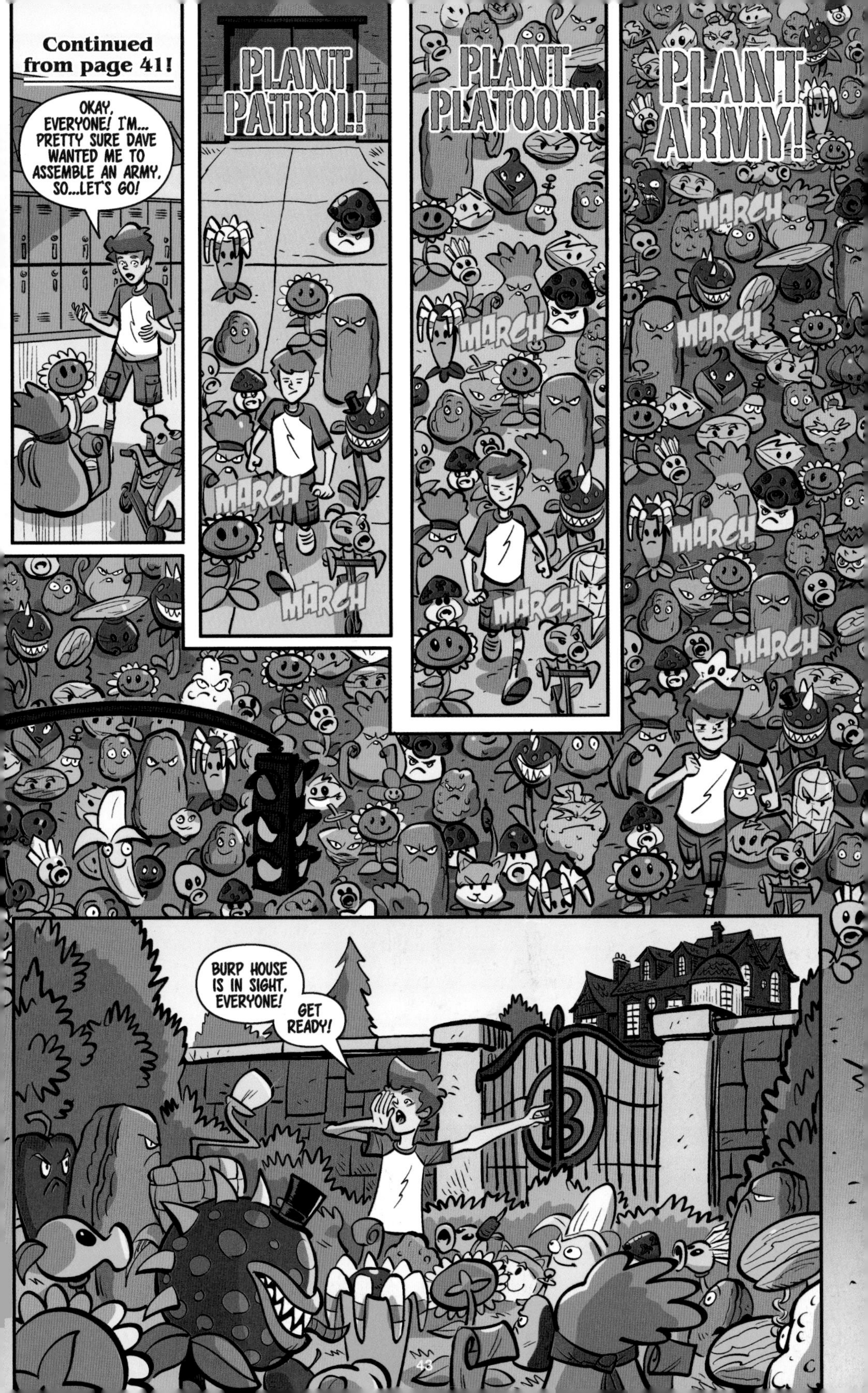
OKAY, EVERYONE! I'M... PRETTY SURE DAVE WANTED ME TO ASSEMBLE AN ARMY, SO...LET'S GO!
PLANT PATROL!
MARCH
MARCH
PLANT PLATOON!
MARCH
MARCH
PLANT ARMY!
MARCH
MARCH
MARCH
MARCH
BURP HOUSE IS IN SIGHT, EVERYONE!
GET READY!

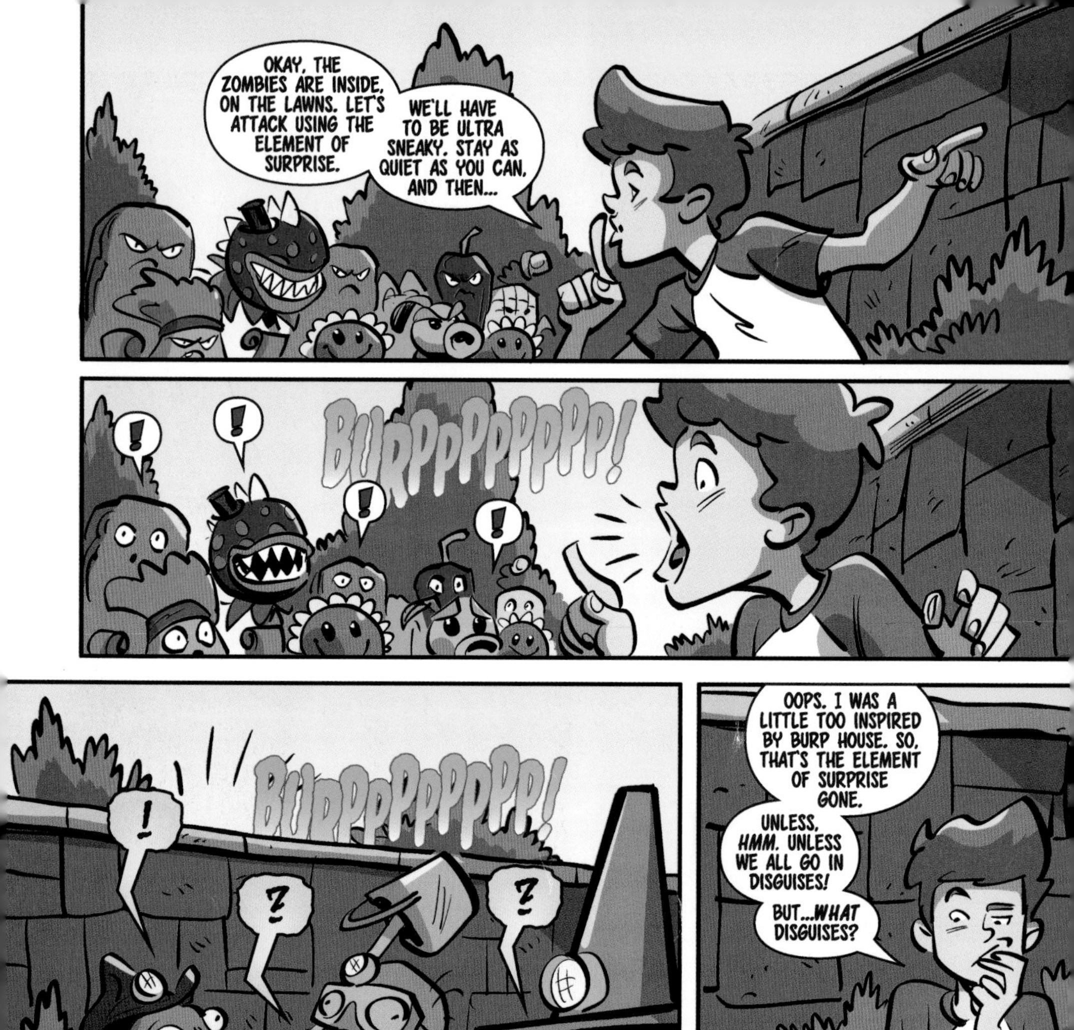
OKAY, THE ZOMBIES ARE INSIDE, ON THE LAWNS. LET'S ATTACK USING THE ELEMENT OF SURPRISE.
WE'LL HAVE TO BE ULTRA SNEAKY. STAY AS QUIET AS YOU CAN, AND THEN...
!
!
BURPPPPPPPP!
!
!
BURPPPPPPPP!
!
?
?
OOPS. I WAS A LITTLE TOO INSPIRED BY BURP HOUSE. SO, THAT'S THE ELEMENT OF SURPRISE GONE.
UNLESS, *HMM.* UNLESS WE ALL GO IN DISGUISES!
BUT...*WHAT* DISGUISES?

FIND THE GARDEN PATH:

Ooh! Disguises! What disguises do YOU think Nate Timely and the plants should wear?

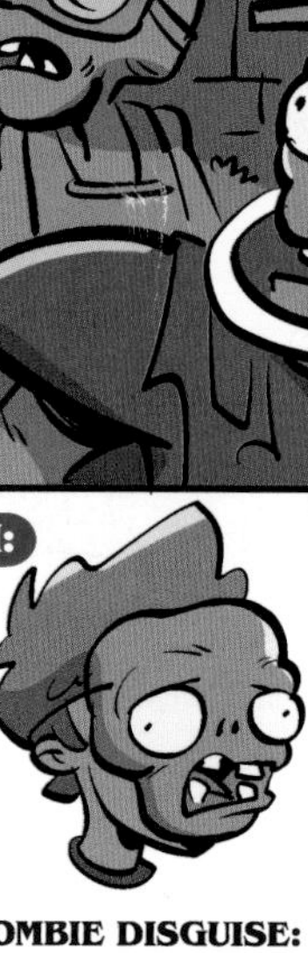

ZOMBIE DISGUISE:
Go to next page!

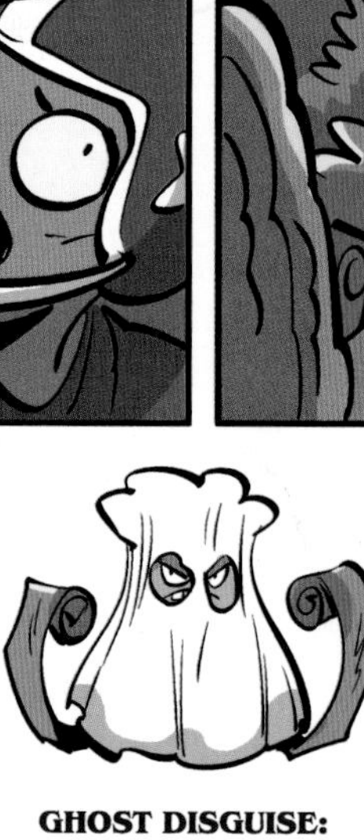

GHOST DISGUISE:
Turn to page 46!

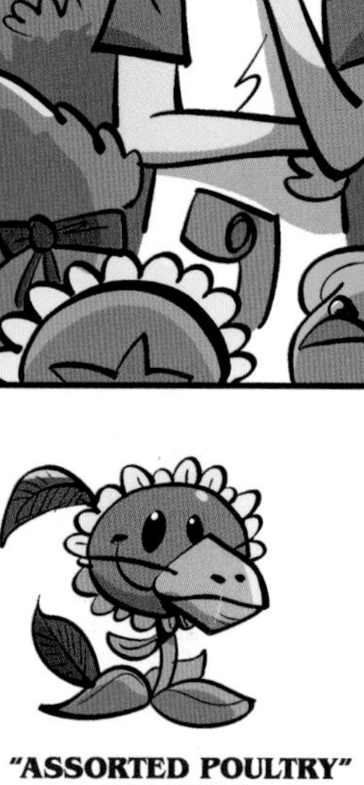

"ASSORTED POULTRY" DISGUISE:
Turn to page 47!

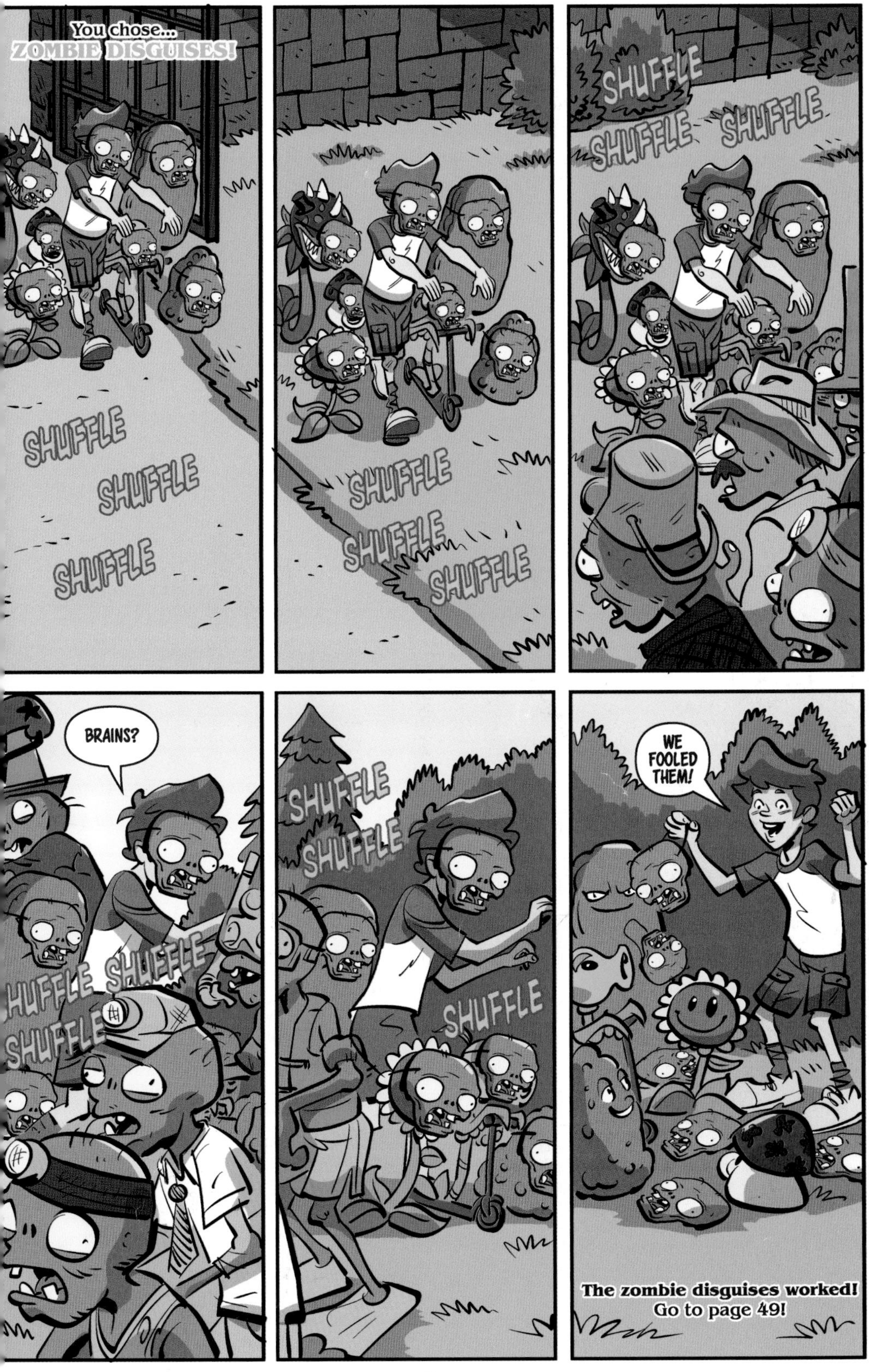
You chose...
ZOMBIE DISGUISES!
SHUFFLE
SHUFFLE
SHUFFLE
SHUFFLE
SHUFFLE
SHUFFLE
SHUFFLE
SHUFFLE
SHUFFLE
BRAINS?
HUFFLE SHUFFLE
SHUFFLE
SHUFFLE
SHUFFLE
SHUFFLE
WE FOOLED THEM!
The zombie disguises worked!
Go to page 49!

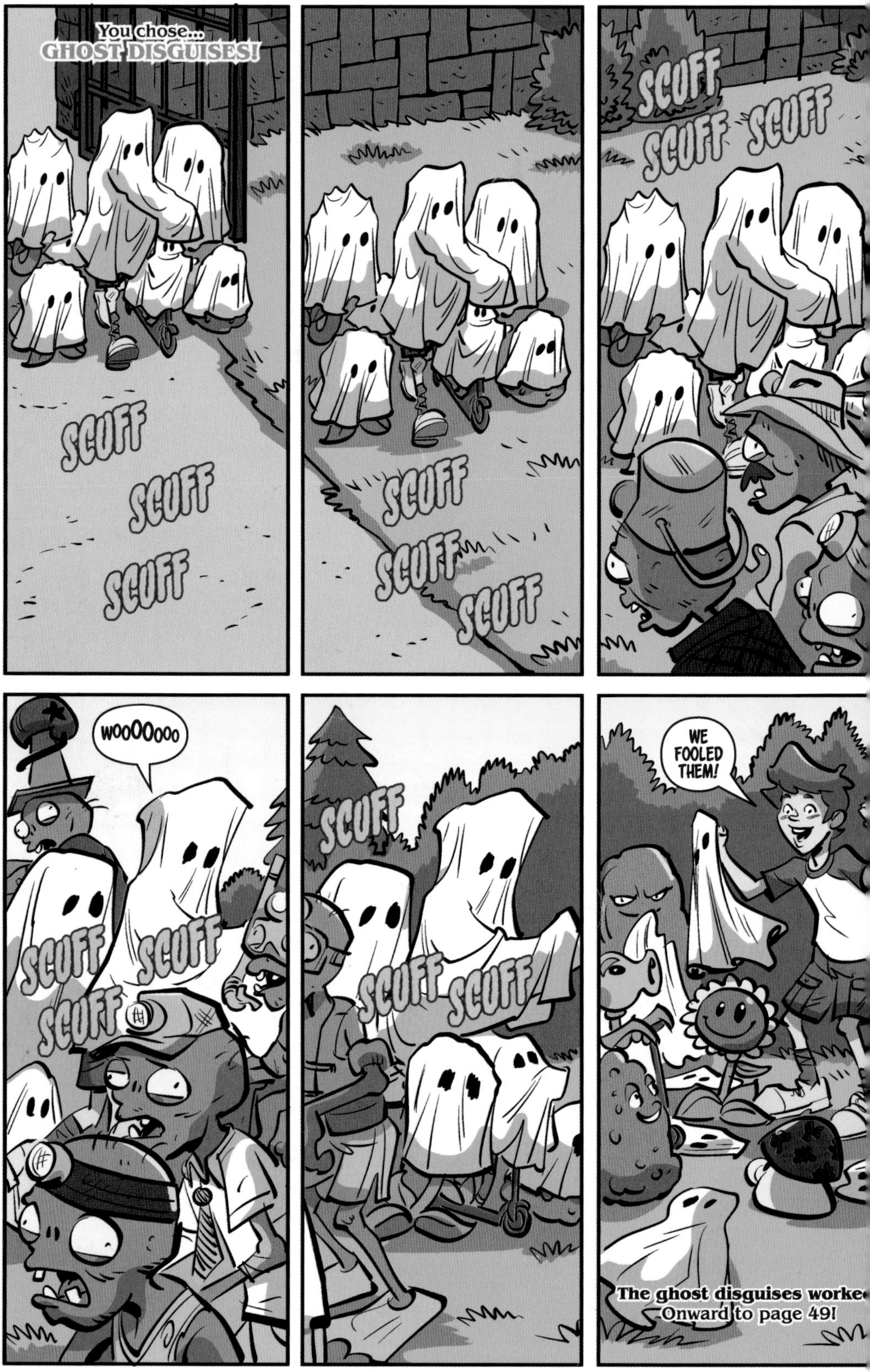
You chose...
GHOST DISGUISES!
SCUFF
SCUFF
SCUFF
SCUFF
SCUFF
SCUFF
SCUFF
SCUFF SCUFF
WOOOOOOO
SCUFF SCUFF
SCUFF
SCUFF
SCUFF SCUFF
WE FOOLED THEM!
The ghost disguises worke
Onward to page 49!

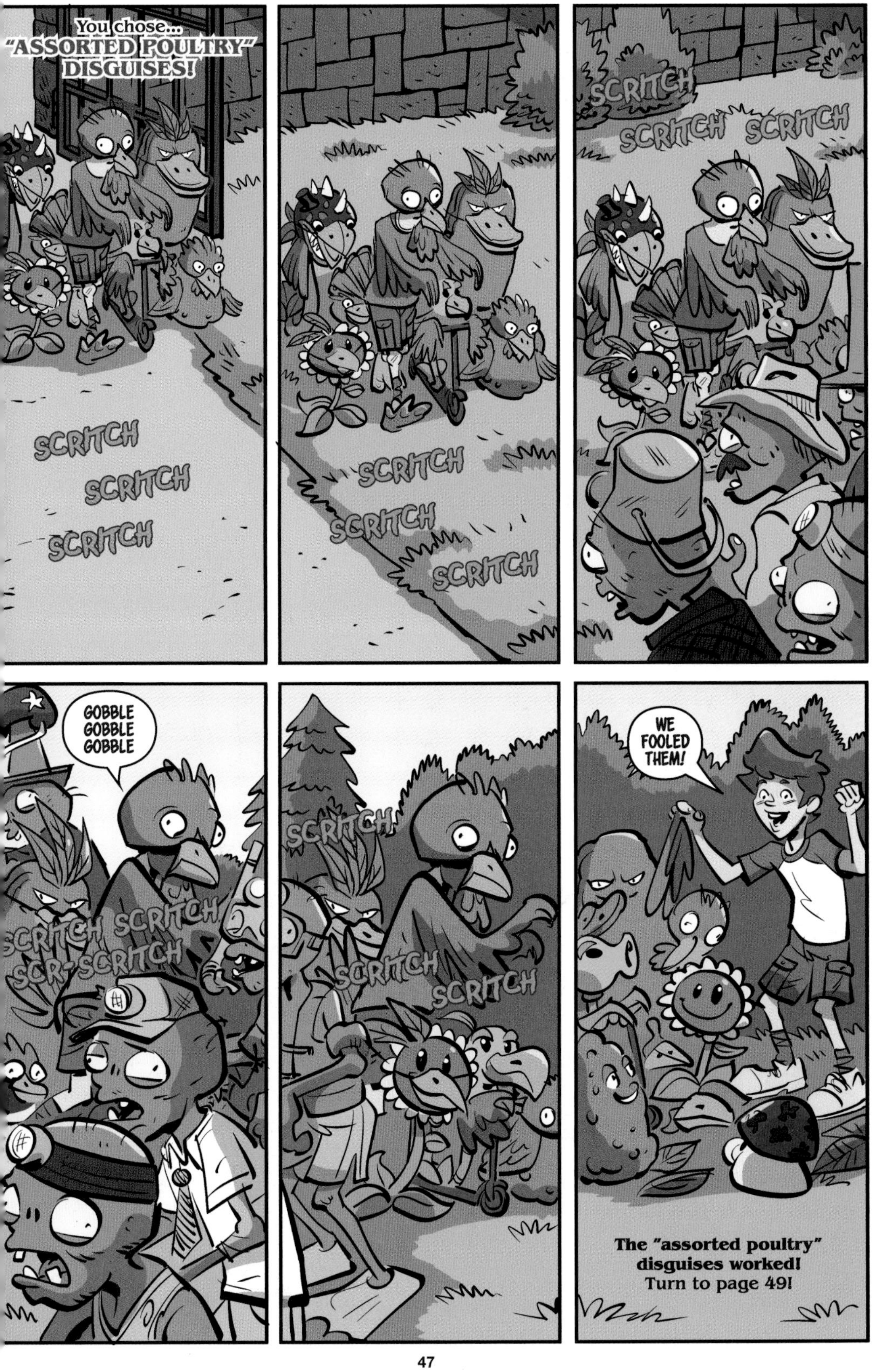
You chose...
"ASSORTED POULTRY" DISGUISES!
SCRITCH
SCRITCH
SCRITCH
SCRITCH
SCRITCH
SCRITCH
SCRITCH
SCRITCH SCRITCH
GOBBLE GOBBLE GOBBLE
SCRITCH SCRITCH
SCR-SCRITCH
SCRITCH
SCRITCH
SCRITCH
WE FOOLED THEM!
The "assorted poultry" disguises worked!
Turn to page 49!

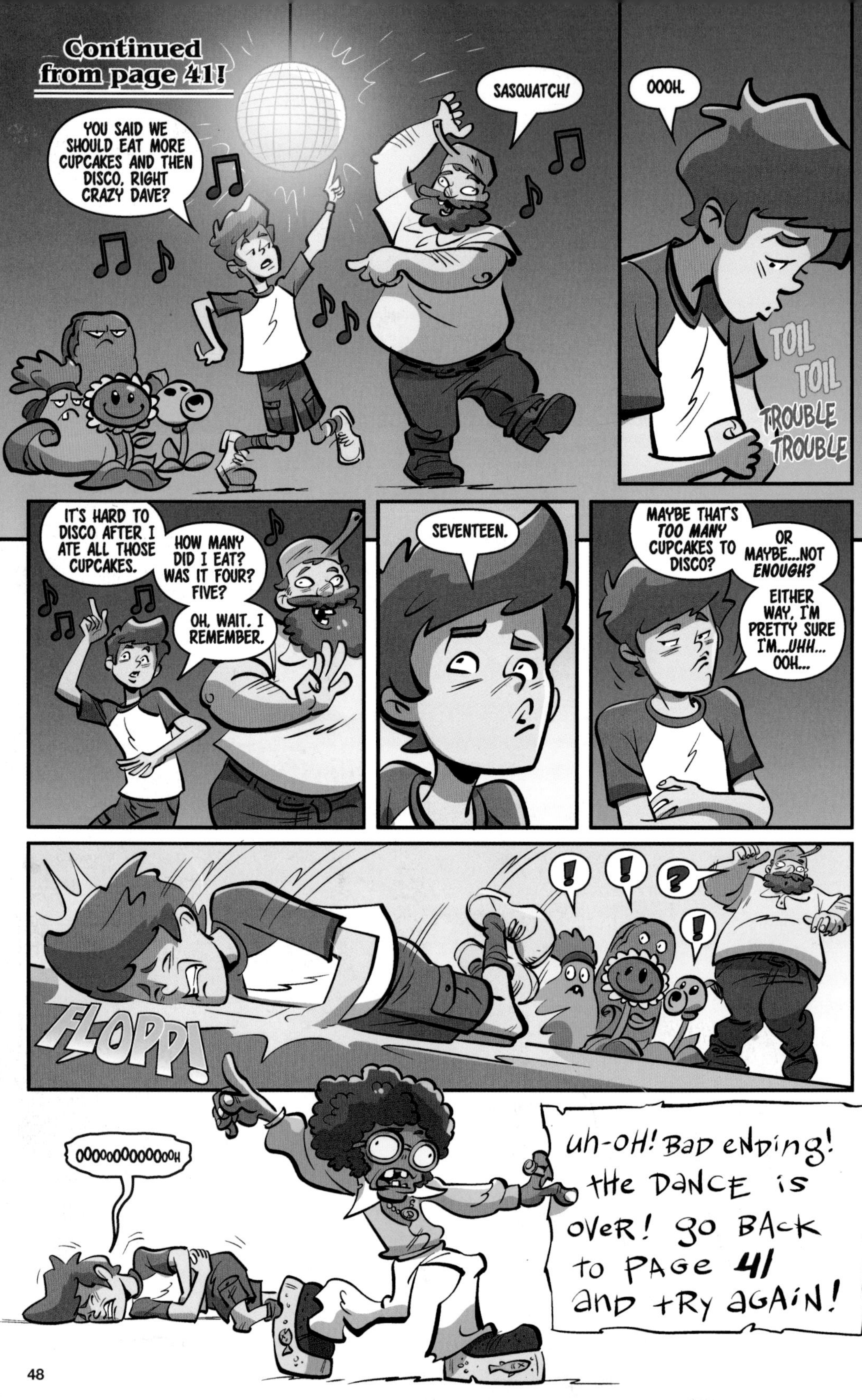

Continued from page 41!
YOU SAID WE SHOULD EAT MORE CUPCAKES AND THEN DISCO, RIGHT CRAZY DAVE?
SASQUATCH!
OOOH.
TOIL TOIL TROUBLE TROUBLE
IT'S HARD TO DISCO AFTER I ATE ALL THOSE CUPCAKES.
HOW MANY DID I EAT? WAS IT FOUR? FIVE?
OH, WAIT. I REMEMBER.
SEVENTEEN.
MAYBE THAT'S TOO MANY CUPCAKES TO DISCO?
OR MAYBE...NOT ENOUGH?
EITHER WAY, I'M PRETTY SURE I'M...UHH... OOH...
!
!
?
!
FLOPP!
OOOOOOOOOOOOOH
UH-OH! BAD ENDING! THE DANCE IS OVER! GO BACK TO PAGE 41 AND TRY AGAIN!

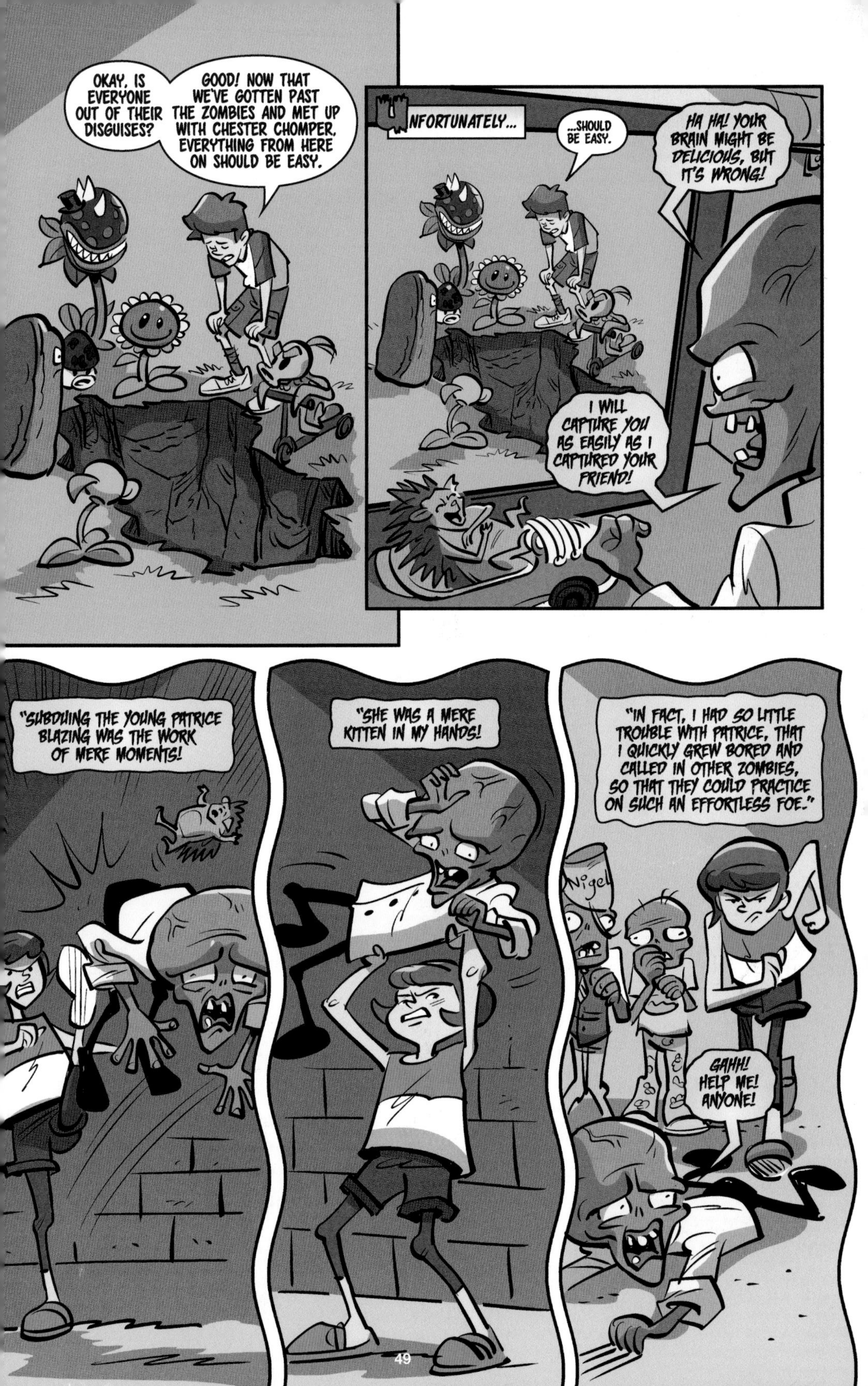
OKAY, IS EVERYONE OUT OF THEIR DISGUISES?
GOOD! NOW THAT WE'VE GOTTEN PAST THE ZOMBIES AND MET UP WITH CHESTER CHOMPER, EVERYTHING FROM HERE ON SHOULD BE EASY.
UNFORTUNATELY...
...SHOULD BE EASY.
HA HA! YOUR BRAIN MIGHT BE DELICIOUS, BUT IT'S WRONG!
I WILL CAPTURE YOU AS EASILY AS I CAPTURED YOUR FRIEND!
"SUBDUING THE YOUNG PATRICE BLAZING WAS THE WORK OF MERE MOMENTS!
"SHE WAS A MERE KITTEN IN MY HANDS!
"IN FACT, I HAD SO LITTLE TROUBLE WITH PATRICE, THAT I QUICKLY GREW BORED AND CALLED IN OTHER ZOMBIES, SO THAT THEY COULD PRACTICE ON SUCH AN EFFORTLESS FOE."
Nigel
GAHH! HELP ME! ANYONE!

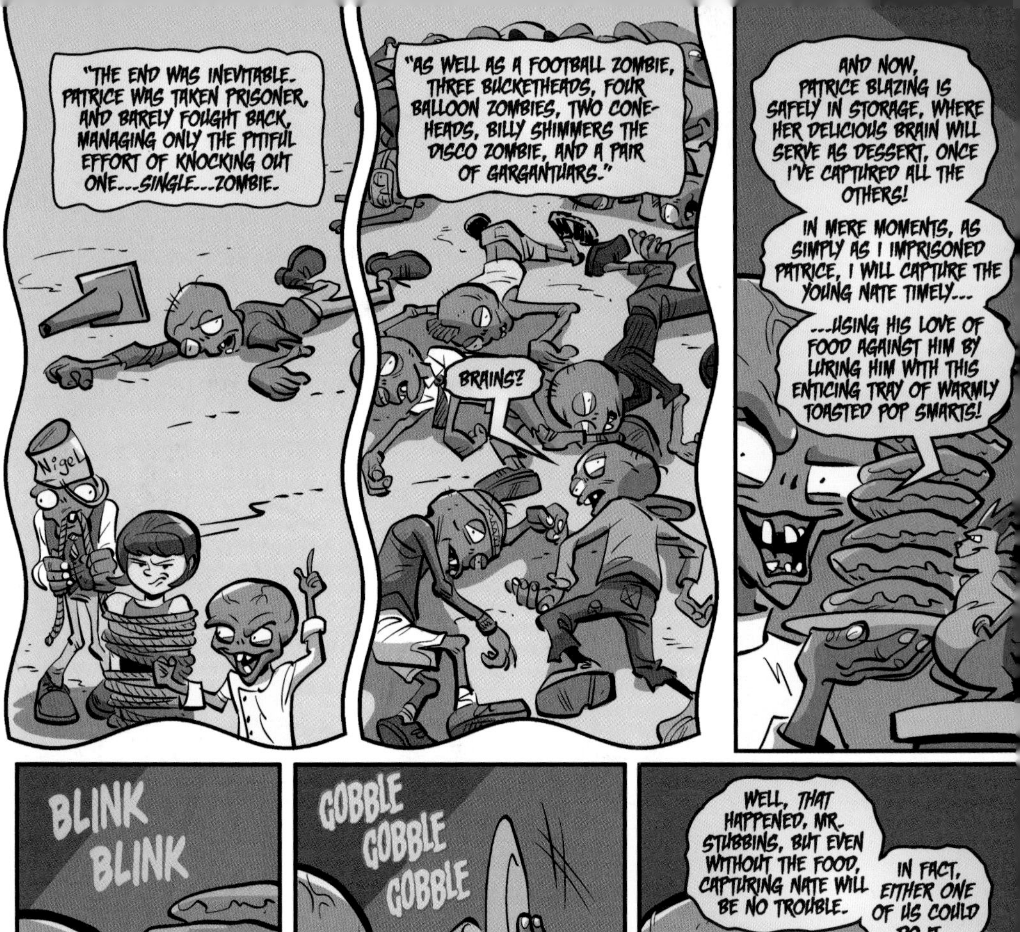
"THE END WAS INEVITABLE. PATRICE WAS TAKEN PRISONER, AND BARELY FOUGHT BACK, MANAGING ONLY THE PITIFUL EFFORT OF KNOCKING OUT ONE...SINGLE...ZOMBIE.
NIGEL
"AS WELL AS A FOOTBALL ZOMBIE, THREE BUCKETHEADS, FOUR BALLOON ZOMBIES, TWO CONE-HEADS, BILLY SHIMMERS THE DISCO ZOMBIE, AND A PAIR OF GARGANTUARS."
BRAINS?
AND NOW, PATRICE BLAZING IS SAFELY IN STORAGE, WHERE HER DELICIOUS BRAIN WILL SERVE AS DESSERT, ONCE I'VE CAPTURED ALL THE OTHERS!
IN MERE MOMENTS, AS SIMPLY AS I IMPRISONED PATRICE, I WILL CAPTURE THE YOUNG NATE TIMELY...
...USING HIS LOVE OF FOOD AGAINST HIM BY LURING HIM WITH THIS ENTICING TRAY OF WARMLY TOASTED POP SMARTS!
BLINK BLINK
GOBBLE GOBBLE GOBBLE
WELL, THAT HAPPENED, MR. STUBBINS, BUT EVEN WITHOUT THE FOOD, CAPTURING NATE WILL BE NO TROUBLE.
IN FACT, EITHER ONE OF US COULD DO IT.
Z

FIND THE GARDEN PATH:

Which one of them should take charge?
The genius leader of all zombies,
or the adorable zombie hedgehog?

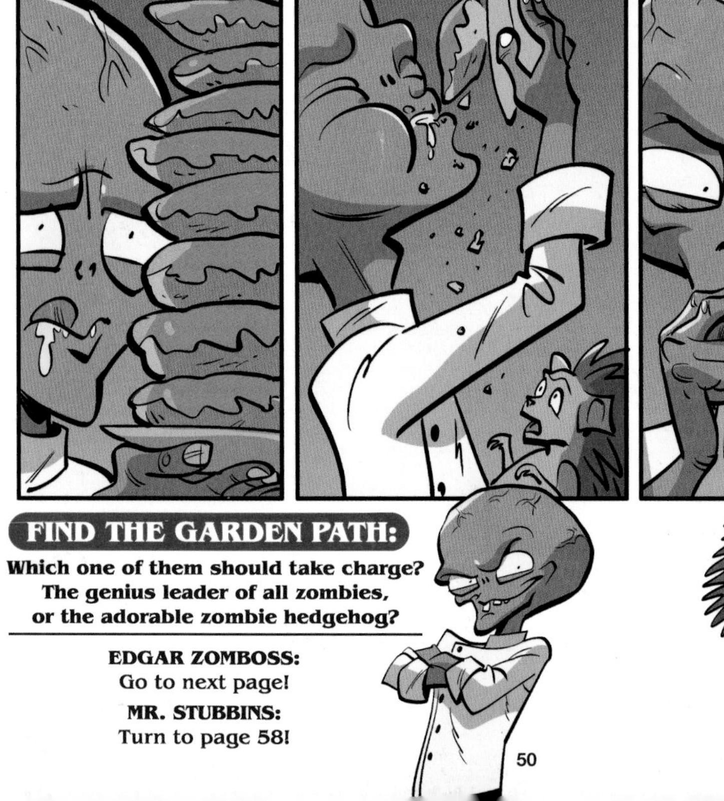

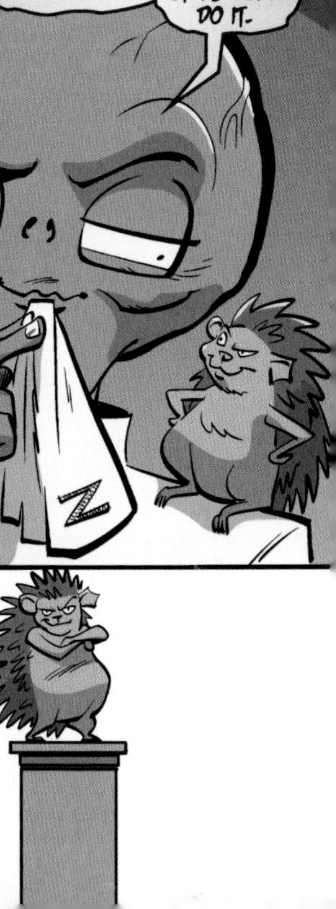

EDGAR ZOMBOSS:
Go to next page!

MR. STUBBINS:
Turn to page 58!

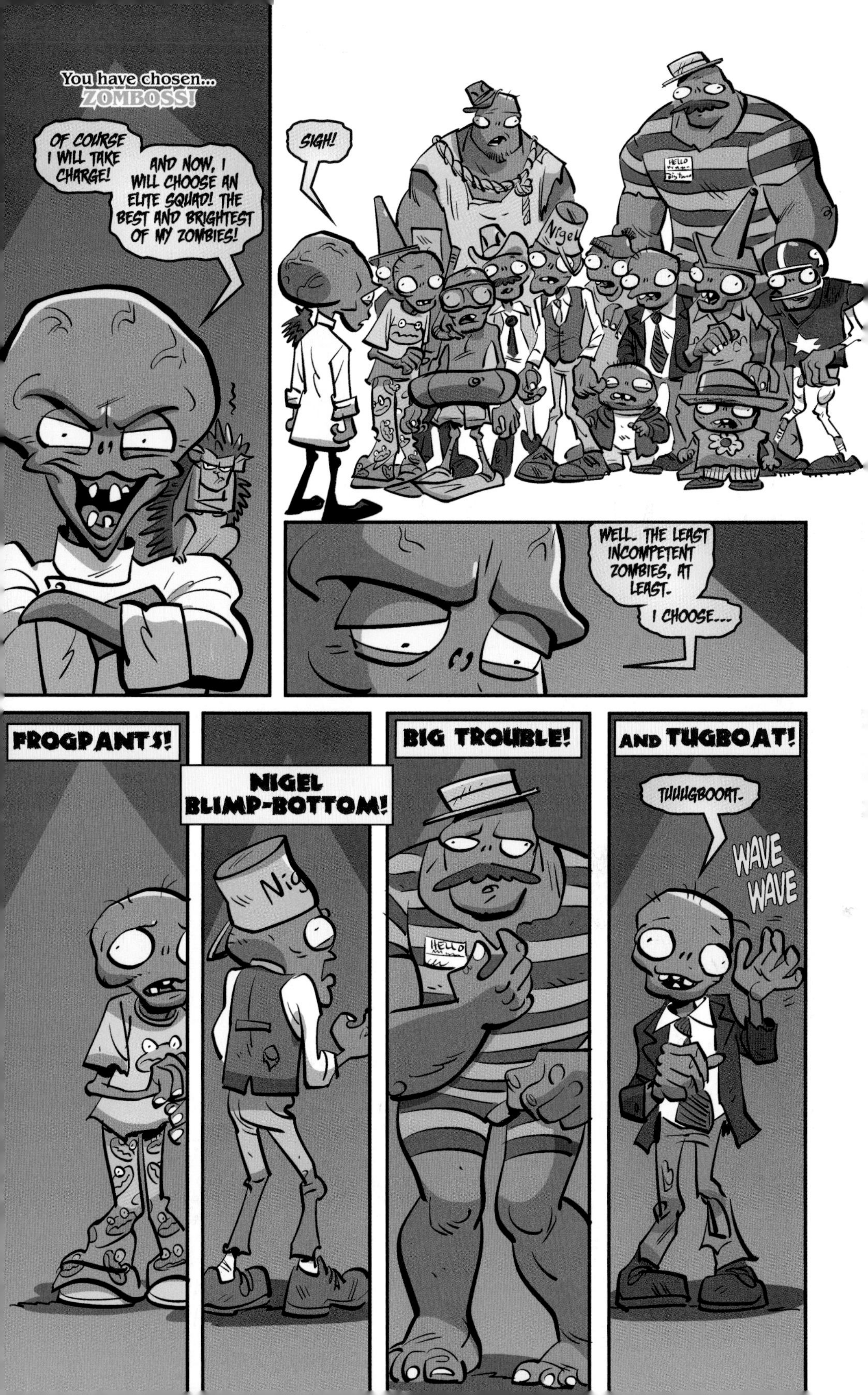

You have chosen...
ZOMBOSS!
OF COURSE I WILL TAKE CHARGE!
AND NOW, I WILL CHOOSE AN ELITE SQUAD! THE BEST AND BRIGHTEST OF MY ZOMBIES!
SIGH!
Nigel
HELLO
WELL. THE LEAST INCOMPETENT ZOMBIES, AT LEAST.
I CHOOSE...
FROGPANTS!
NIGEL BLIMP-BOTTOM!
Nig
BIG TROUBLE!
HELLO
AND TUGBOAT!
THUUGBOOAT.
WAVE
WAVE

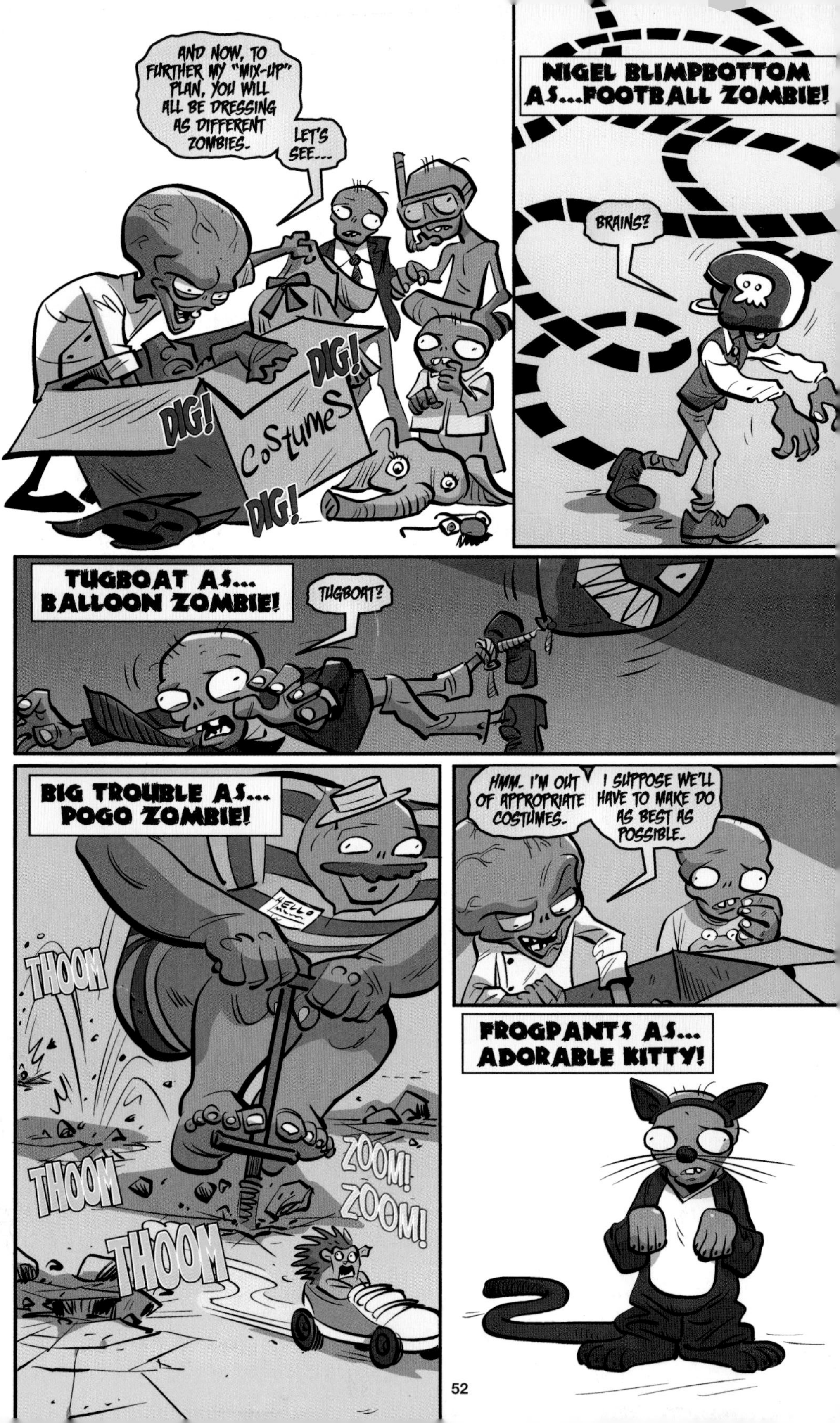
AND NOW, TO FURTHER MY "MIX-UP" PLAN, YOU WILL ALL BE DRESSING AS DIFFERENT ZOMBIES.
LET'S SEE...
DIG!
DIG!
DIG!
COSTUMES
NIGEL BLIMPBOTTOM AS...FOOTBALL ZOMBIE!
BRAINS?
TUGBOAT AS... BALLOON ZOMBIE!
TUGBOAT?
BIG TROUBLE AS... POGO ZOMBIE!
HELLO
THOOM
THOOM
THOOM
ZOOM!
ZOOM!
HMM. I'M OUT OF APPROPRIATE COSTUMES.
I SUPPOSE WE'LL HAVE TO MAKE DO AS BEST AS POSSIBLE.
FROGPANTS AS... ADORABLE KITTY!

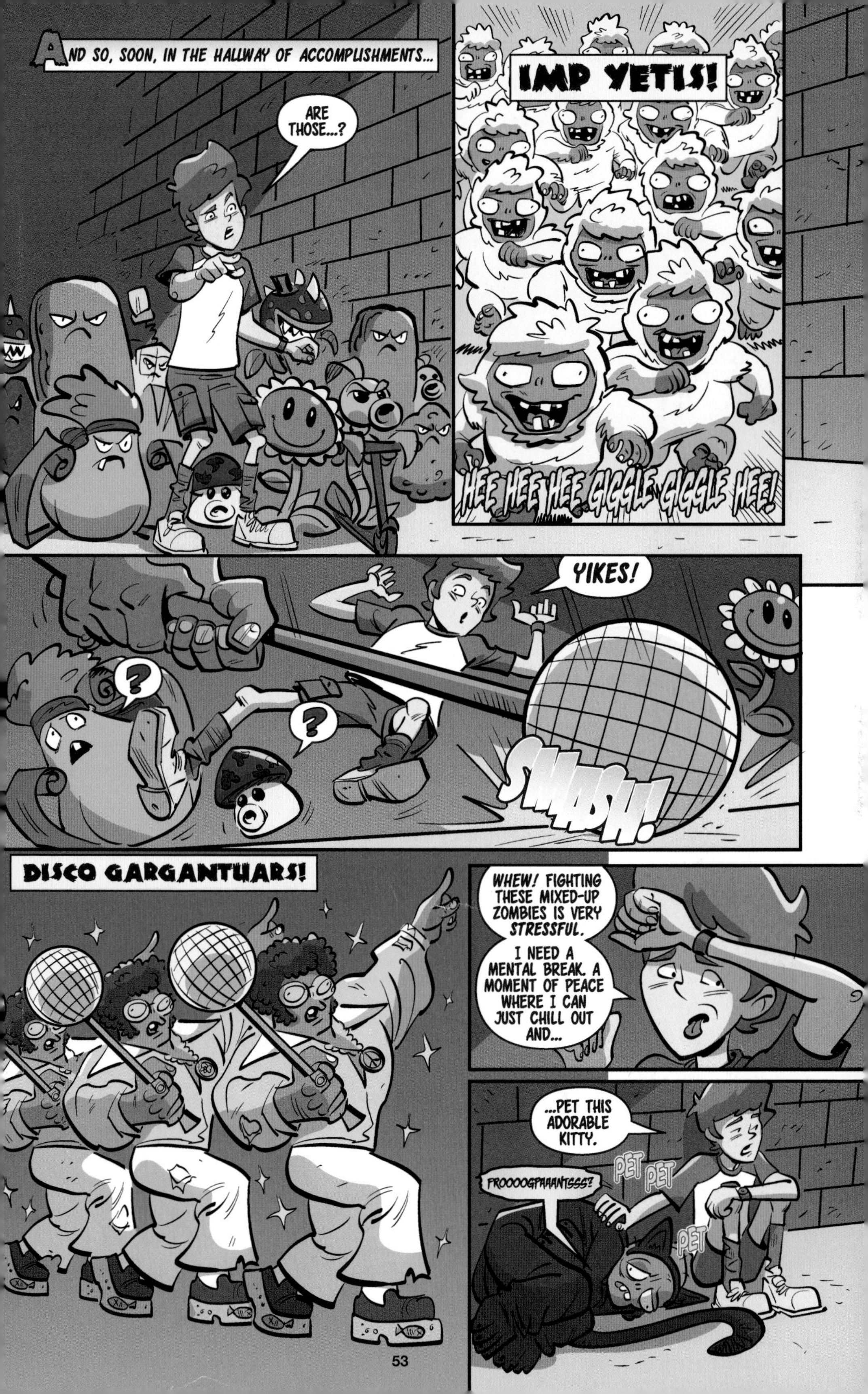
AND SO, SOON, IN THE HALLWAY OF ACCOMPLISHMENTS...
ARE THOSE...?
IMP YETIS!
HEE HEE HEE GIGGLE GIGGLE HEE!
YIKES!
?
?
SMASH!
DISCO GARGANTUARS!
WHEW! FIGHTING THESE MIXED-UP ZOMBIES IS VERY STRESSFUL.
I NEED A MENTAL BREAK. A MOMENT OF PEACE WHERE I CAN JUST CHILL OUT AND...
...PET THIS ADORABLE KITTY.
PET PET
FROOOOGPHAAANTSSS?
PET

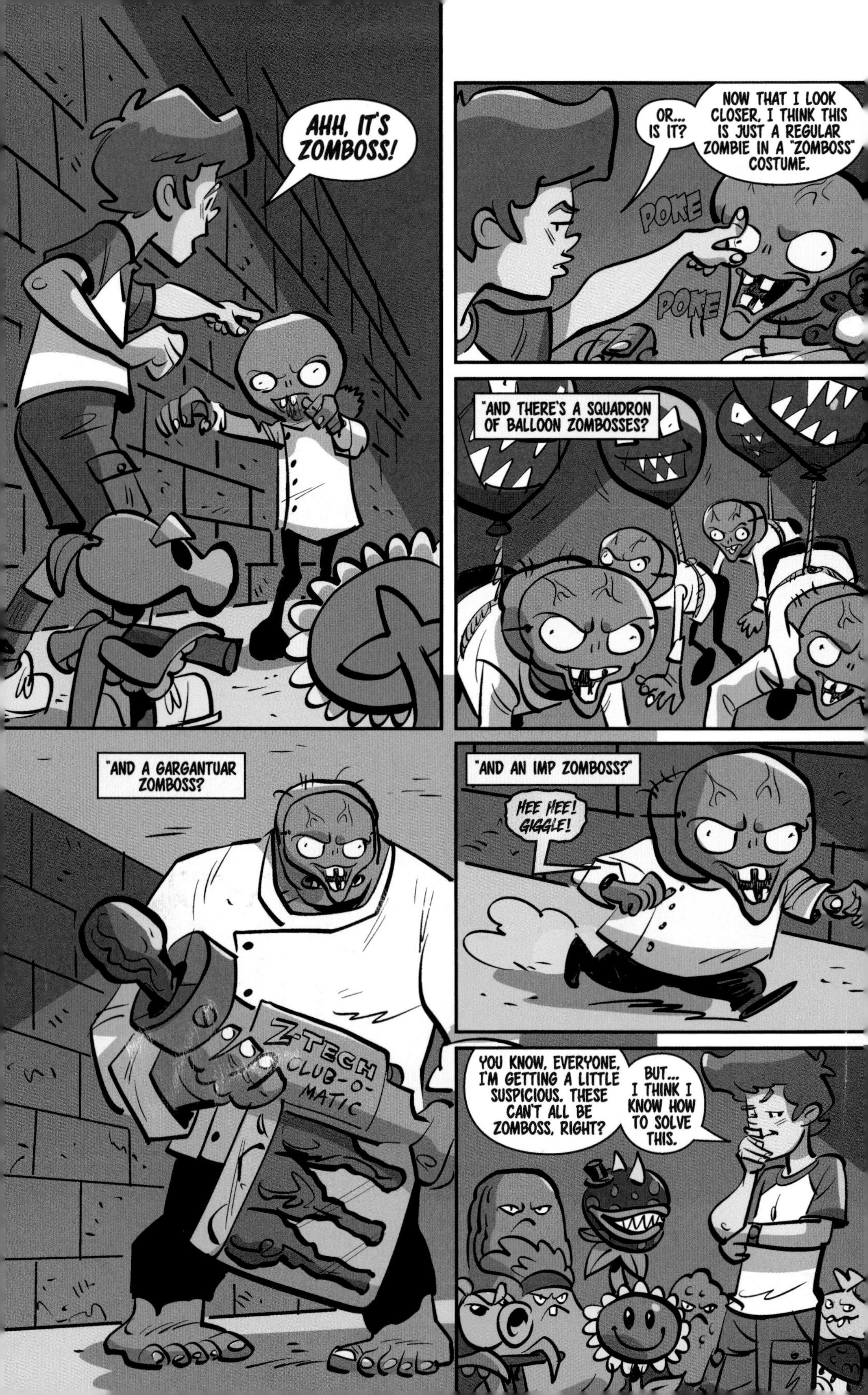
AHH, IT'S ZOMBOSS!
OR... IS IT?
NOW THAT I LOOK CLOSER, I THINK THIS IS JUST A REGULAR ZOMBIE IN A "ZOMBOSS" COSTUME.
POKE
POKE
"AND THERE'S A SQUADRON OF BALLOON ZOMBOSSES?
"AND A GARGANTUAR ZOMBOSS?
Z-TECH CLUB-O-MATIC
"AND AN IMP ZOMBOSS?"
HEE HEE! GIGGLE!
YOU KNOW, EVERYONE, I'M GETTING A LITTLE SUSPICIOUS. THESE CAN'T ALL BE ZOMBOSS, RIGHT?
BUT... I THINK I KNOW HOW TO SOLVE THIS.

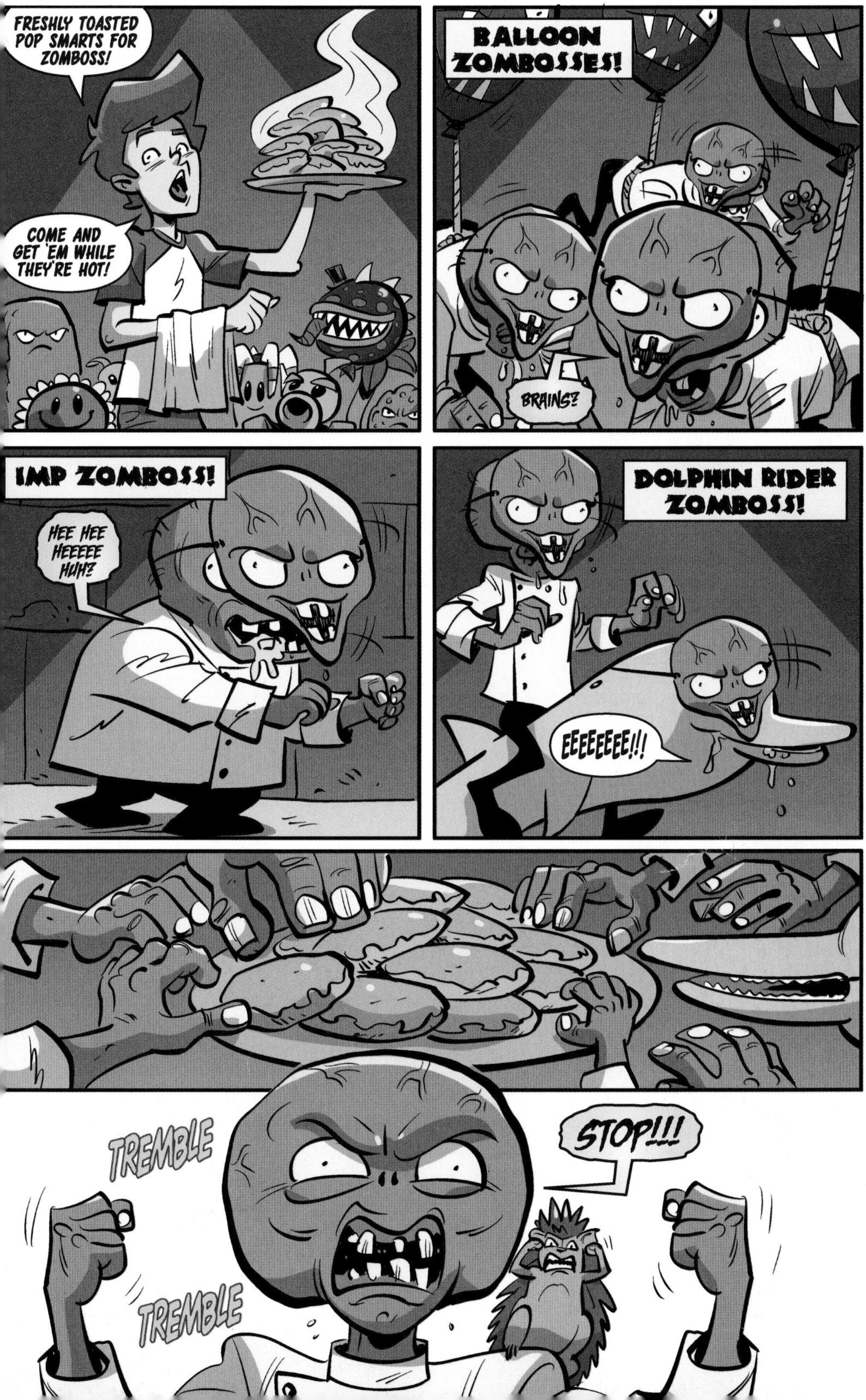
FRESHLY TOASTED POP SMARTS FOR ZOMBOSS!
COME AND GET 'EM WHILE THEY'RE HOT!
BALLOON ZOMBOSSES!
BRAINS?
IMP ZOMBOSS!
HEE HEE HEEEEE HUH?
DOLPHIN RIDER ZOMBOSS!
EEEEEEEE!!!
TREMBLE
TREMBLE
STOP!!!

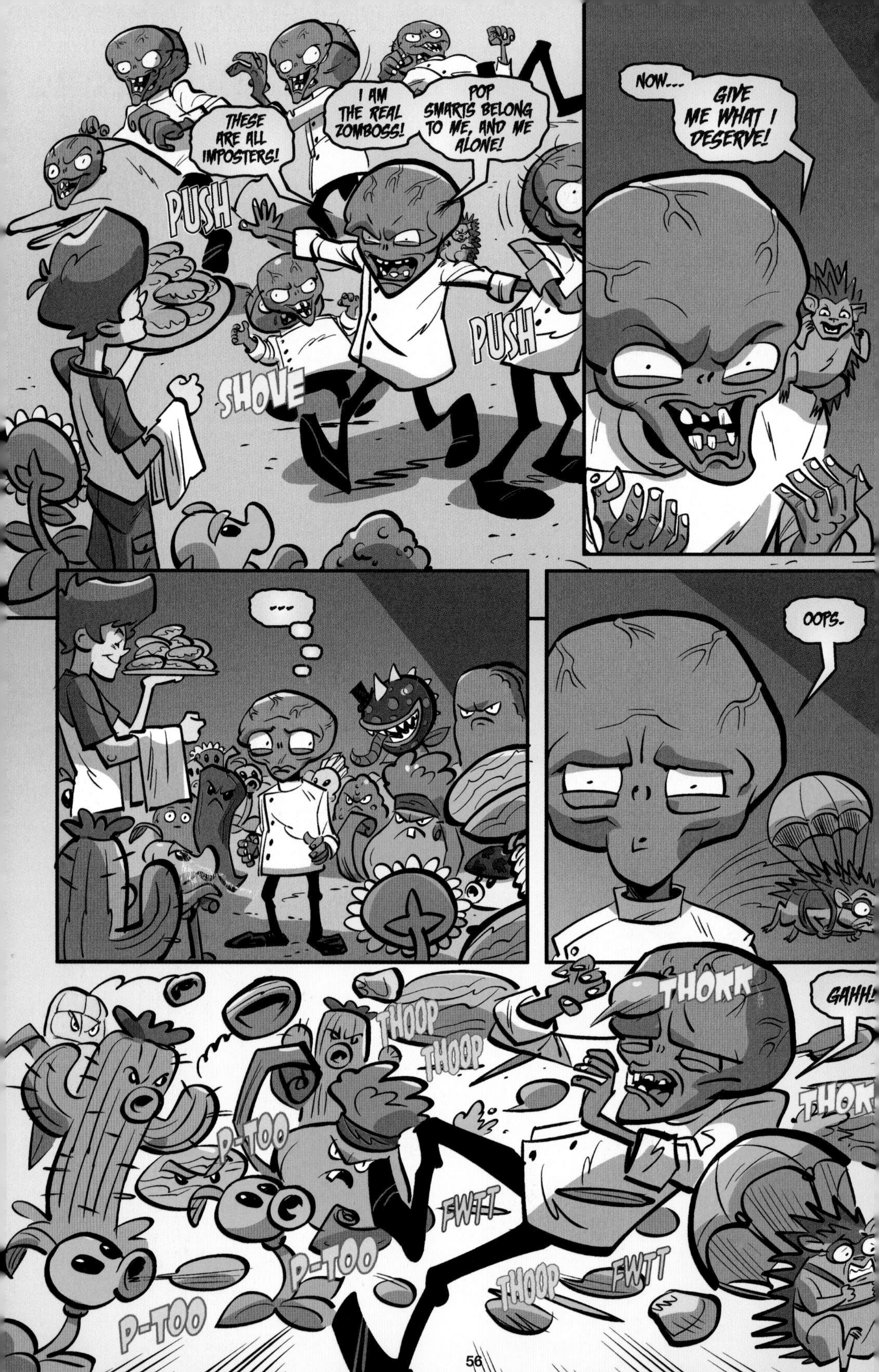
THESE ARE ALL IMPOSTERS!
I AM THE REAL ZOMBOSS!
POP SMARTS BELONG TO ME, AND ME ALONE!
PUSH
PUSH
SHOVE
NOW...
GIVE ME WHAT I DESERVE!
...
OOPS.
THORK
GAHH!
THOOP
THOOP
THORK
P-TOO
FWTT
P-TOO
THOOP
FWTT
P-TOO

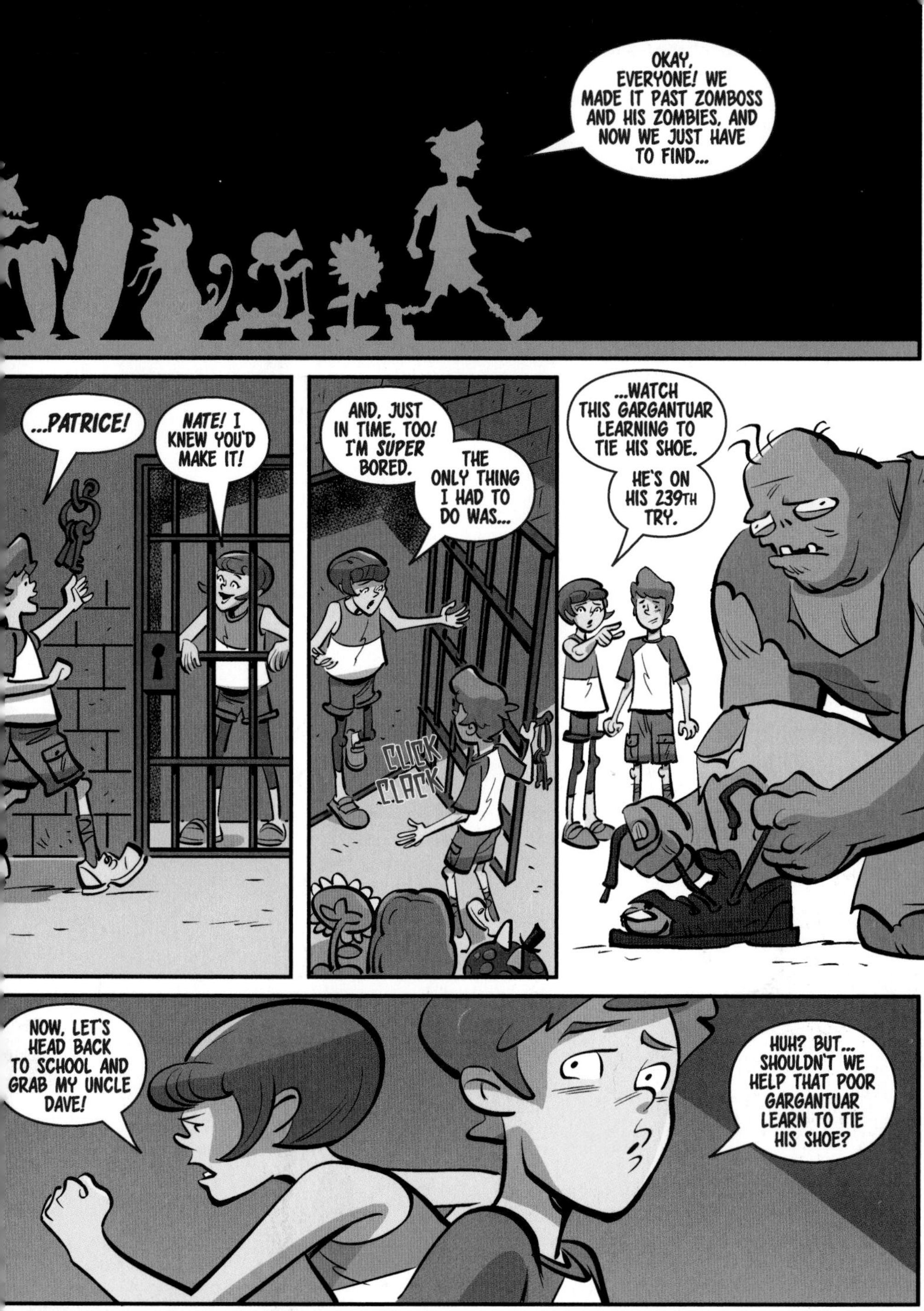
OKAY, EVERYONE! WE MADE IT PAST ZOMBOSS AND HIS ZOMBIES, AND NOW WE JUST HAVE TO FIND...
...PATRICE!
NATE! I KNEW YOU'D MAKE IT!
AND, JUST IN TIME, TOO! I'M SUPER BORED.
THE ONLY THING I HAD TO DO WAS...
CLICK CLACK
...WATCH THIS GARGANTUAR LEARNING TO TIE HIS SHOE.
HE'S ON HIS 239TH TRY.
NOW, LET'S HEAD BACK TO SCHOOL AND GRAB MY UNCLE DAVE!
HUH? BUT... SHOULDN'T WE HELP THAT POOR GARGANTUAR LEARN TO TIE HIS SHOE?

IND THE GARDEN PATH:

Stay and help the Gargantuar, or go back to school?

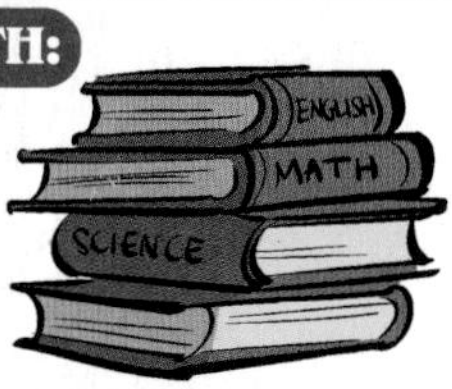
ENGLISH
MATH
SCIENCE

BACK TO SCHOOL:
Turn to page 60!

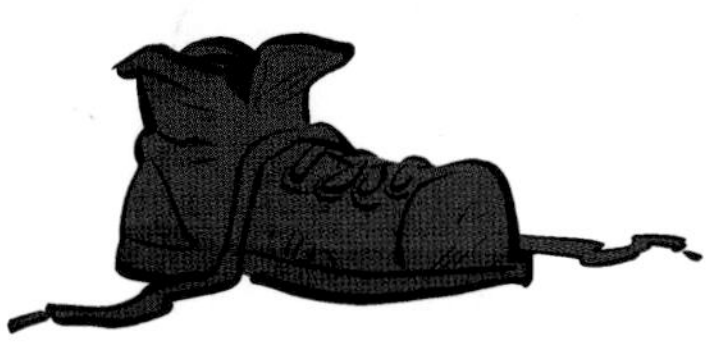

TEACH GARGANTUAR:
Turn to page 63!

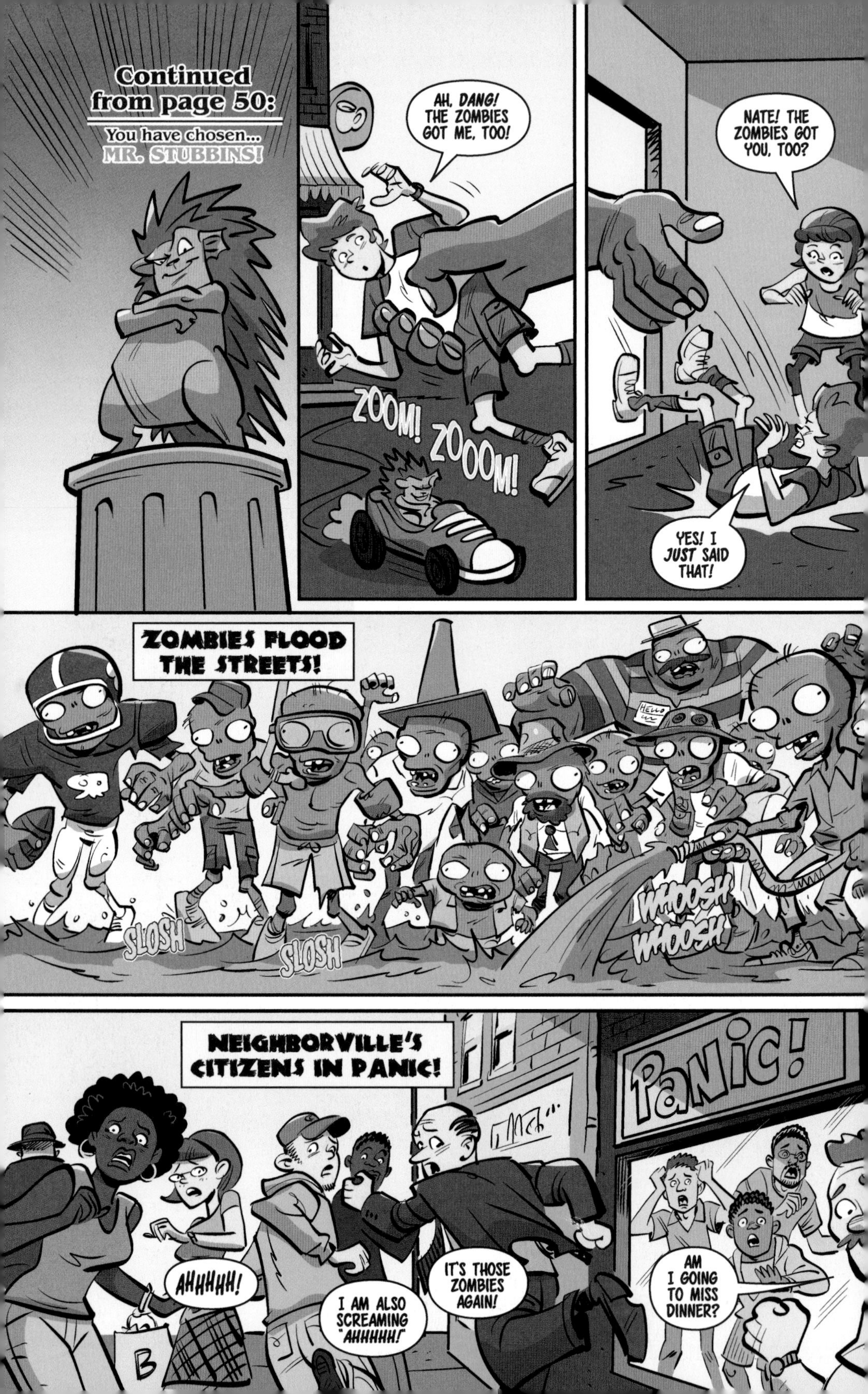
Continued from page 50:
You have chosen... MR. STUBBINS!
AH, DANG! THE ZOMBIES GOT ME, TOO!
ZOOM! ZOOOM!
NATE! THE ZOMBIES GOT YOU, TOO?
YES! I JUST SAID THAT!
ZOMBIES FLOOD THE STREETS!
HELLO
SLOSH
SLOSH
WHOOSH WHOOSH
NEIGHBORVILLE'S CITIZENS IN PANIC!
PANIC!
AHHHHH!
I AM ALSO SCREAMING "AHHHHH!"
IT'S THOSE ZOMBIES AGAIN!
AM I GOING TO MISS DINNER?
B

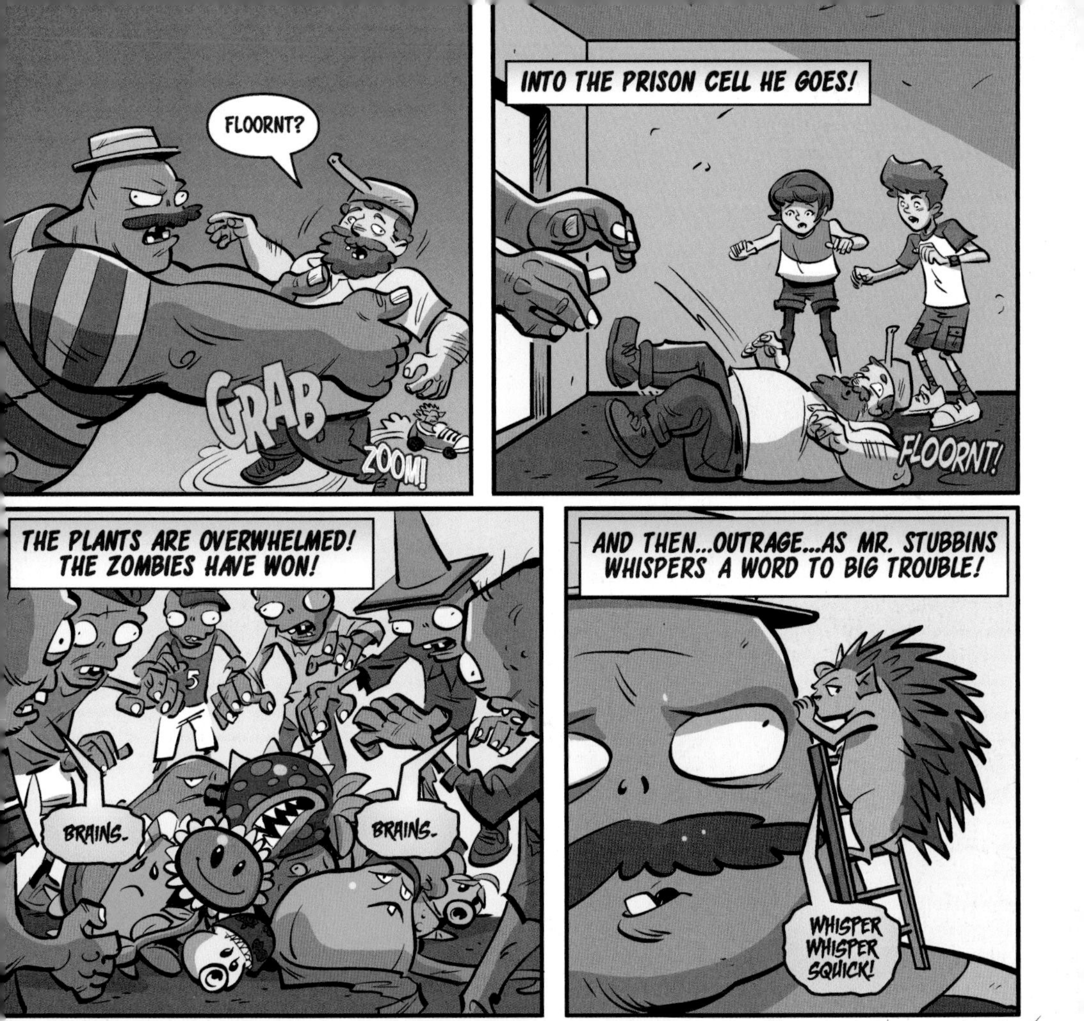
FLOORNT?
GRAB
ZOOM!
INTO THE PRISON CELL HE GOES!
FLOORNT!
THE PLANTS ARE OVERWHELMED! THE ZOMBIES HAVE WON!
BRAINS.
BRAINS.
AND THEN...OUTRAGE...AS MR. STUBBINS WHISPERS A WORD TO BIG TROUBLE!
WHISPER WHISPER SQUICK!

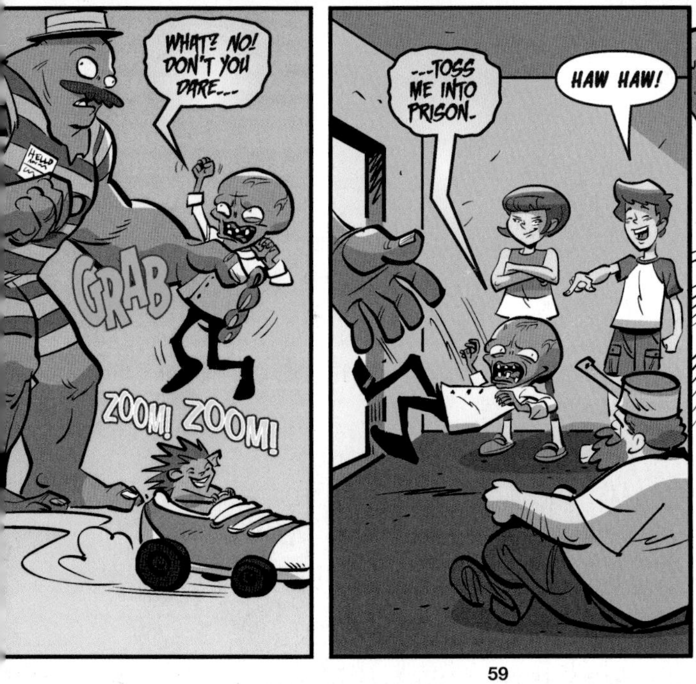
WHAT? NO! DON'T YOU DARE...
GRAB
ZOOM! ZOOM!
...TOSS ME INTO PRISON.
HAW HAW!

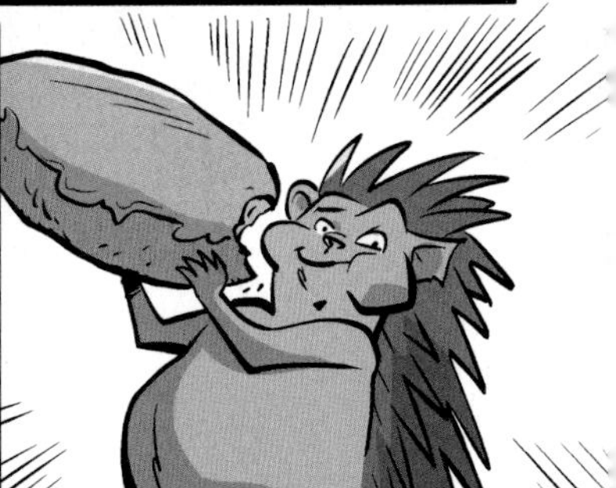

It's total victory for our adorable hedgehog zombie! And that means... TOTALLY BAD ENDING!

Go back to page 50 and try again!

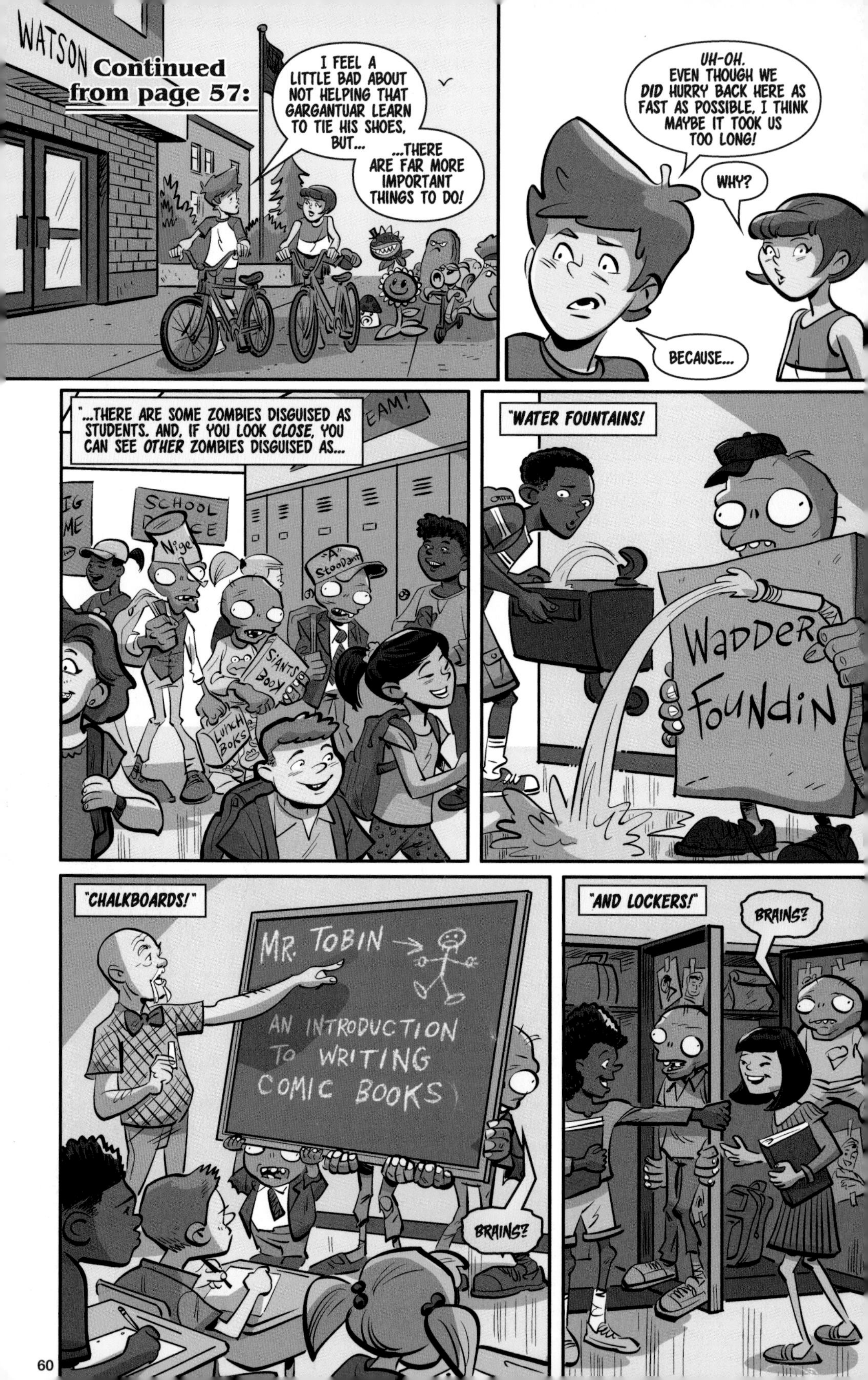
WATSON
Continued from page 57:
I FEEL A LITTLE BAD ABOUT NOT HELPING THAT GARGANTUAR LEARN TO TIE HIS SHOES, BUT...
...THERE ARE FAR MORE IMPORTANT THINGS TO DO!
UH-OH. EVEN THOUGH WE DID HURRY BACK HERE AS FAST AS POSSIBLE, I THINK MAYBE IT TOOK US TOO LONG!
WHY?
BECAUSE...
"...THERE ARE SOME ZOMBIES DISGUISED AS STUDENTS. AND, IF YOU LOOK CLOSE, YOU CAN SEE OTHER ZOMBIES DISGUISED AS...
SCHOOL
Nige
A StooDant
SIANTS BOOK
LUNCH BOKS
"WATER FOUNTAINS!
WADDER FOUNDIN
"CHALKBOARDS!"
MR. TOBIN
AN INTRODUCTION TO WRITING COMIC BOOKS
BRAINS?
"AND LOCKERS!"
BRAINS?

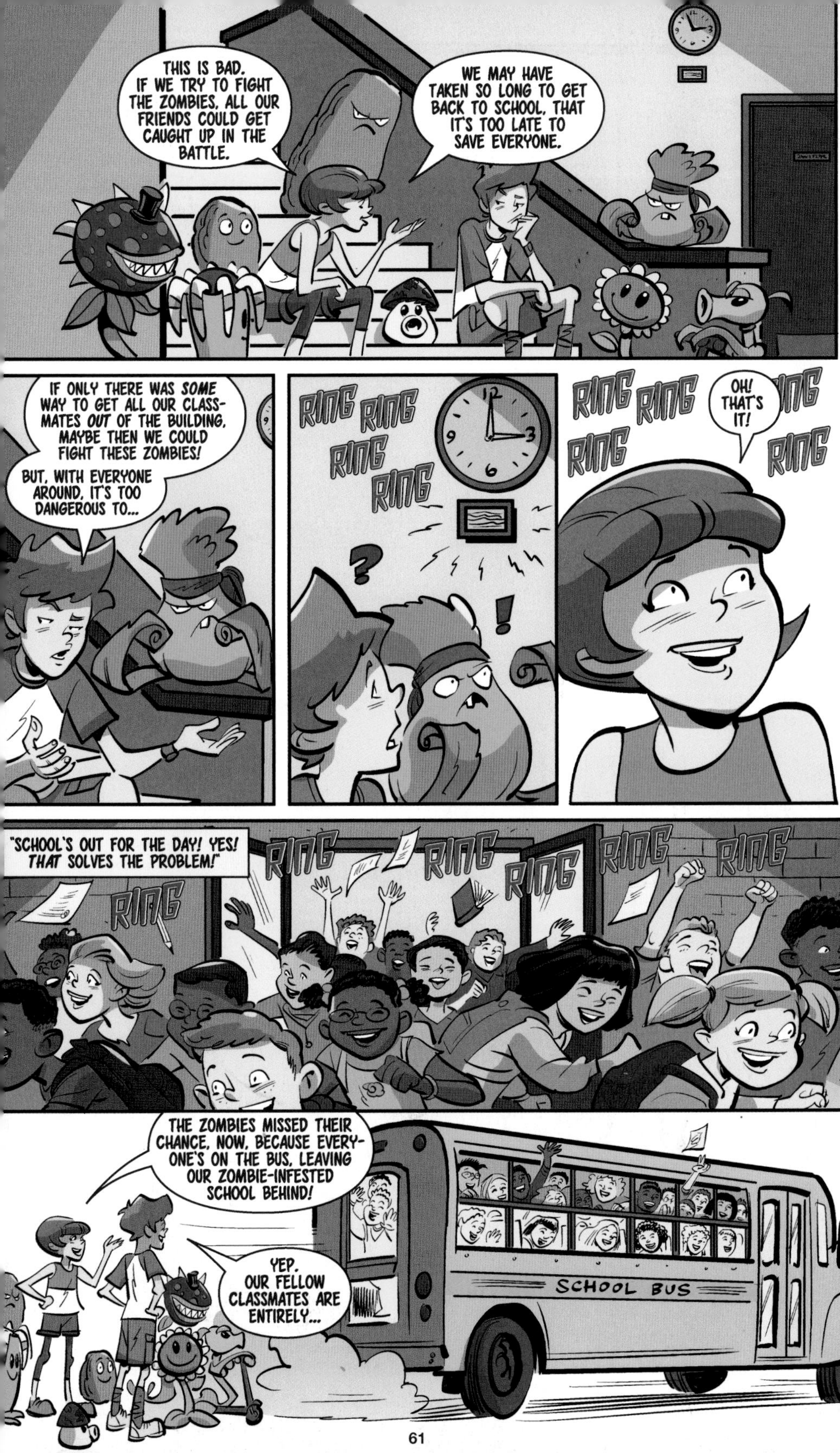
THIS IS BAD. IF WE TRY TO FIGHT THE ZOMBIES, ALL OUR FRIENDS COULD GET CAUGHT UP IN THE BATTLE.
WE MAY HAVE TAKEN SO LONG TO GET BACK TO SCHOOL, THAT IT'S TOO LATE TO SAVE EVERYONE.
IF ONLY THERE WAS *SOME* WAY TO GET ALL OUR CLASSMATES *OUT* OF THE BUILDING, MAYBE THEN WE COULD FIGHT THESE ZOMBIES!
BUT, WITH EVERYONE AROUND, IT'S TOO DANGEROUS TO...
RING RING RING RING
RING RING RING
OH! THAT'S IT!
RING RING
"SCHOOL'S OUT FOR THE DAY! YES! *THAT* SOLVES THE PROBLEM!"
RING RING RING RING RING RING
THE ZOMBIES MISSED THEIR CHANCE, NOW, BECAUSE EVERYONE'S ON THE BUS, LEAVING OUR ZOMBIE-INFESTED SCHOOL BEHIND!
SCHOOL BUS
YEP. OUR FELLOW CLASSMATES ARE ENTIRELY...

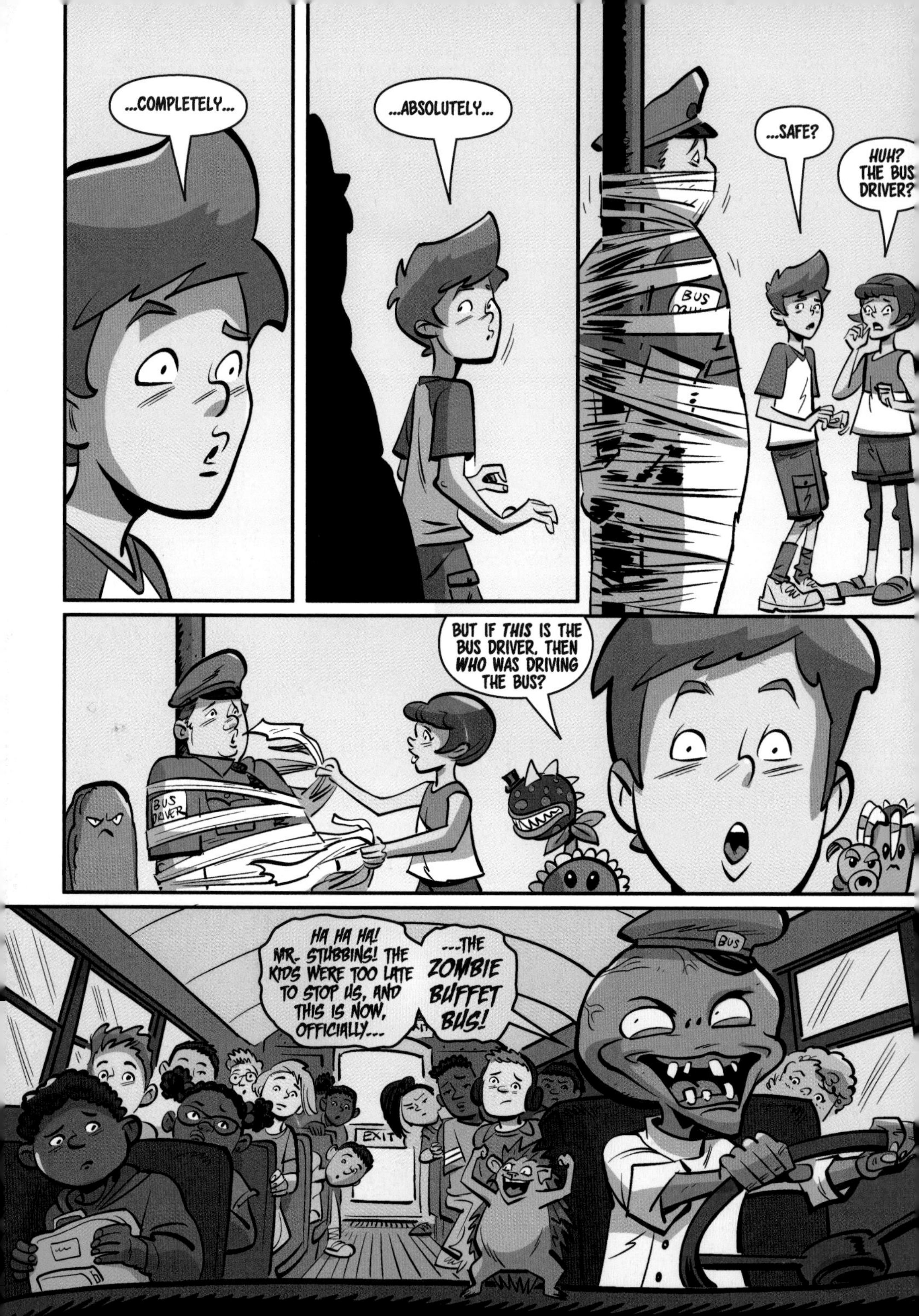
...COMPLETELY...
...ABSOLUTELY...
...SAFE?
HUH? THE BUS DRIVER?
BUT IF *THIS* IS THE BUS DRIVER, THEN *WHO* WAS DRIVING THE BUS?
BUS DRIVER
HA HA HA! MR. STUBBING! THE KIDS WERE TOO LATE TO STOP US, AND THIS IS NOW, OFFICIALLY...
...THE ZOMBIE BUFFET BUS!
BUS
EXIT

OH, NO! BAD ENDING! YOU WERE LATE FOR SCHOOL! IF ONLY THERE WAS SOME WAY TO GET THERE QUICKER!

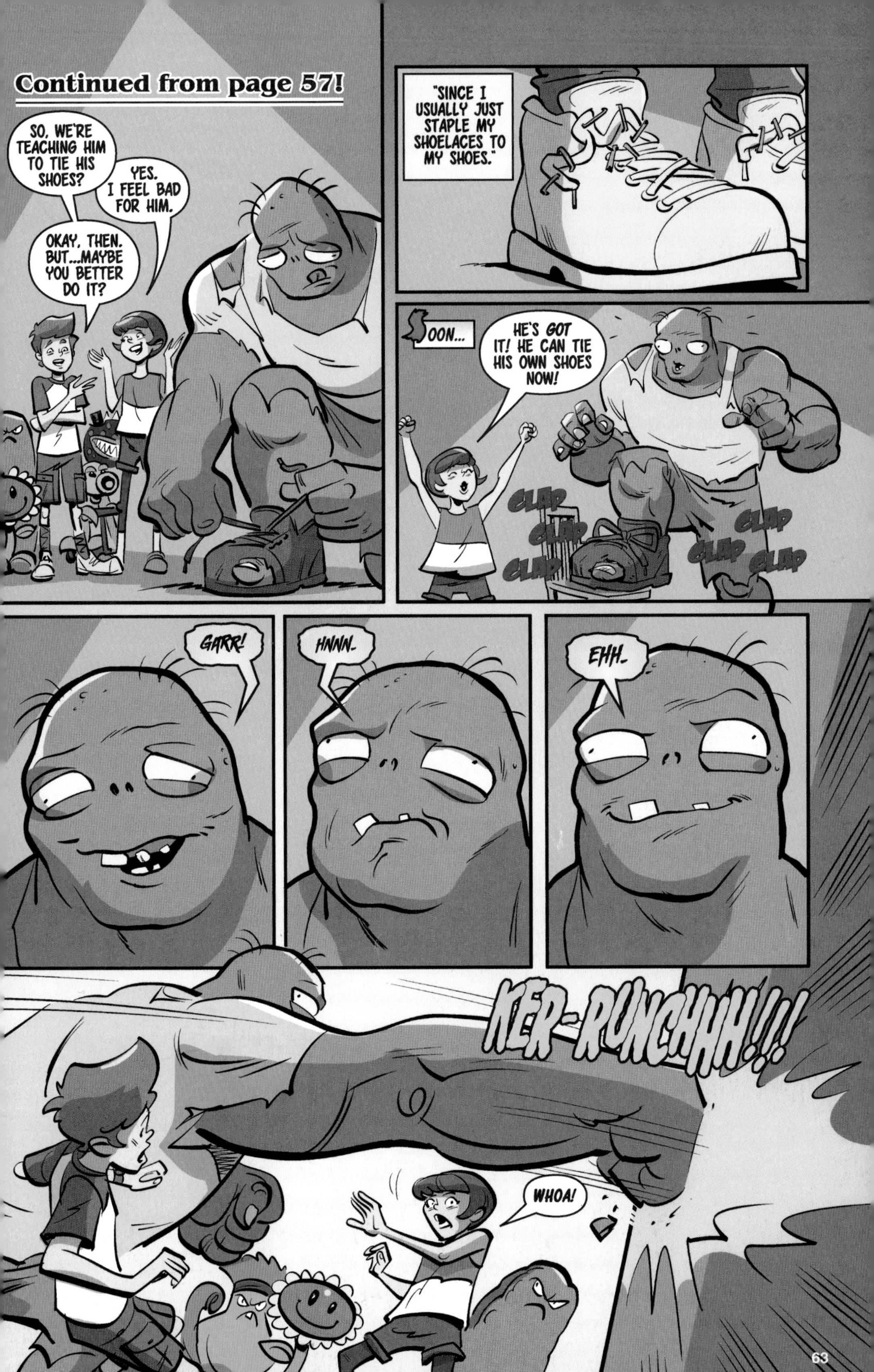
Continued from page 57!
SO, WE'RE TEACHING HIM TO TIE HIS SHOES?
YES. I FEEL BAD FOR HIM.
OKAY, THEN. BUT...MAYBE YOU BETTER DO IT?
"SINCE I USUALLY JUST STAPLE MY SHOELACES TO MY SHOES."
SOON...
HE'S GOT IT! HE CAN TIE HIS OWN SHOES NOW!
CLAP CLAP CLAP
CLAP CLAP CLAP
GARR!
HNNN...
EHH...
KER-RUNCHHH!!!
WHOA!

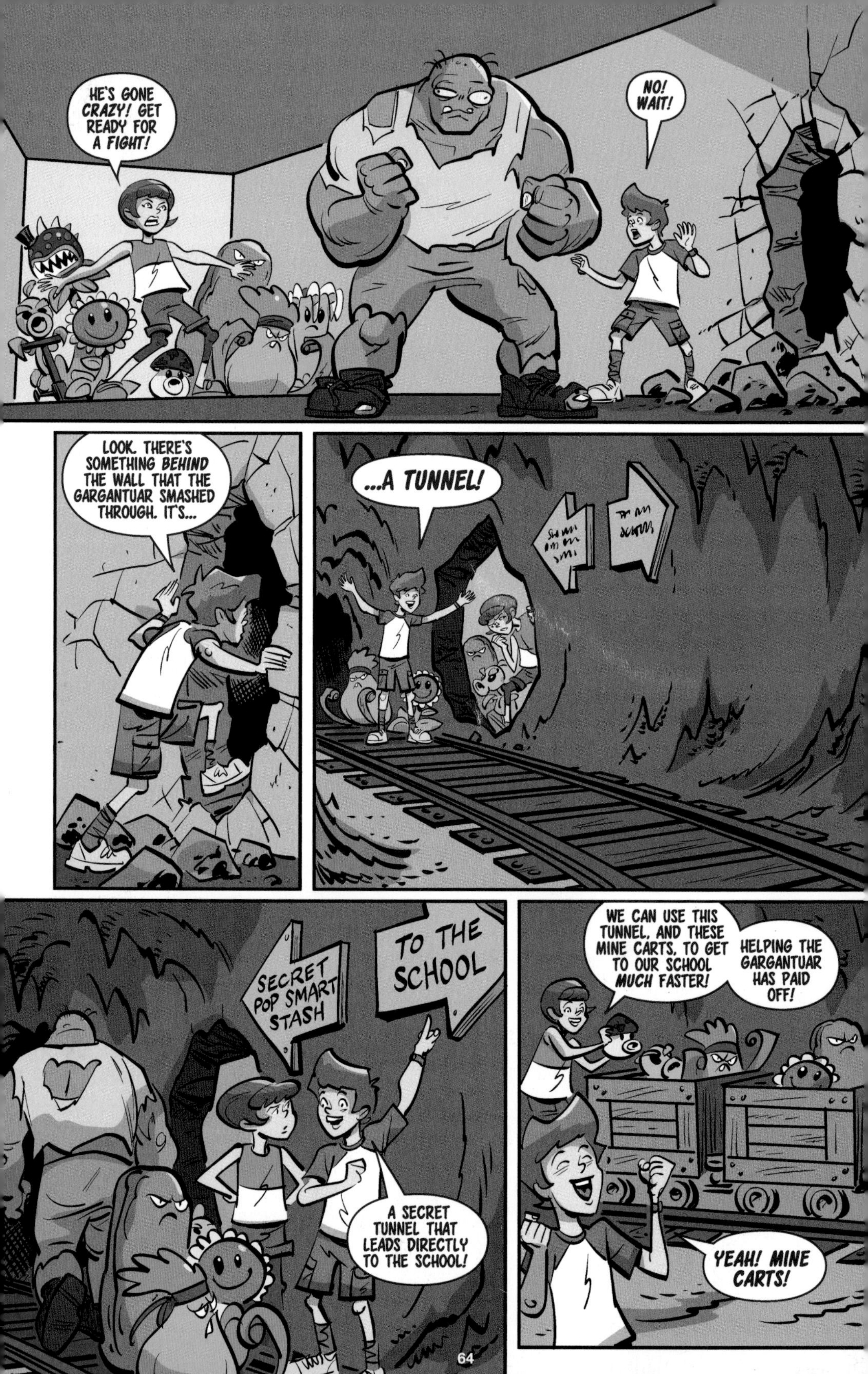
HE'S GONE CRAZY! GET READY FOR A FIGHT!
NO! WAIT!
LOOK. THERE'S SOMETHING BEHIND THE WALL THAT THE GARGANTUAR SMASHED THROUGH. IT'S...
...A TUNNEL!
SECRET POP SMART STASH
TO THE SCHOOL
A SECRET TUNNEL THAT LEADS DIRECTLY TO THE SCHOOL!
WE CAN USE THIS TUNNEL, AND THESE MINE CARTS, TO GET TO OUR SCHOOL MUCH FASTER!
HELPING THE GARGANTUAR HAS PAID OFF!
YEAH! MINE CARTS!

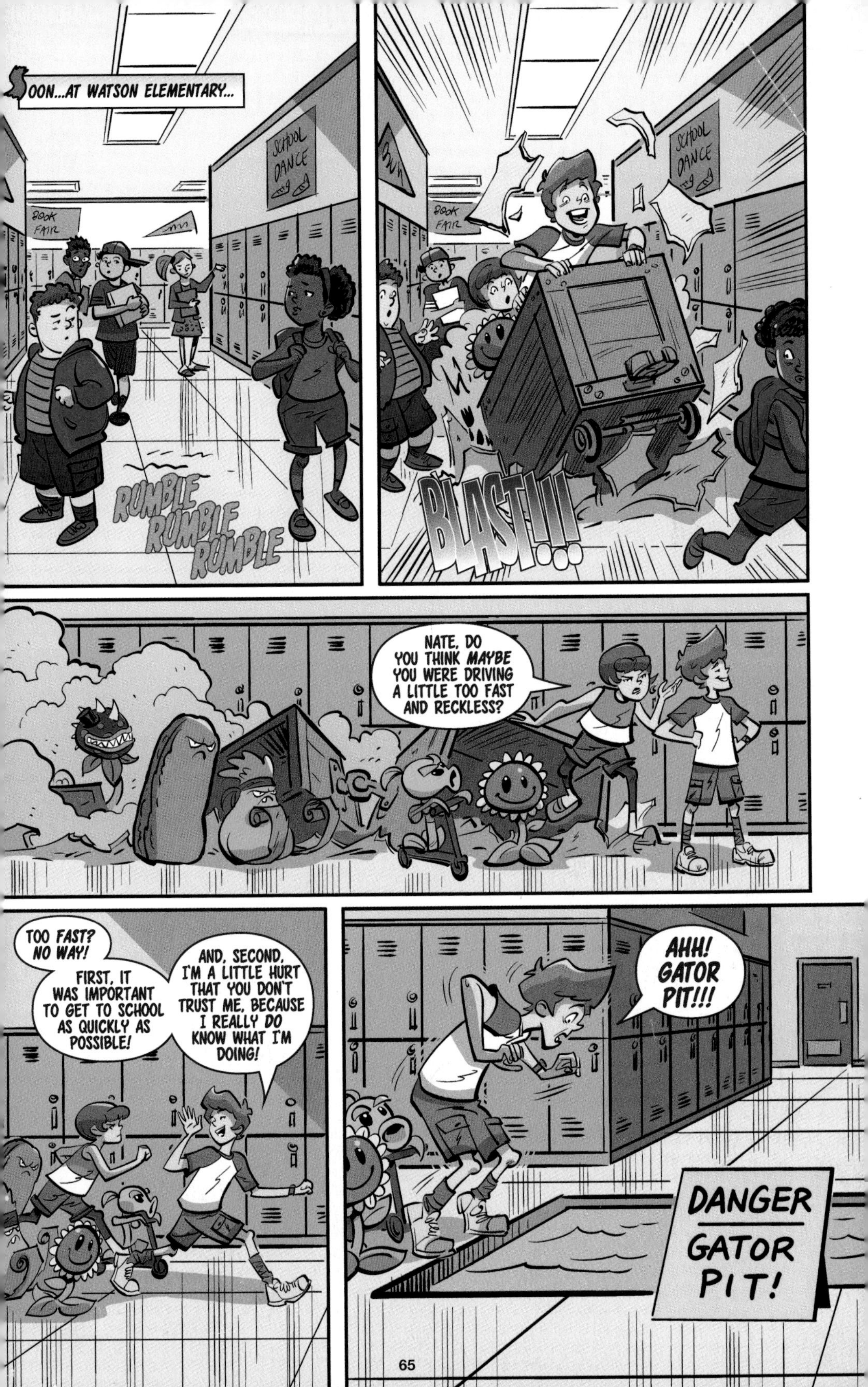
SOON...AT WATSON ELEMENTARY...
SCHOOL DANCE
BOOK FAIR
RUMBLE RUMBLE RUMBLE
SCHOOL DANCE
BOOK FAIR
BLAST!!!
NATE, DO YOU THINK MAYBE YOU WERE DRIVING A LITTLE TOO FAST AND RECKLESS?
TOO FAST? NO WAY!
FIRST, IT WAS IMPORTANT TO GET TO SCHOOL AS QUICKLY AS POSSIBLE!
AND, SECOND, I'M A LITTLE HURT THAT YOU DON'T TRUST ME, BECAUSE I REALLY DO KNOW WHAT I'M DOING!
AHH! GATOR PIT!!!
DANGER GATOR PIT!

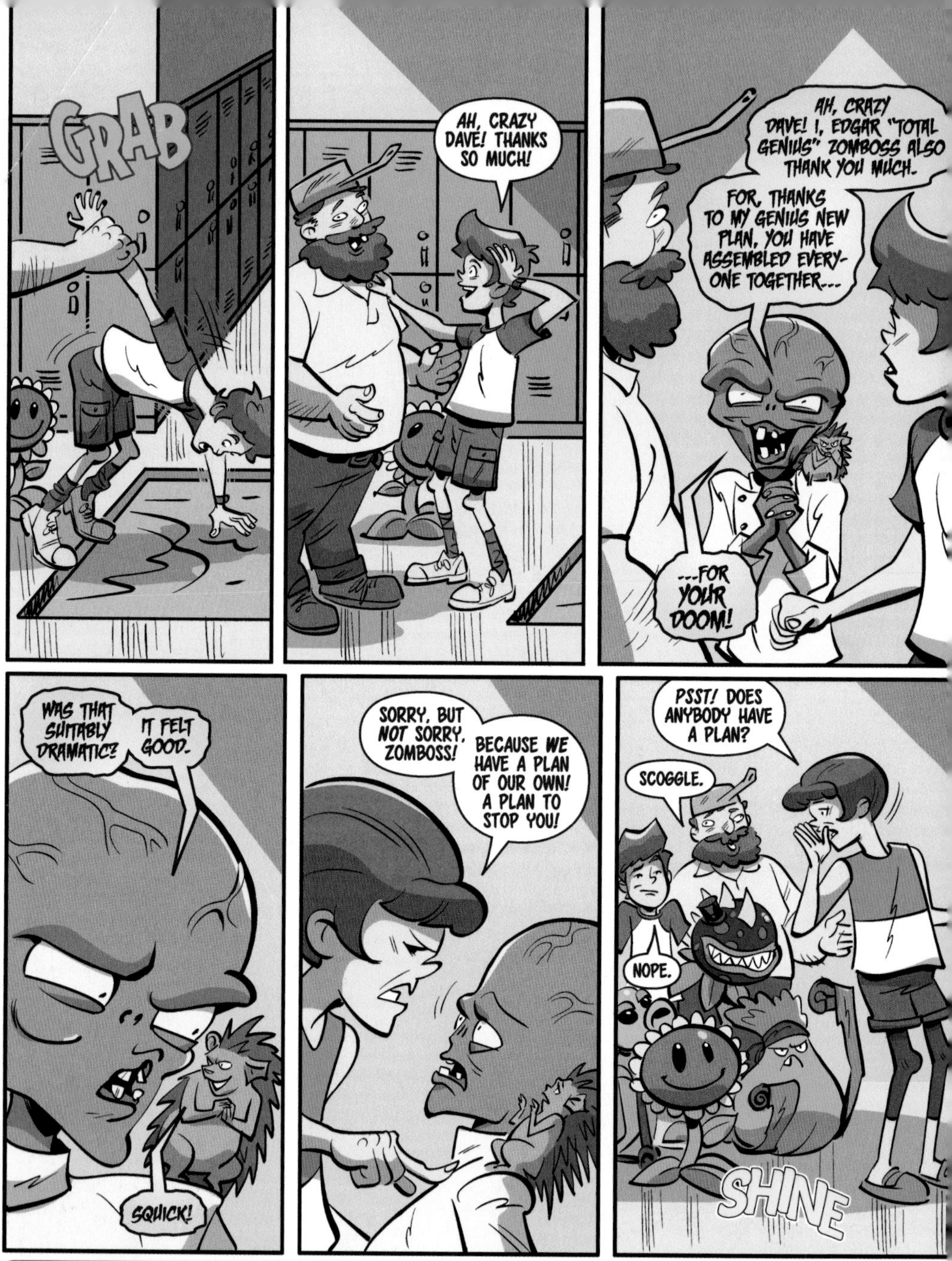
GRAB
AH, CRAZY DAVE! THANKS SO MUCH!
AH, CRAZY DAVE! I, EDGAR "TOTAL GENIUS" ZOMBOSS ALSO THANK YOU MUCH.
FOR, THANKS TO MY GENIUS NEW PLAN, YOU HAVE ASSEMBLED EVERYONE TOGETHER...
...FOR YOUR DOOM!
WAS THAT SUITABLY DRAMATIC?
IT FELT GOOD.
SQUICK!
SORRY, BUT NOT SORRY, ZOMBOSS!
BECAUSE WE HAVE A PLAN OF OUR OWN! A PLAN TO STOP YOU!
PSST! DOES ANYBODY HAVE A PLAN?
SCOGGLE.
NOPE.
SHINE

FIND THE GARDEN PATH:

Oh, no! Help Crazy Dave and the plants put an end to Zomboss!

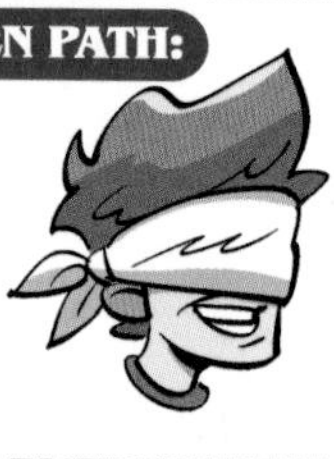

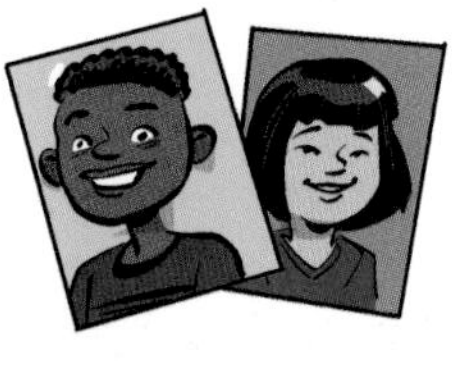

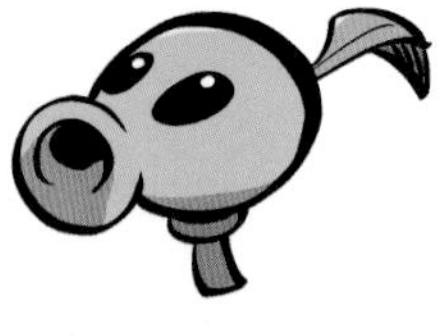

FIGHT WHILE BLINDFOLDED! (The zombies aren't visually confusing when you can't see them.):
Go to next page!

GET THE REST OF THE STUDENTS TO FIGHT:
Go to page 68!

TRUST THE PLANTS:
Go to page 69!

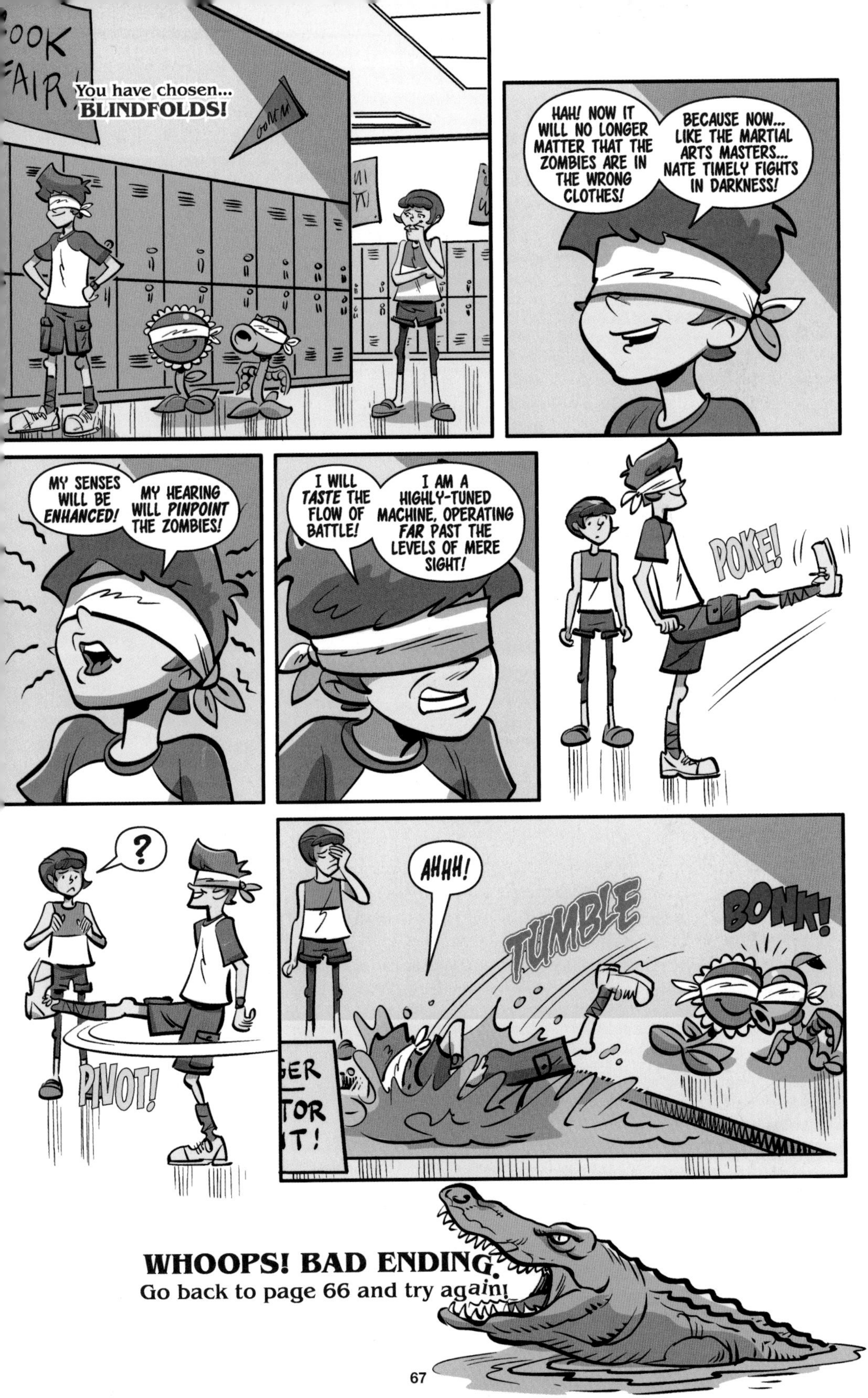
BOOK FAIR!
You have chosen...
BLINDFOLDS!
HAH! NOW IT WILL NO LONGER MATTER THAT THE ZOMBIES ARE IN THE WRONG CLOTHES!
BECAUSE NOW... LIKE THE MARTIAL ARTS MASTERS... NATE TIMELY FIGHTS IN DARKNESS!
MY SENSES WILL BE ENHANCED!
MY HEARING WILL PINPOINT THE ZOMBIES!
I WILL TASTE THE FLOW OF BATTLE!
I AM A HIGHLY-TUNED MACHINE, OPERATING FAR PAST THE LEVELS OF MERE SIGHT!
POKE!
?
PIVOT!
AHHH!
TUMBLE
BONK!
WHOOPS! BAD ENDING.
Go back to page 66 and try again!

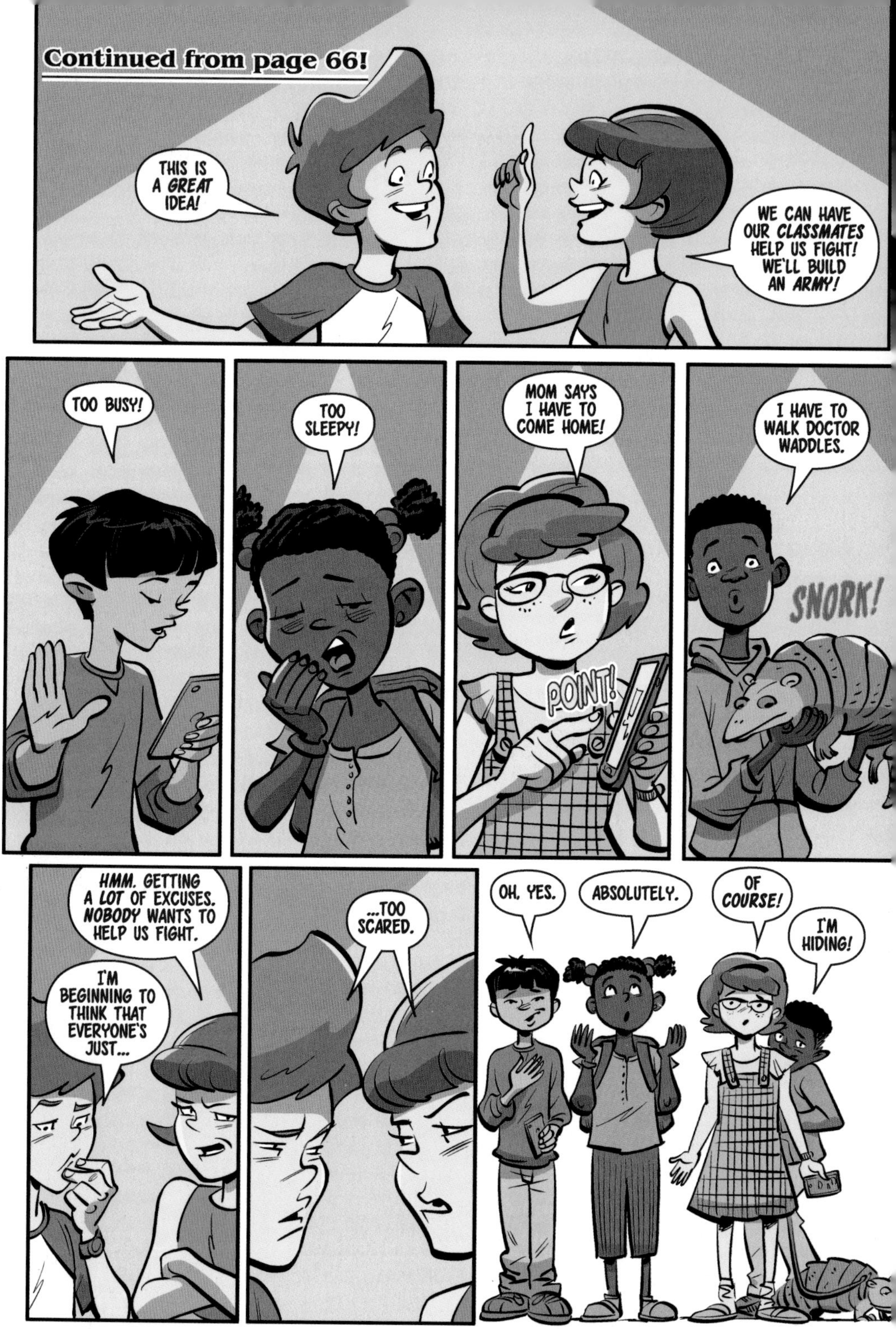
Continued from page 66!
THIS IS A GREAT IDEA!
WE CAN HAVE OUR CLASSMATES HELP US FIGHT! WE'LL BUILD AN ARMY!
TOO BUSY!
TOO SLEEPY!
MOM SAYS I HAVE TO COME HOME!
POINT!
I HAVE TO WALK DOCTOR WADDLES.
SNORK!
HMM. GETTING A LOT OF EXCUSES. NOBODY WANTS TO HELP US FIGHT.
I'M BEGINNING TO THINK THAT EVERYONE'S JUST...
...TOO SCARED.
OH, YES.
ABSOLUTELY.
OF COURSE!
I'M HIDING!

Well, THAT didn't work. Go back to page 66 and try again!

ontinued from page 66:

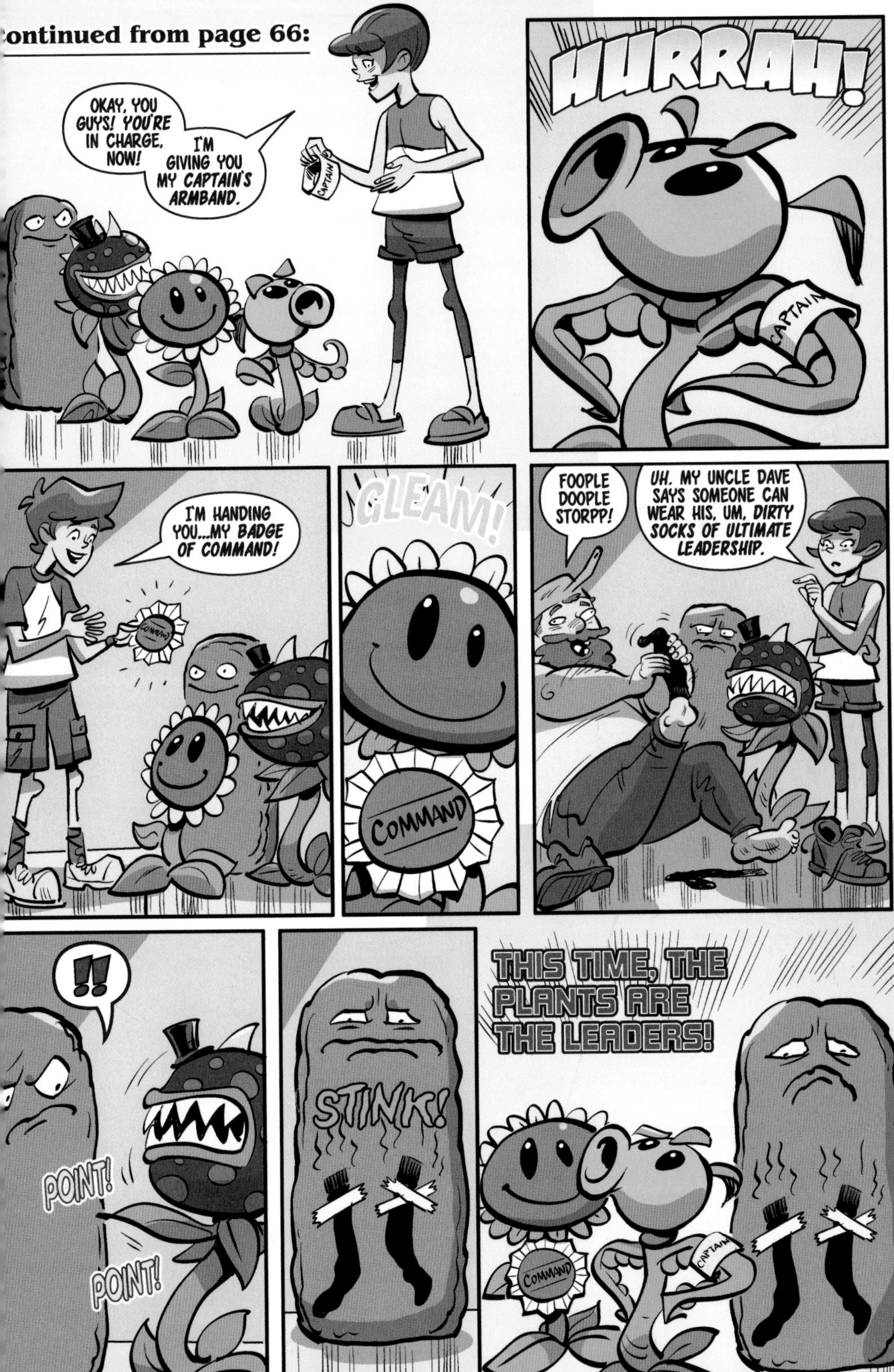
OKAY, YOU GUYS! YOU'RE IN CHARGE, NOW!
I'M GIVING YOU MY CAPTAIN'S ARMBAND.
CAPTAIN
HURRAH!
CAPTAIN
I'M HANDING YOU...MY BADGE OF COMMAND!
COMMAND
GLEAM!
COMMAND
FOOPLE DOOPLE STORPP!
UH. MY UNCLE DAVE SAYS SOMEONE CAN WEAR HIS, UM, DIRTY SOCKS OF ULTIMATE LEADERSHIP.
!!
POINT!
POINT!
STINK!
THIS TIME, THE PLANTS ARE THE LEADERS!
COMMAND
CAPTAIN

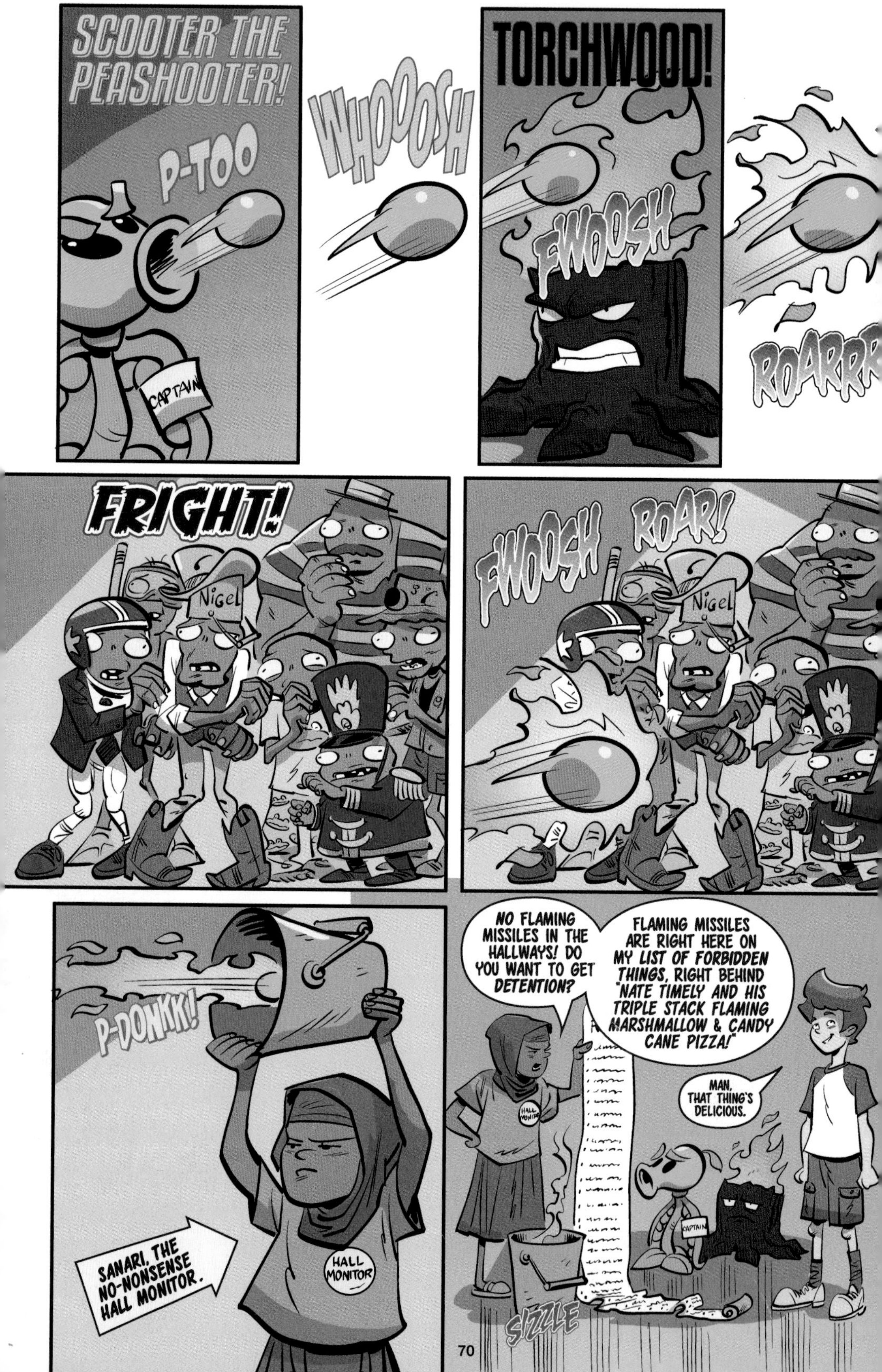
SCOOTER THE PEASHOOTER!
P-TOO
CAPTAIN
WHOOOSH
TORCHWOOD!
FWOOSH
ROARRR
FRIGHT!
Nigel
FWOOSH
ROAR!
Nigel
P-DONKK!
SANARI, THE NO-NONSENSE HALL MONITOR.
HALL MONITOR
NO FLAMING MISSILES IN THE HALLWAYS! DO YOU WANT TO GET DETENTION?
FLAMING MISSILES ARE RIGHT HERE ON MY LIST OF FORBIDDEN THINGS, RIGHT BEHIND "NATE TIMELY AND HIS TRIPLE STACK FLAMING MARSHMALLOW & CANDY CANE PIZZA!"
MAN, THAT THING'S DELICIOUS.
SIZZLE

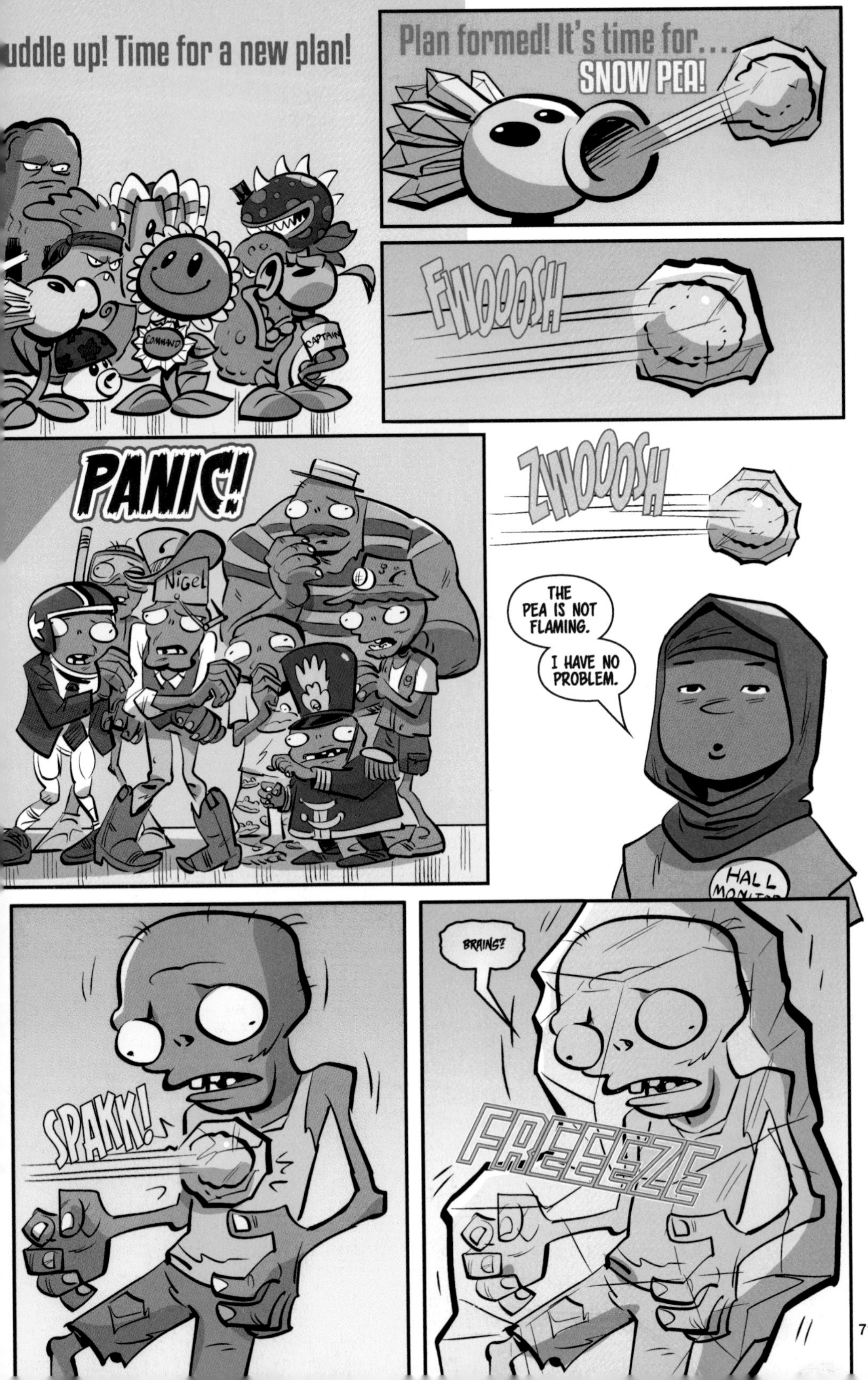
uddle up! Time for a new plan!
COMMAND
CAPTAIN
Plan formed! It's time for...
SNOW PEA!
FWOOOSH
PANIC!
Nigel
ZWOOOSH
THE PEA IS NOT FLAMING.
I HAVE NO PROBLEM.
HALL MONITOR
SPAKK!
BRAINS?
FREEEZE

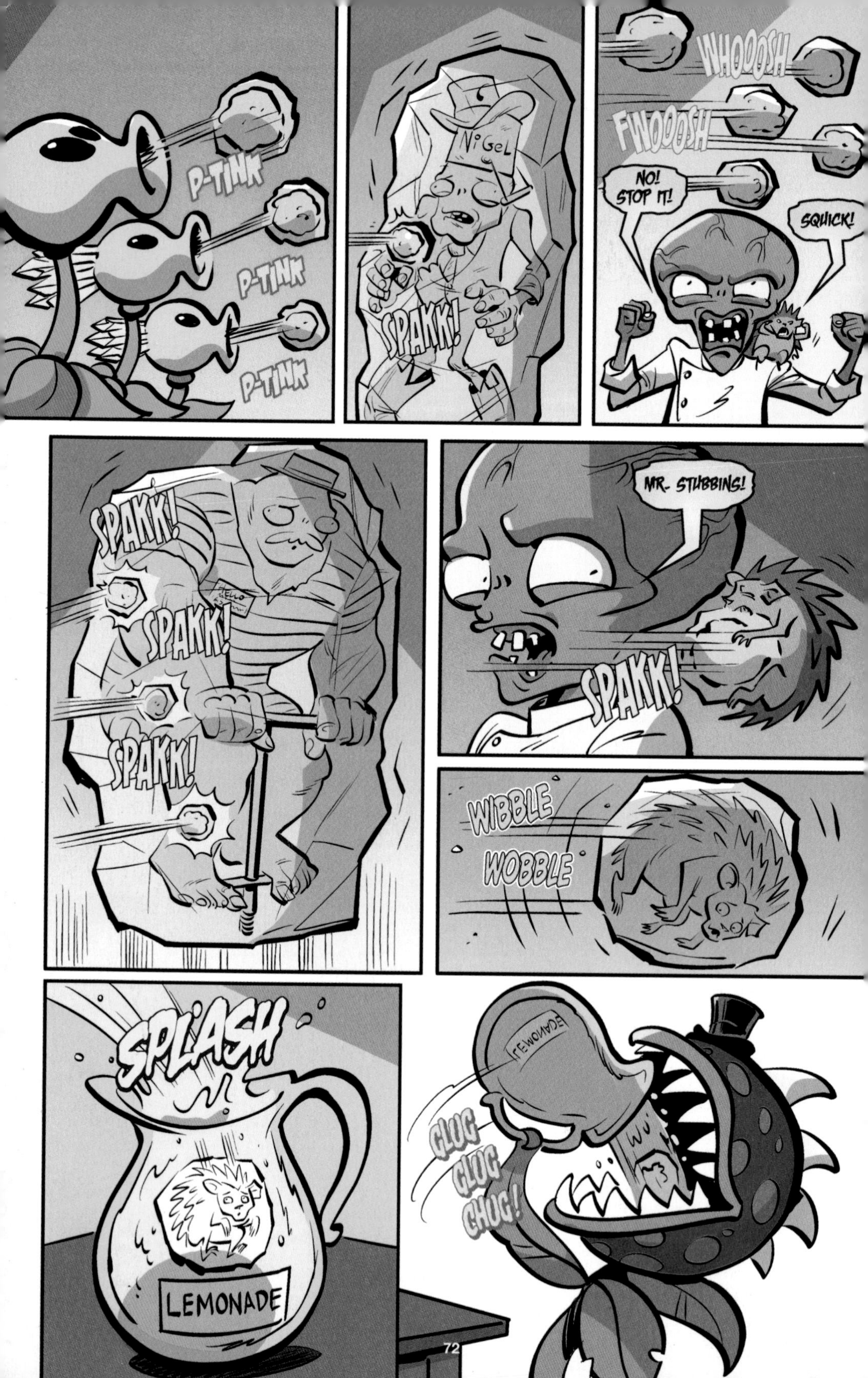

P-TINK
P-TINK
P-TINK
NiGeL
SPAKK!
WHOOOSH
FWOOOSH
NO! STOP IT!
SQUICK!
SPAKK!
HELLO
SPAKK!
SPAKK!
MR. STUBBINS!
SPAKK!
WIBBLE
WOBBLE
SPLASH
LEMONADE
LEMONADE
GLUG
GLUG
CHUG!

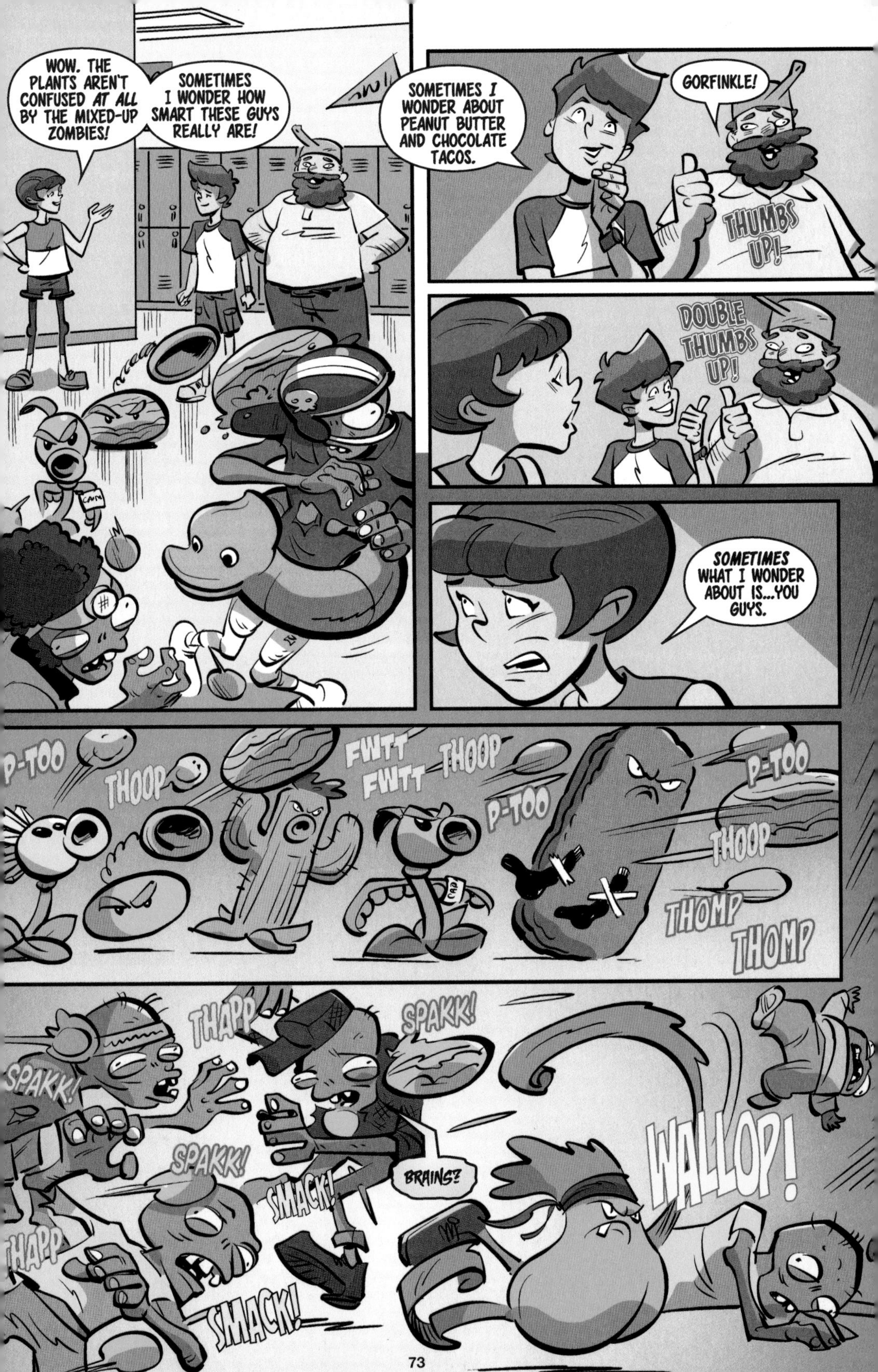

WOW. THE PLANTS AREN'T CONFUSED AT ALL BY THE MIXED-UP ZOMBIES!
SOMETIMES I WONDER HOW SMART THESE GUYS REALLY ARE!
SOMETIMES I WONDER ABOUT PEANUT BUTTER AND CHOCOLATE TACOS.
GORFINKLE!
THUMBS UP!
DOUBLE THUMBS UP!
SOMETIMES WHAT I WONDER ABOUT IS...YOU GUYS.
P-TOO
THOOP
FWTT
FWTT
THOOP
P-TOO
P-TOO
THOOP
THOMP
THOMP
THAPP
SPAKK!
SPAKK!
SPAKK!
BRAINS?
SMACK!
WALLOP!
THAPP
SMACK!

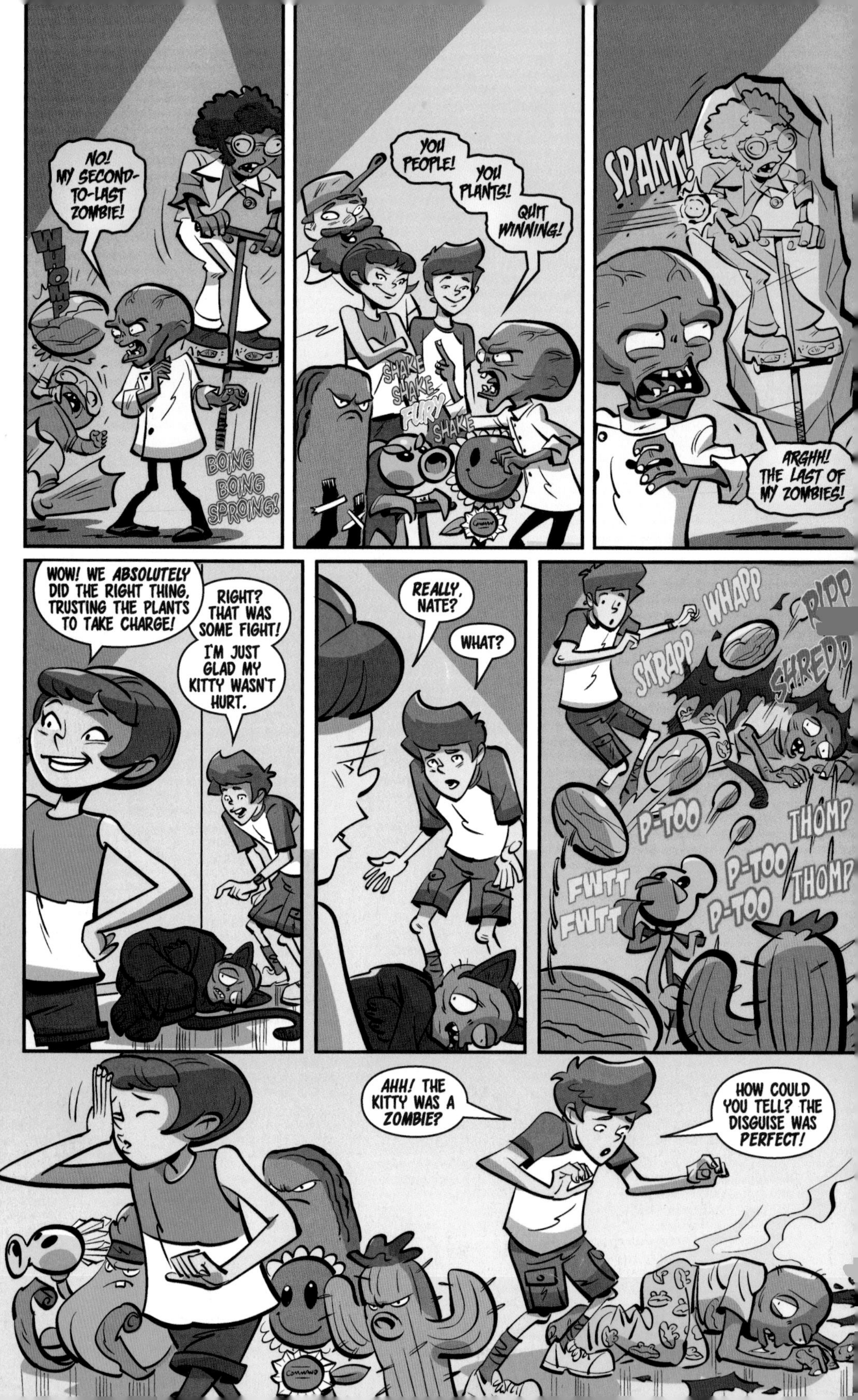
NO! MY SECOND-TO-LAST ZOMBIE!
WHOMP
BOING BOING SPROING!
YOU PEOPLE!
YOU PLANTS!
QUIT WINNING!
SHAKE SHAKE FURY SHAKE
SPAKK!
ARGHH! THE LAST OF MY ZOMBIES!
WOW! WE ABSOLUTELY DID THE RIGHT THING, TRUSTING THE PLANTS TO TAKE CHARGE!
RIGHT? THAT WAS SOME FIGHT!
I'M JUST GLAD MY KITTY WASN'T HURT.
REALLY, NATE?
WHAT?
WHAPP
RIPP
SKRAPP
SHREDD
P-TOO
THOMP
FWTT FWTT
P-TOO P-TOO
THOMP
AHH! THE KITTY WAS A ZOMBIE?
HOW COULD YOU TELL? THE DISGUISE WAS PERFECT!

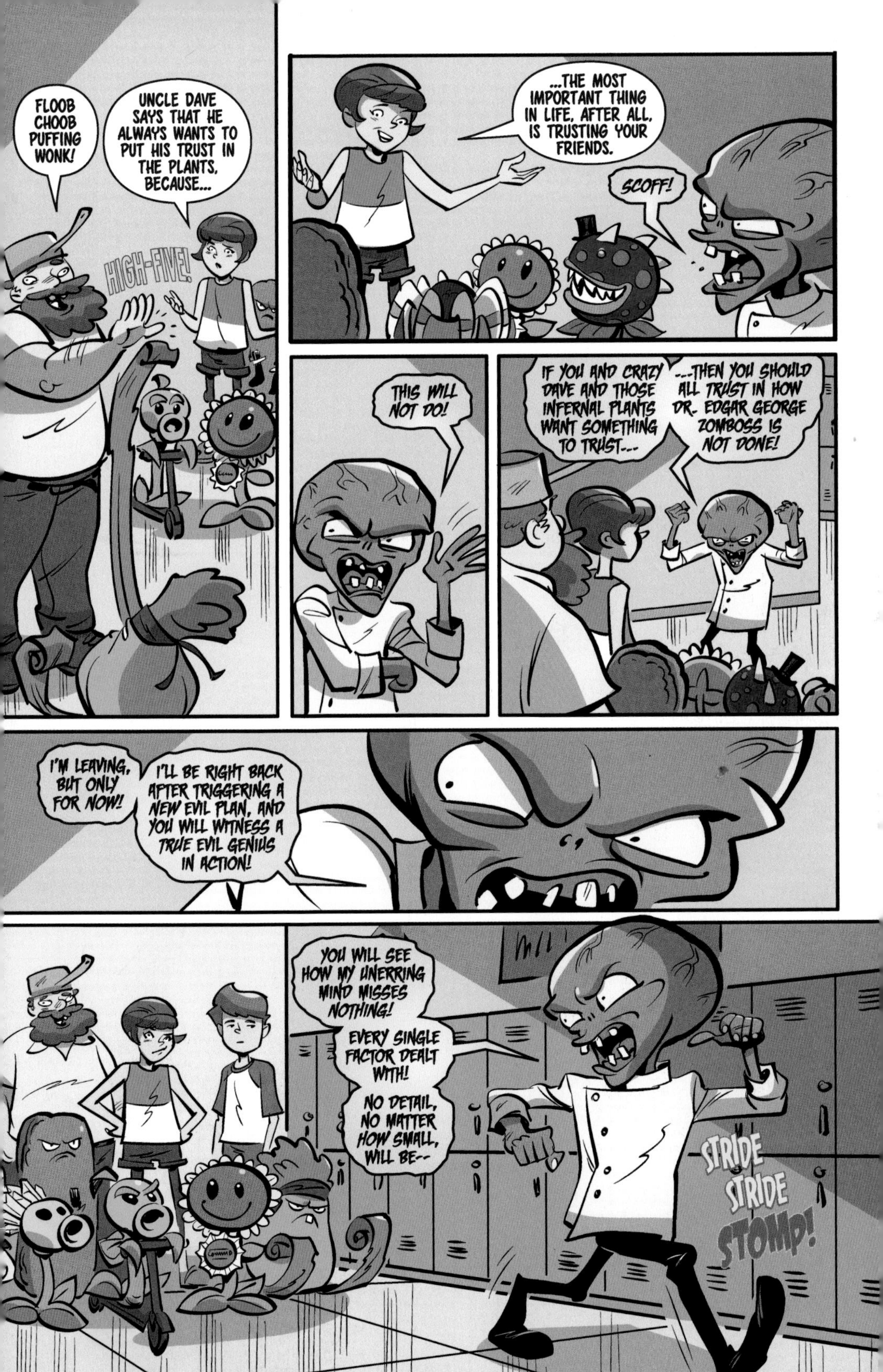
FLOOB CHOOB PUFFING WONK!
UNCLE DAVE SAYS THAT HE ALWAYS WANTS TO PUT HIS TRUST IN THE PLANTS, BECAUSE...
HIGH-FIVE!
...THE MOST IMPORTANT THING IN LIFE, AFTER ALL, IS TRUSTING YOUR FRIENDS.
SCOFF!
THIS WILL NOT DO!
IF YOU AND CRAZY DAVE AND THOSE INFERNAL PLANTS WANT SOMETHING TO TRUST...
...THEN YOU SHOULD ALL TRUST IN HOW DR. EDGAR GEORGE ZOMBOSS IS NOT DONE!
I'M LEAVING, BUT ONLY FOR NOW!
I'LL BE RIGHT BACK AFTER TRIGGERING A NEW EVIL PLAN, AND YOU WILL WITNESS A TRUE EVIL GENIUS IN ACTION!
YOU WILL SEE HOW MY UNERRING MIND MISSES NOTHING!
EVERY SINGLE FACTOR DEALT WITH!
NO DETAIL, NO MATTER HOW SMALL, WILL BE--
STRIDE
STRIDE
STOMP!

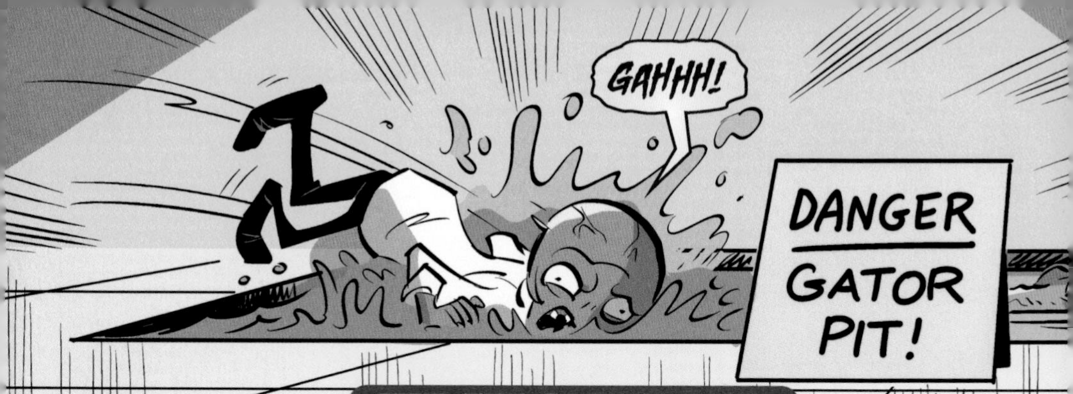
GAHHH!
DANGER
GATOR PIT!

FIND THE GARDEN PATH:

Uh-oh! Zomboss fell into the gator pit! Choose someone to decide if Zomboss should be rescued!

- **CRAZY DAVE:** He's a fellow genius! Go to the next panel!
- **PATRICE BLAZING:** Good judge of character! Go to the next panel!
- **NATE TIMELY:** Unfortunately, not paying attention! Go to the next panel!
- **THE PLANTS:** They're merciful, right? Go to the next panel!

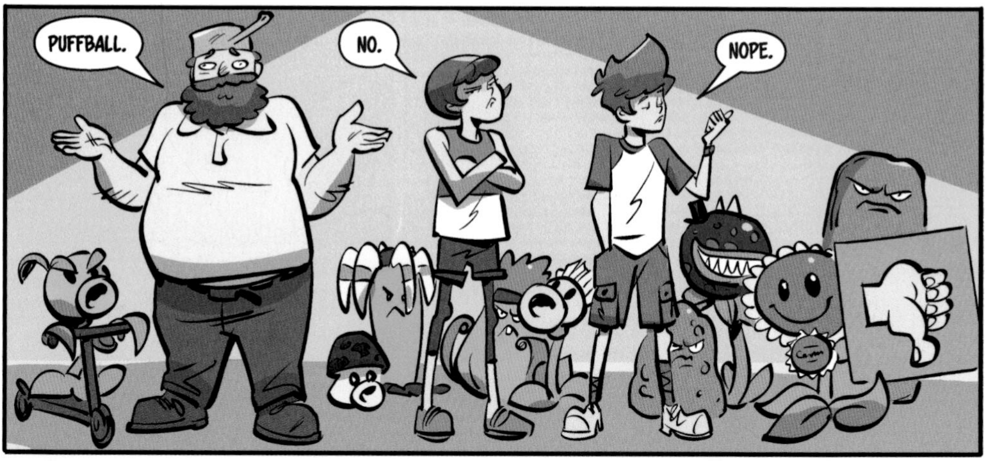
PUFFBALL.
NO.
NOPE.

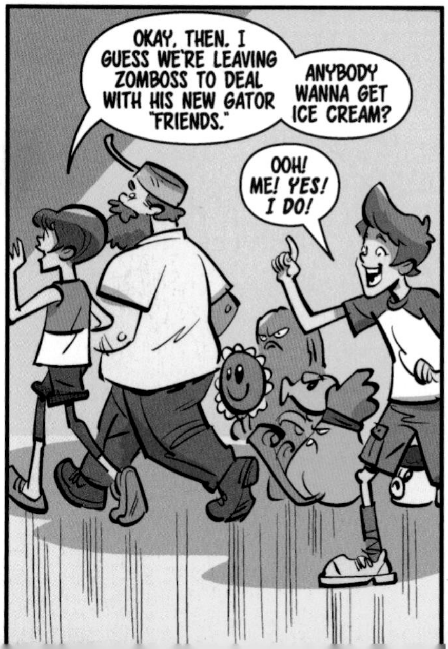
OKAY, THEN. I GUESS WE'RE LEAVING ZOMBOSS TO DEAL WITH HIS NEW GATOR "FRIENDS."
ANYBODY WANNA GET ICE CREAM?
OOH! ME! YES! I DO!

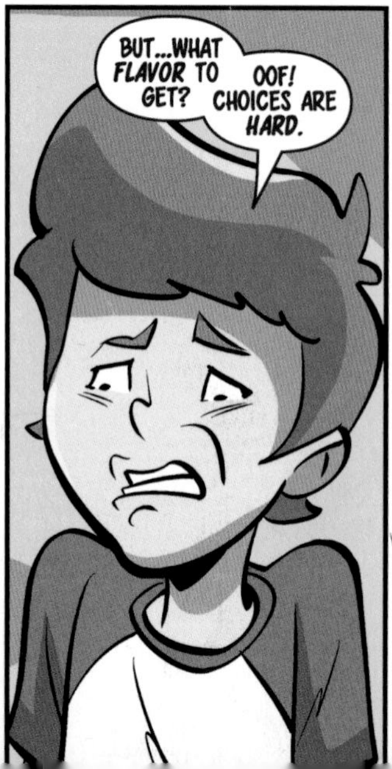
BUT...WHAT FLAVOR TO GET?
OOF! CHOICES ARE HARD.

Thanks for reading, everyone! We hope you enjoyed our crazy tale, and, remember...make good choices out there!

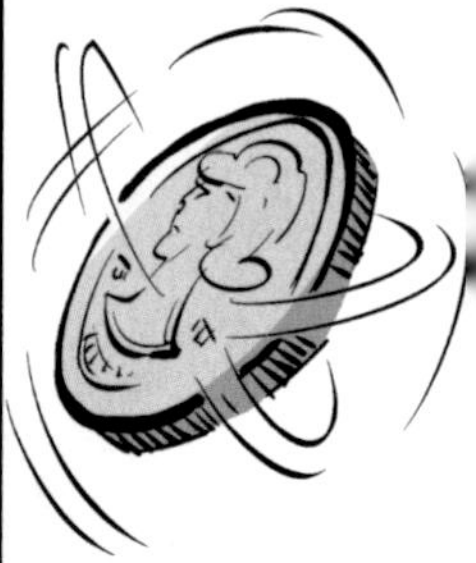

THE END

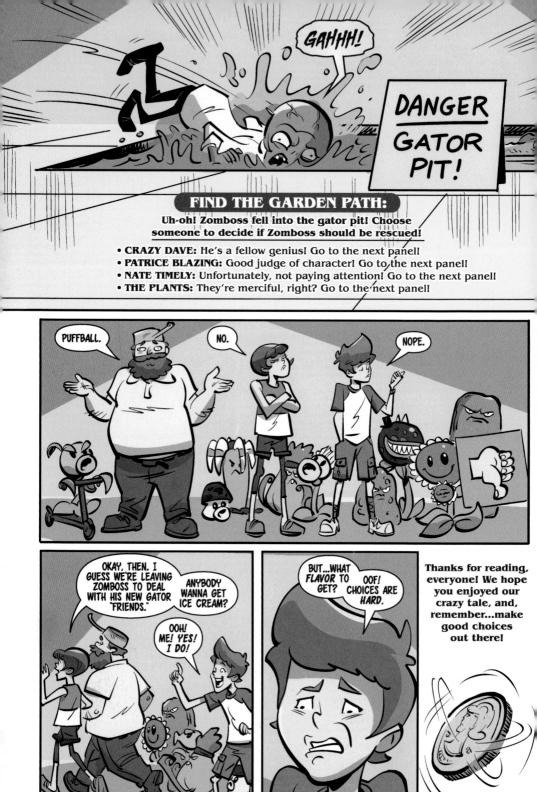

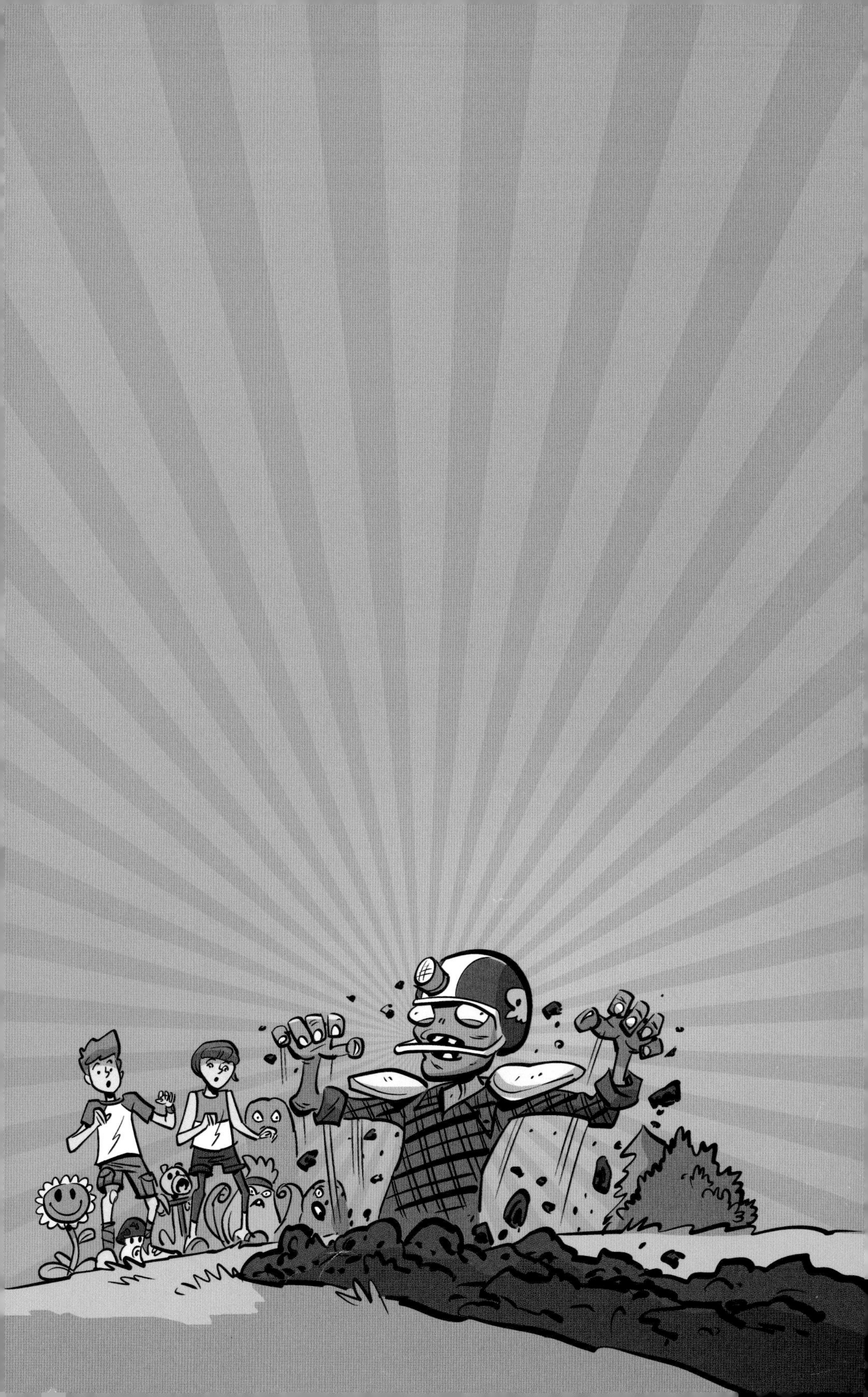

PLANTS VS. ZOMBIES: THE GARDEN PATH
COVER PENCILS BY KIERON DWYER

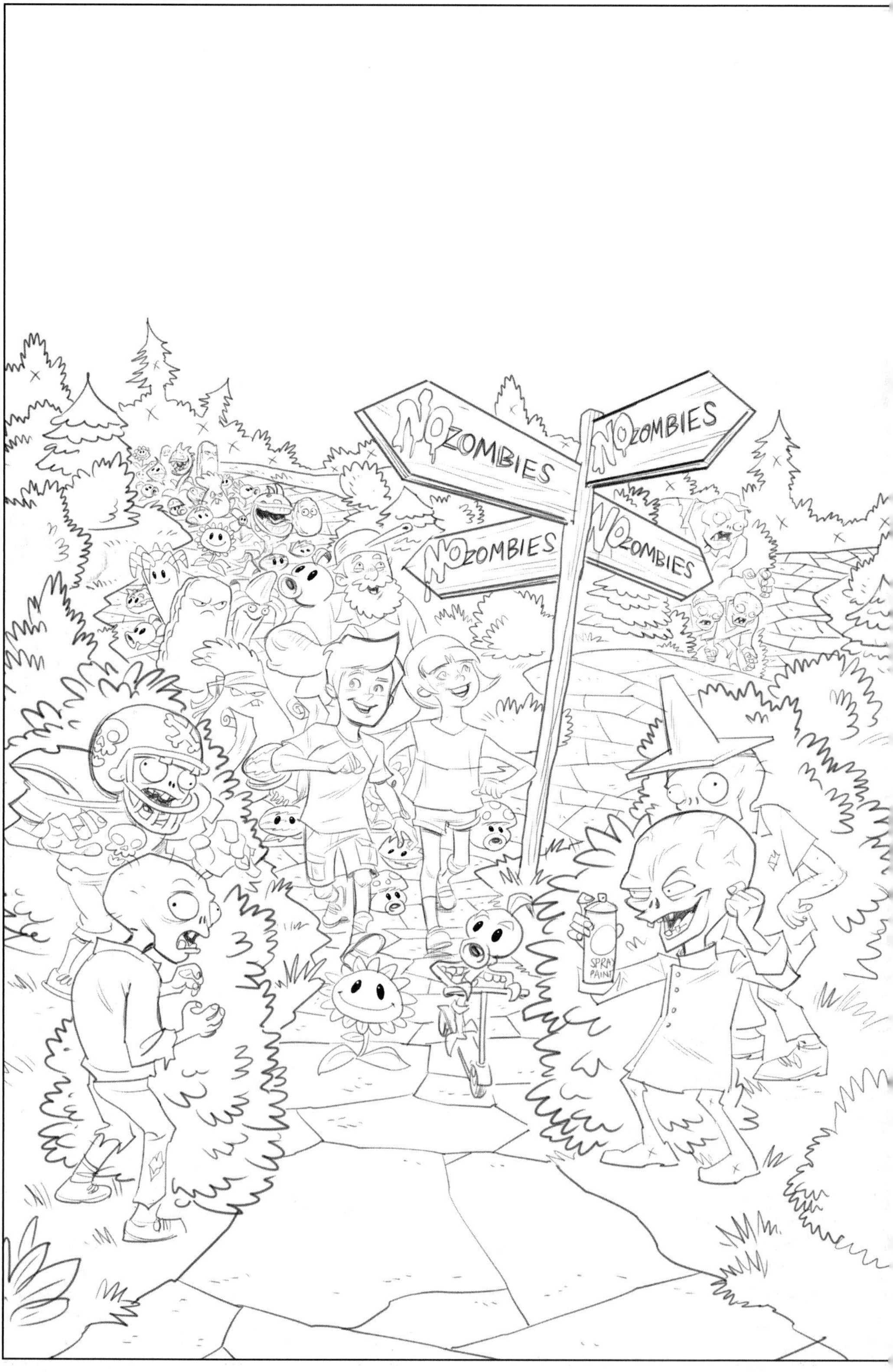
NO ZOMBIES
NO ZOMBIES
NO ZOMBIES
NO ZOMBIES
SPRAY PAINT

PLANTS VS. ZOMBIES: THE GARDEN PATH
COVER INKS BY KIERON DWYER

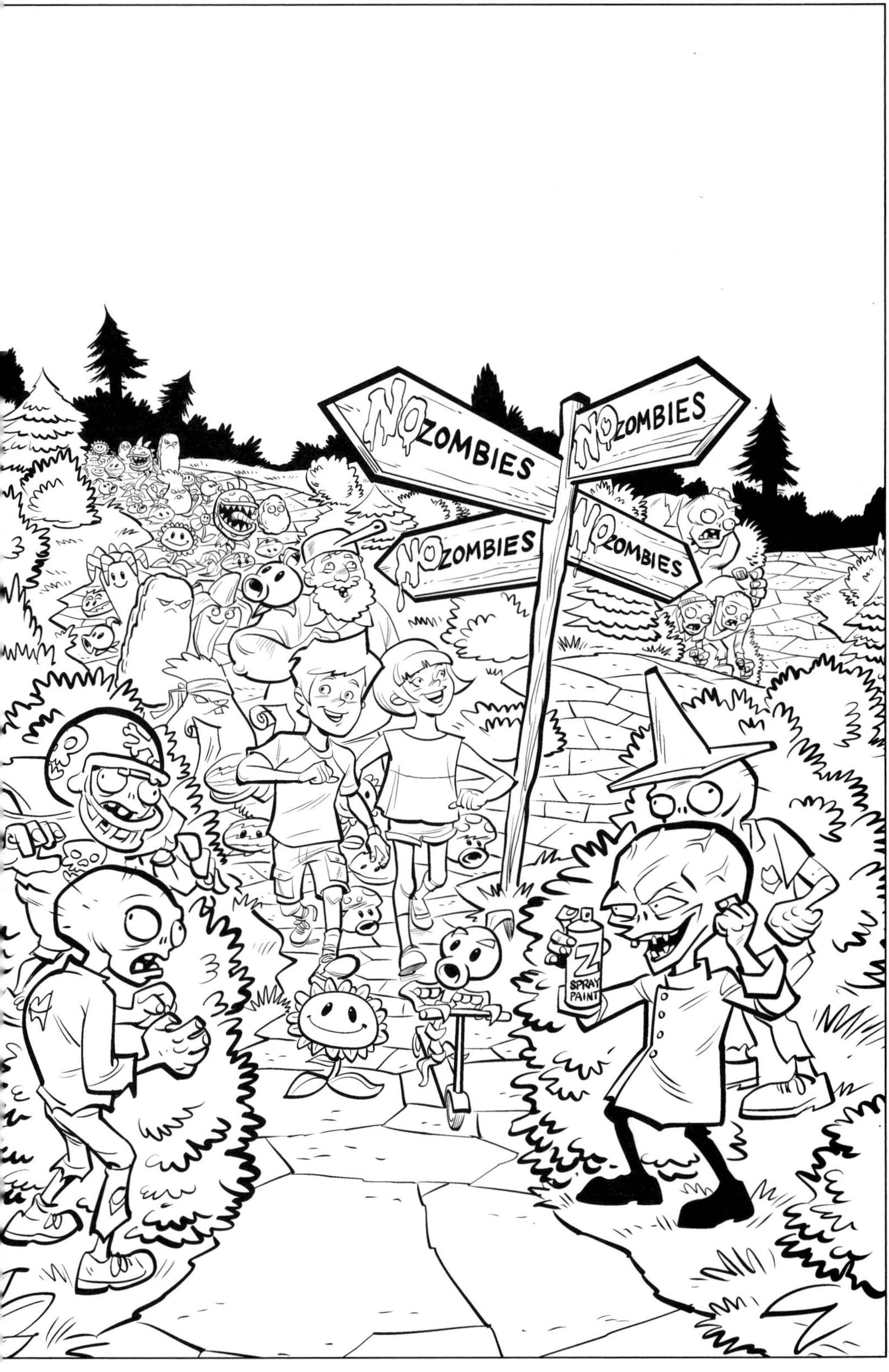
NO ZOMBIES
NO ZOMBIES
NO ZOMBIES
NO ZOMBIES
Z SPRAY PAINT

LINE ART FROM *THE GARDEN PATH* PAGES 26–29 BY ARTIST KIERON DWYER!

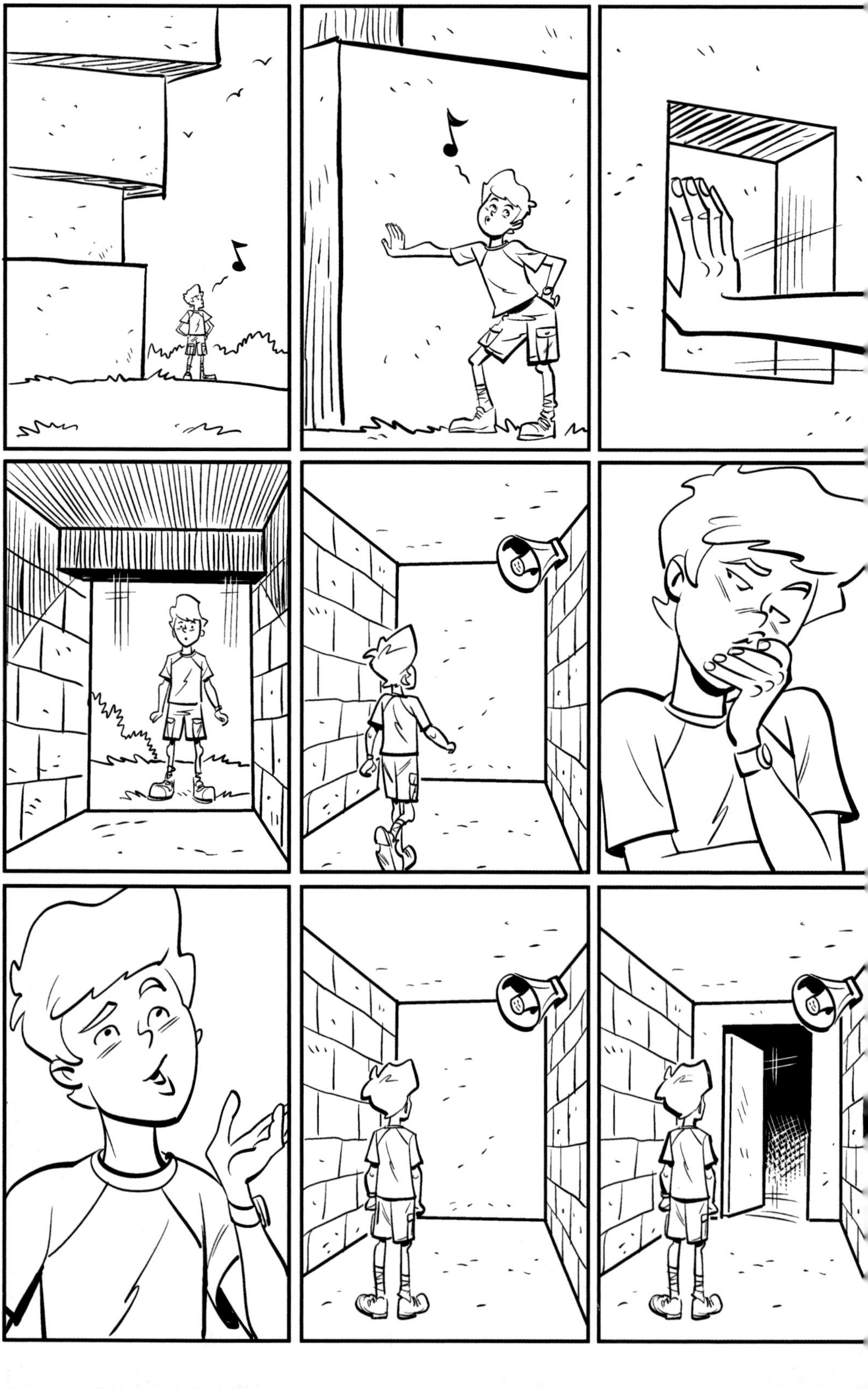

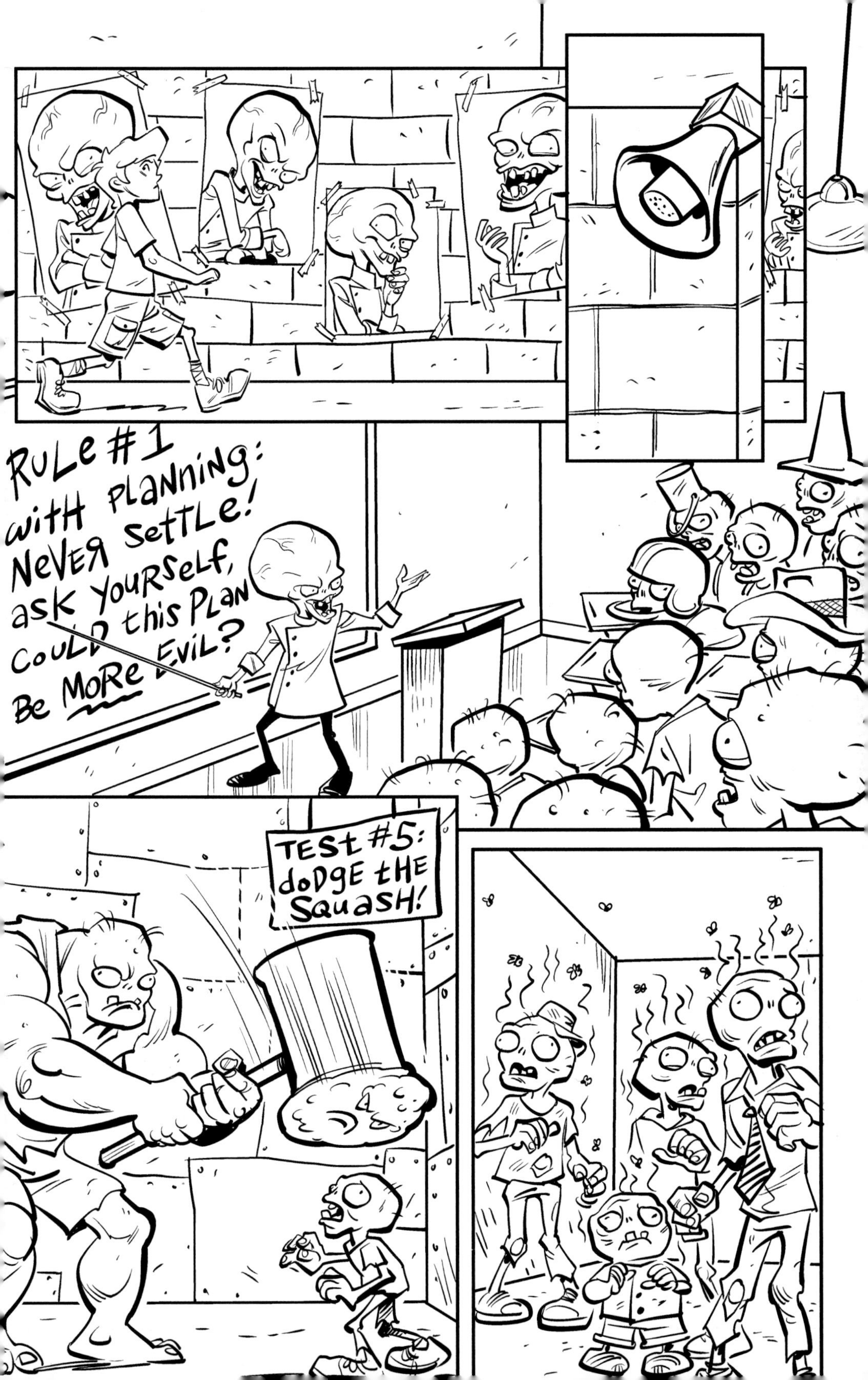
RULE #1
WITH PLANNING:
NEVER SETTLE!
ASK YOURSELF,
COULD THIS PLAN
BE MORE EVIL?
TEST #5:
DODGE THE
SQUASH!

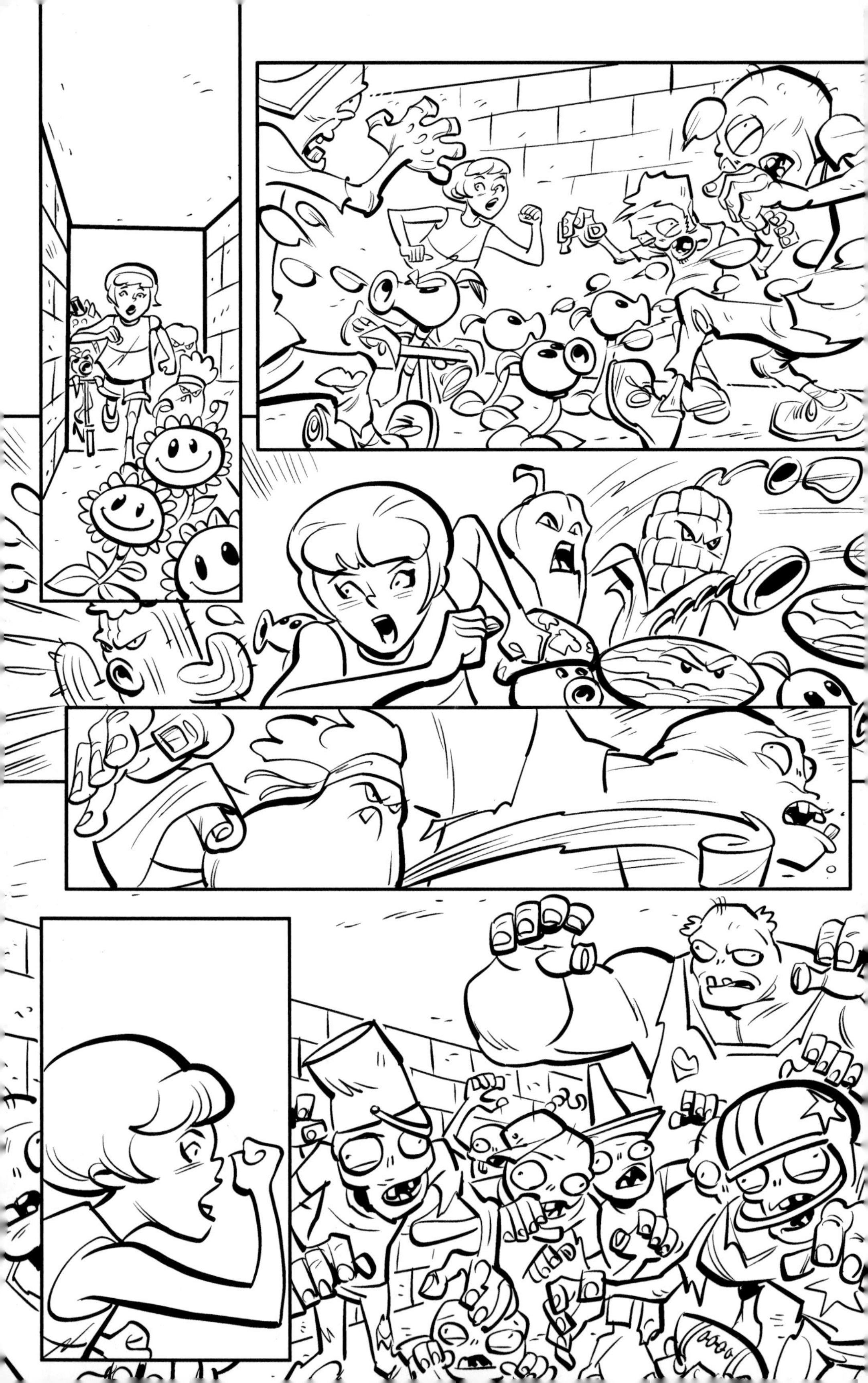

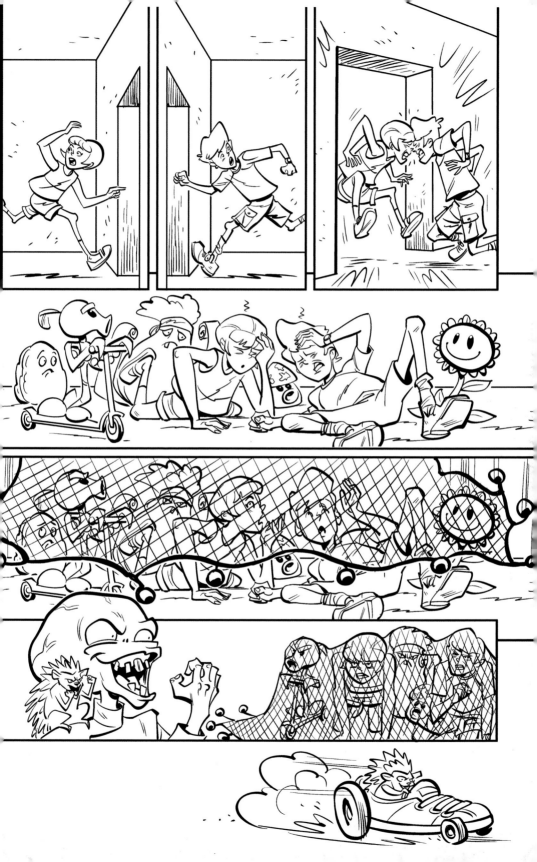

CREATOR BIOS

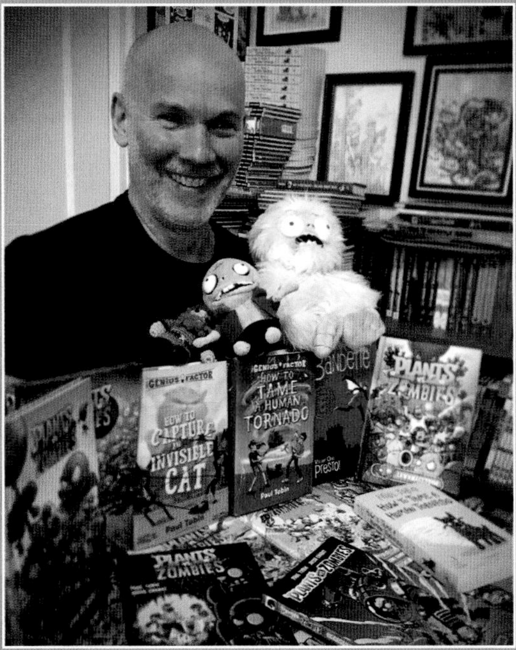
GENIUS FACTOR
HOW TO CAPTURE AN INVISIBLE CAT
GENIUS FACTOR
HOW TO TAME A HUMAN TORNADO
Paul Tobin
Bandette
Presto!
PLANTS vs. ZOMBIES
PLANTS vs. ZOMBIES

Paul Tobin

PAUL TOBIN is a 12th level writer and a 15th level cookie eater. He begins each morning in the manner we all do, by battling those zombies that have strayed too close to his pillow fort. Between writing all the *Plants vs. Zombies* comics and taking four naps a day, he's also found time to write the *Genius Factor* series of novels, the ape-filled *Banana Sunday* graphic novel, the award-winning *Bandette* series, the upcoming *Wrassle Castle* and *Earth Boy* graphic novels, and many other works. He has ridden a giant turtle and an elephant on purpose, and a tornado by accident.

Heather Breckel

HEATHER BRECKEL went to the Columbus College of Art and Design for animation. She decided animation wasn't for her, so she switched to comics. She's been working as a colorist for nearly ten years and has worked for nearly every major comics publisher out there. When she's not burning the midnight oil in a deadline crunch, she's either dying a bunch in videogames or telling her cats to stop running around at two in the morning.

Steve Dutro

STEVE DUTRO is an Eisner Award-nominated comic-book letterer from Redding, California, who can also drive a tractor. He graduated from the Kubert School and has been lettering comics since the days when foil-embossed covers were cool, working for Dark Horse (*The Fifth Beatle*, *I Am a Hero*, *Planet of the Apes*, *Star Wars*), Viz, Marvel, and DC. He has submitted a request to the Department of Homeland Security that in the event of a zombie apocalypse he be put in charge of all digital freeway signs so citizens can be alerted to avoid nearby brain-eatings and the like. He finds the *Plants vs. Zombies* game to be a real stress-fest, but highly recommends the *Plants vs. Zombies* table on *Pinball FX2* for game-room hipsters.

ALSO AVAILABLE FROM DARK HORSE!

THE HIT VIDEO GAME CONTINUES ITS COMIC BOOK INVASION!

PLANTS VS. ZOMBIES: LAWNMAGEDDON
Crazy Dave—the babbling-yet-brilliant inventor and top-notch neighborhood defender—helps young adventurer Nate fend off a zombie invasion that threatens to overrun the peaceful town of Neighborville in *Plants vs. Zombies: Lawnmageddon*! Their only hope is a brave army of chomping, squashing, and pea-shooting plants! A wacky adventure for zombie zappers young and old!
ISBN 978-1-61655-192-6 | $10.99

THE ART OF PLANTS VS. ZOMBIES
Part zombie memoir, part celebration of zombie triumphs, and part anti-plant screed, *The Art of Plants vs. Zombies* is a treasure trove of never-before-seen concept art, character sketches, and surprises from PopCap's popular *Plants vs. Zombies* games!
ISBN 978-1-61655-331-9 | $9.99

PLANTS VS. ZOMBIES: TIMEPOCALYPSE
Crazy Dave helps Patrice and Nate Timely fend off Zomboss' latest attack in *Plants vs. Zombies: Timepocalypse*! This new standalone tale will tickle your funny bones and thrill your brains through any timeline!
ISBN 978-1-61655-621-1 | $9.99

PLANTS VS. ZOMBIES: BULLY FOR YOU
Patrice and Nate are ready to investigate a strange college campus to keep the streets safe from zombies!
ISBN 978-1-61655-889-5 | $10.99

PLANTS VS. ZOMBIES: GARDEN WARFARE VOLUME 1
Based on the hit video game, this comic tells the story leading up to the events in *Plants vs. Zombies: Garden Warfare 2*!
ISBN 978-1-61655-946-5 | $10.99

VOLUME 2
ISBN 978-1-50670-548-4 | $9.99

VOLUME 3
ISBN 978-1-50670-837-9 | $9.99

PLANTS VS. ZOMBIES: GROWN SWEET HOME
With newfound knowledge of humanity, Dr. Zomboss strikes at the heart of Neighborville . . . sparking a series of plant-versus-zombie brawls!
ISBN 978-1-61655-971-7 | $10.99

PLANTS VS. ZOMBIES: PETAL TO THE METAL
Crazy Dave takes on the tough *Don't Blink* video game—and challenges Dr. Zomboss to a race to determine the future of Neighborville!
ISBN 978-1-61655-999-1 | $9.99

PLANTS VS. ZOMBIES: BOOM BOOM MUSHROOM
The gang discover Zomboss' secret plan for swallowing the city of Neighborville whole! A rare mushroom must be found in order to save the humans aboveground!
ISBN 978-1-50670-037-3 | $10.99

PLANTS VS. ZOMBIES: BATTLE EXTRAVAGONZO
Zomboss is back, hoping to buy the same factory that Crazy Dave is eyeing! Will Crazy Dave and his intelligent plants beat Zomboss and his zombie army to the punch?
ISBN 978-1-50670-189-9 | $9.99

PLANTS VS. ZOMBIES: LAWN OF DOOM
With Zomboss filling everyone's yards with traps and specia soldiers, will he and his zombie army turn Halloween into thei zanier Lawn of Doom celebration?!
ISBN 978-1-50670-204-9 | $10.99

PLANTS VS. ZOMBIES: THE GREATEST SHOW UNEARTHED
Dr. Zomboss believes that all humans hold a secret desire to run away and join the circus, so he aims to use his "Big Z's Adequately Amazing Flytrap Circus" to lure Neighborville's citizens to their doom!
ISBN 978-1-50670-298-8 | $9.99

PLANTS VS. ZOMBIES: RUMBLE AT LAKE GUMBO
The battle for clean water begins! Nate, Patrice, and Crazy Dave spot trouble and grab all the Tangle Kelp and Party Crabs they can to quell another zombie attack!
ISBN 978-1-50670-497-5 | $10.99

PLANTS VS. ZOMBIES: WAR AND PEAS
When Dr. Zomboss and Crazy Dave find themselves members of the same book club, a literary war is inevitable! The position of leader of the book club opens up and Zomboss and Crazy Dave compete for the top spot in a scholarly scuffle for the ages
ISBN 978-1-50670-677-1 | $9.99

PLANTS VS. ZOMBIES: DINO-MIGHT
Dr. Zomboss sets his sights on destroying the yards in town and rendering the plants homeless—and his plans include dogs cats, rabbits, hammock sloths, and, somehow, dinosaurs . . .
ISBN 978-1-50670-838-6 | $9.99

PLANTS VS. ZOMBIES: SNOW THANKS
Dr. Zomboss invents a Cold Crystal capable of freezing Neighborville, burying the town in snow and ice! It's up to the humans and the fieriest plants to save Neighborville—with the help of pirates!
ISBN 978-1-50670-839-3 | $10.99

PLANTS VS. ZOMBIES: A LITTLE PROBLEM
Will an invasion of teeny-tiny miniature zombies mean the party for Crazy Dave's two-hundred-year-old pants gets canceled?
ISBN 978-1-50670-840-9 | $10.99

PLANTS VS. ZOMBIES: BETTER HOMES AND GUARDENS
Nate and Patrice try thwarting zombie attacks by putting defending "Guardens" plants *inside* homes as well as in yards But as soon as Dr. Zomboss finds out, he's determined to circumvent this plan with an epically evil one of his own . . .
ISBN 978-1-50671-305-2 | $9.99

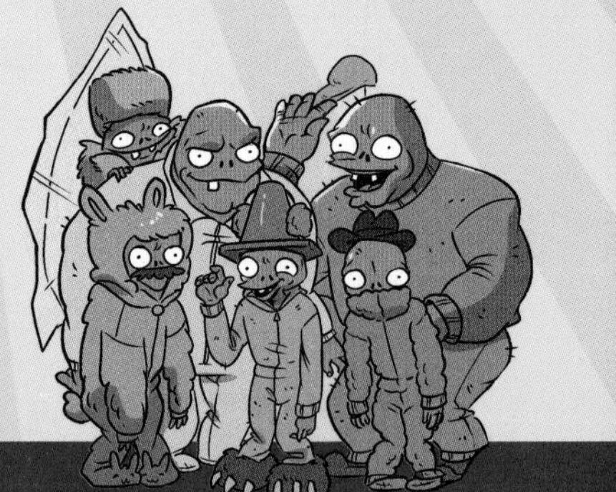

AVAILABLE AT YOUR LOCAL COMICS SHOP OR BOOKSTORE
To find a comics shop in your area, visit comicshoplocator.com. For more information or to order direct, visit **DarkHorse.com**

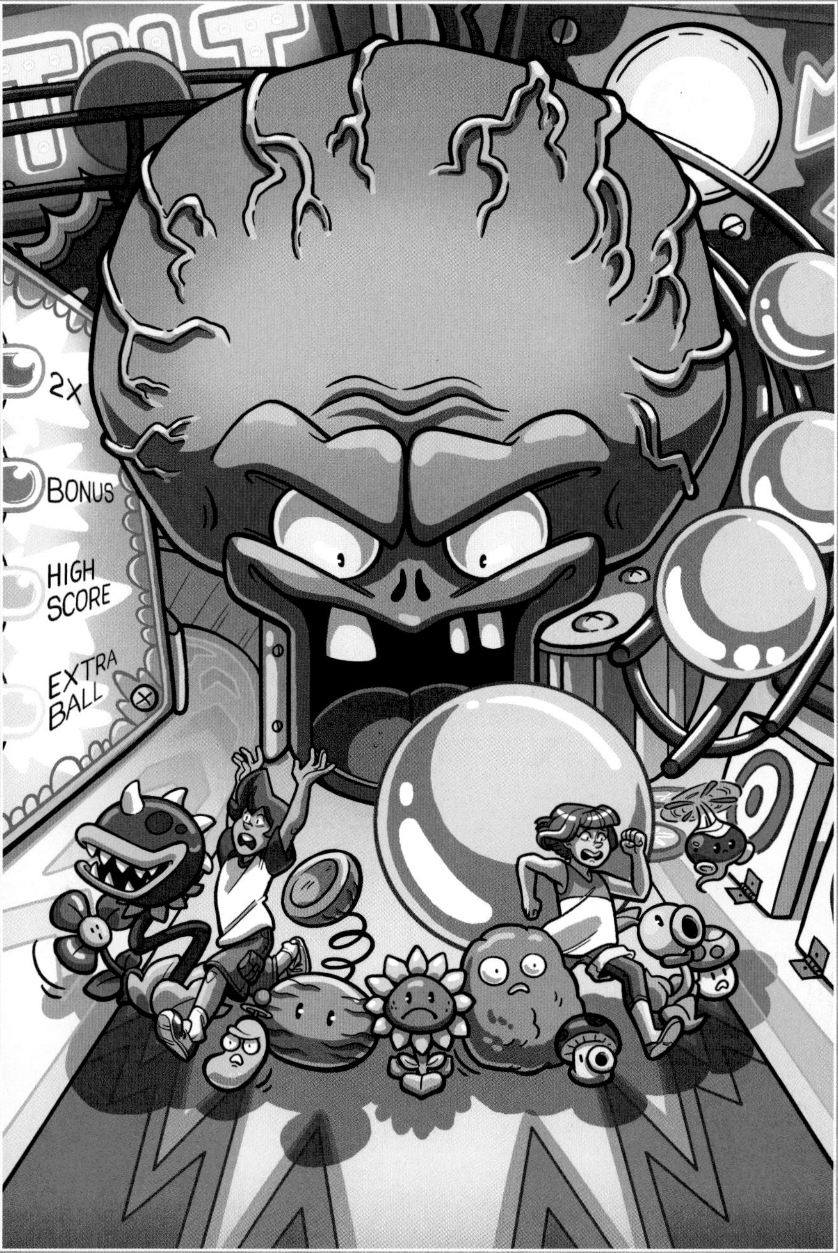
2X
BONUS
HIGH SCORE
EXTRA BALL

Will Flora the Sunflower and Neighborville's plant platoon hit a triple-bonus combo or will their efforts ride the outlanes to certain loss?

Plunge into another battle between plants and zombies as Dr. Zomboss turns the entirety of Neighborville into a giant, fully-functional pinball machine! With bumpers, flippers, and pegs meticulously scattered across town by the zombie pinball wizard himself, Nate, Patrice, and their plant posse must find a way to revert Neighborville to its normal state and halt this uniquely horrifying zombie invasion. With every ball and bumper set against them, will they hit a run of zombie knock-out skill shots—or will the battle go *full tilt zombies*?! Eisner Award-winning writer Paul Tobin (*Bandette*, *Genius Factor*) collaborates with artist Christianne Gillenardo-Goudreau (*Plants vs. Zombies: Better Homes and Guardens*) for a brand-new *Plants vs. Zombies* journey!